After No God

TOM MILES

Copyright © 2021 Tom Miles

All rights reserved.

ISBN-13: 979-8-542601-44-1

For Gelareh, by Gad xxx

Volume the First

I

MR CHARLES BARRATT was a gentleman of good height, with an upper frame that was both broad and deep, like a blanket box, so that when he coughed, as he occasionally did, having recently given up the pipe on the advice of Smith, the apothecary, clouds of startled sparrows would emerge from the trees, and piglets would squeal in their pens as if the Earth itself had trembled. He suffered from a certain indelicacy of manner, or rather he did not suffer at all, since this quality, or lack thereof, was merely observed by the residents of B_____, the small town to which he had recently removed, and not perceived by Barratt himself. He tried to reconcile an instinct for honesty with an appreciation of the value of kindness which had come slowly to him; he was now in his fiftieth year. He found that the results of this attempted synthesis, in polite discourse at least, were uneven and frequently difficult to predict, nevertheless it was a course he was determined to follow, since it offered the greatest likelihood of not being misunderstood and of presenting himself as he wished to be seen. If *Ecce Homo* were to be one's motto, he reasoned, then the man to be beheld ought to be a fair representation of that person's best self. His voice was not meant for drawing room chatter, he was seemingly incapable of conversing in pleasantries and he had not lived his entire life in B_____, so butcher, baker and chandler, and the greater society of the town, came to refer to him as the gentleman from the City.

Barratt was a widower of some fortune, and childless, so his arrival in the town brought before it light winds of excitement amongst the womenfolk, which occasionally concerted into something like a storm, as when cartfuls of fine dark furniture rolled in stately procession twice along the high street, executing a full turn by the bridge (the driver of the first cart having lost his bearings) and stopping outside the grand house, built in the time of our last Queen, at its northernmost reach. The subsequent arrival of the gentleman from the City, with his intimidating stature, mercantile directness, and powerful mode of speaking, seemed to quieten the weather entirely. His voice and his person would surely fill the Red House, large as it was, and leave no space whatsoever for another wife.

He was invited into the homes of B_____'s more eminent families and was politely asked his opinion about this and that. Impolitely, he offered this opinion unvarnished by any consciousness that his interlocutor might think differently, presuming that if someone asked what he thought they did so in good faith or in ignorance, that what they required was counsel or information, rather than flattery. He was not a stupid man, however, and after a small number of misunderstandings of this sort he began to disqualify himself from speaking on matters of opinion, at least, if not matters of fact. Nor did Barratt fail to notice that his habit of correcting the misinformed assertions of others was not as well tolerated here in the country, where fiction and rumour seemed to be the very backbone of civil discourse, than it was in London, and with no insignificant struggle he discontinued the practice. This left him with very little to say, however, so those hosts whose invitations he accepted first, who were taken aback by his unusual frankness of expression were confused to learn from those upon whom he called later in the year that they found Mr Barratt rather a reserved fellow, despite the resounding nature of his voice, who could barely be persuaded to speak at all.

Barratt recorded and then dutifully returned the invitations he received, waiting until the spring to do so, reasoning that drier weather would ensure less inconvenience for those wishing to visit the Red House. In fact this frustrated those who might otherwise have pleaded that winter's inclemency prevented them from attending and thus taxed their ingenuity in a way that was adjudged thoughtless or even manipulative. Most excused him from his obligation. Those who did dine with Mr Barratt, unable to overcome their natural human curiosity about what the inside of such a man's house might look like, found that he was better company as host than hosted. Both his cook and cellar were excellent, and he was inevitably more relaxed surrounded by his own things. An awkwardness still prevailed at these gatherings, and a kind of sobriety, despite the superior claret. Barratt remained unskilled at inconsequential talk and the dining table was overlooked by a large portrait of a woman, the late Mrs Barratt it was assumed, who, if it were a truthful likeness, must have been a person of considerable beauty. She was dressed in a white gown and her hair, honey-coloured, was elaborately arranged. The background of the painting was a dark crimson and the wall on which it hung a similar shade, so that the woman seemed to float in space between the ceiling and the chair where her surviving beloved sat, an effect which served to limit the jollity of the occasion.

In truth the majority of his visitors found him to be remarkable only in the degree to which he maintained an appearance of self-containment. It was as if the extremes of emotional capacity that one might remark in a young man, his enthusiasm, curiosity or disdain, had been largely eroded in Mr Barratt's case, or suppressed perhaps, so that the sentiments which he expressed, and the passion with which he expressed them, stood in muted contrast to the great volume of sound produced in doing so. If a fellow diner were to praise the duck, to insist that it was the finest he had eaten in many a year, and to enquire where such splendid birds could possibly be procured, Barratt might answer "My cook is very capable, yes, you'd have to ask them," and further conversation regarding poultry in general or the duck in particular would be curbed in a subtle, yet final fashion. There were one or two gentlemen of a complementary temperament who continued to exchange suppers with Barratt, but as the days lengthened and the distractions of summer unfurled like a rich Persian carpet before the people of B_____, interest in the Red House and its current occupant dissipated completely.

There our story might end, with Mr Charles Barratt seeing out the remainder of his days amongst his books and his wine and his fine, dark furniture, untroubled by any slight change in circumstance. Or perhaps we might imagine him returning to London, never to be heard of again. We could sensibly part company with him in either eventuality, at this point, but we must stay with the gentleman a little longer, because his circumstances did indeed change, the change was not trifling, and its origins can be traced back to a specific incident, involving the Reverend Archer and a wasp.

II

B   HAD GROWN sufficiently populous during the reign of the second King George that it was deemed necessary to divide the town and its immediate environs into two separate parishes. The richer of these livings had been awarded most recently to young Reverend Archer, a nephew of the Duke of Rutland. The church of St Andrew was several hundred years old, with a square tower rather than a spire, and the churchyard was planted with yew and trees which produced small, sweet apples, which were freely scrumped by local children.

Some half-remembered protocol insisted that the second left pew of the old church belonged to the occupants of the Red House. On the first Sunday following his removal to the town Mr Charles Barratt walked past the font and looked for a place to sit close to the back of the nave. A series of glances redirected him towards the altar and his allocated spot, which he occupied alone and in a state of mild embarrassment. The next week he made sure to take his cook and valet with him. Johnson, his man, was not a person of unusual stature, but Barratt's broad back and the considerable girth of the cook and her extensive finery meant that the pew was almost full.

The Rectory stood across the high street from the Red House, and Reverend Archer was also Barratt's opposite in a number of other regards. He was a short, slight man with a gentle disposition, fair-skinned, straw-haired and rather witty. He spoke softly, even from the pulpit, meaning that his congregation seemed always to be leaning forward to catch the last word God had spoken. The two men saw each other often, entering or leaving their proximate residences, or out in their carriages. From time to time they would speak, though their converse natures meant that these exchanges were almost as one-sided without the chapel walls as within them. Nothing so definite as a friendship developed between them, but they always acknowledged one another with a gesture of some sort, and when Barratt was absent from his pew one Sunday in May, having travelled to London on business, Reverend Archer sent a letter across the street enquiring after the older man's health. Mr Barratt was moved by the gesture, moved enough, at any rate, to send a note of reassurance along with a block of Somerset cheese upon his return.

The wasp appeared in late September, drawn by the scent of windfalls rotting on the graves, perhaps, but ushered into the church by a drift of leafsmoke. Reverend Archer was offering his modest reflections on Chapter 15 of St John's Gospel, I am the true vine and my father is the husbandman. The Rector's introductory remarks had just concluded when the wasp flew into his mouth and nestled its tail into his tongue. Reverend Archer registered his distress with a piratical sort of exclamation and then, somewhat misguidedly, closed his mouth. The wasp, seeking egress and observing no obvious mechanism whereby this might be readily achieved, did what wasps do when imperilled, and stung again. The Rector loosed another short, guttural squawk and the wasp made its escape, high above the heads of the pious parishioners there gathered.

Mr Charles Barratt was a learned man, and he had read of incidents such as this concluding with the fatal self-suffocation of the victim. Accordingly he rushed to the clergyman's aid, causing almost universal consternation amongst his flock by pinching Reverend Archer's nose so that his mouth opened once more. He pulled at the Rector's tongue in an extraordinarily violent fashion until, satisfied apparently that he could not remove it altogether, he let go.

"People have been known to choke," Barratt explained, walking the Rector down from the pulpit. Reverend Archer, who had suffered several indignities in quick succession and who remained in some discomfort, simply nodded. The two men sat beside one another for a moment in Barratt's pew. The congregation waited. Reverend Archer handed a sheaf of paper to Mr Barratt and placed a hand on his shoulder. Barratt, as we have noted, was not quite as obtuse as his neighbours determined him to be, and he grasped the meaning of these gestures. He stood and walked from the pew while young women clustered instantly around the stricken cleric. Barratt stood beside the pulpit, tall enough already to be seen from any recess in the small church. He cleared his throat, and the horses beyond the lychgate twitched at their tethers. His eyes passed over the part of the manuscript he had already heard.

"Why does God need us?" he began. "Jesus tells the disciples, 'If ye abide in me, and my words abide in you, ye shall ask what ye will, and it shall be done unto you.' God will grant you anything if you simply choose to live in His light. God will love you forever if you let Him abide in your heart." The sacred, reverberate walls of St Andrew's pulsed with each syllable, and the worshippers sat back on their benches as he spoke. Reverend Archer's Oxford rhetoric was reshaped by Barratt into something comprehensible, and unprecedentedly audible. His rich baritone drew images in the perfumed air, and the Rector's argument, which was simple in essence, though a degree less limpid in construction, was compelled into the minds of all who heard it, as if it were a conclusion that they had reached themselves through instinct. Mr Barratt never whispered anywhere but in church, and now he realised that he ought not to constrain himself *a capella*. This was the one place where his being made sense. He became conscious of the attention focused upon him, and found that he rather enjoyed it, his general lack of vanity notwithstanding. He reached the end of the sermon, "Our first responsibility as Christians is to love God as He loves us," appended an "Amen" and then sat down once more, next to the Rector, when two of the younger gentleman's impromptu nurses made way for him. Reverend Archer shook Barratt's hand and tried to offer his thanks, but his tongue was still too sore to form words.

It is to the credit of the ladies of B_____ that in the most general terms Mr Barratt's newly unearthed talent for oratory made as great an impression upon them as his rumoured wealth had, though we might also note here that the former quality did notreplace the latter, but rather laid atop it, like marzipan on a Madeira cake.The bell rang repeatedly in the grand vestibule of the Red House from

Sunday afternoon onwards and Barratt, with some reluctance, ventured once more in to B_____ society. In this narrowest of milieus he was handed from one host to another like a parcel in the children's game and at some point during each afternoon or evening he would be asked to recount how he had rescued the luckless Reverend Archer (there was always another guest who had not witnessed this exploit) and he would oblige, scrupulously minimising his own role and emphasising the admirable stoicism of the young Rector. Then someone would ask, "Was it really necessary to pull his tongue?" and Barratt would explain what he had learned about the venom of certain flying insects and the sudden inflammation that might be caused and obstruction of the airway, until the young ladies present were almost green.

On the Friday after All Soul's a note arrived from the Rectory inviting Barratt to dine the following evening with Reverend Archer and some others. Barratt was already tired of his sudden celebrity but felt that the one person he could not refuse was the protagonist in their small drama. He sent Johnson across the street with a letter and a small caddy of tea.

Barratt knocked at the Rectory at seven the following evening. The church loomed beside the house like a great, dark ship. Lottie, the Rector's occasional maid, opened the door and directed him through to the library. Two women sat laughing on a chaise in front of the curtained windows, somehow managing not to notice Barratt, though he almost filled the doorway. Entering the room he turned and saw Reverend Archer juggling four oranges with remarkable skill.

"So that is what they teach you at Oxford," Barratt said, much more loudly, as ever, than intended. The ladies started, both levitating briefly from the sofa but the Rector, who had become accustomed to his neighbour's sonorous exclamations, was unfazed. He managed to deftly trap two fruit in each hand before placing them alongside another of their kin in a canoe-shaped bowl on an empty bookshelf.

"Mr Barratt, how good of you to come!" said the Rector, who seemed surprised and thrilled that his new guest had made an appearance, though the effort involved in doing so was negligible, and in spite of the fact that the gentleman concerned had made his intentions absolutely clear, in writing, just a few hours previously.

"I'm delighted to be here," said Barratt, bowing slightly. He then turned to the sofa and bowed again, with an exaggerated formality, one arm bent across his waist and the other stiff at his side, as if he were paying obsequy to a dead king. He straightened, and in doing so registered the appearances of the two women for the first time. One was just a girl, about sixteen years of age, he guessed, and pretty of face, in the soft, unformed way of the very young. It was evident that she found Barratt tremendously amusing, though she was genteel enough to attempt to disguise the fact. The other woman was closer to Barratt in age than to the young Rector. She was particularly well-dressed, he thought. Barratt knew very little about fashion and cared less, but he was not an unworldly man and he recognised expensive fabric and decent craftsmanship when he encountered these things. She had an open, intelligent face, her nose was perhaps a little large, but Barratt found himself fascinated by her eyes, which looked upon him with a kind of even curiosity, as if examining an unfamiliar flower. They were of an indeterminate colour, green-brown, or brown-green or grey but whatever their true pigment Barratt remarked only the physical effect that their calm gaze had upon his person, a confusion of sensations, distantly familiar, like a poem learned by heart in adolescence and long since forgotten.

III

"MR BARRATT," the Rector began, "allow me to introduce my cousin, Mrs Walker, and her daughter Lucy. Ladies, this is Mr Charles Barratt."

"The man of the hour!" Lucy said, enraptured. Barratt found himself bowing again and searching for some morsel of wit with which to deprecate his own achievements but the plate was bare.

"I feel, yes," he said, and Miss Lucy immediately concluded that it was her epithet which had caught the handsome old man off guard. She giggled softly to herself and for a moment an uneasy silence ruled, until Mrs Walker spoke.

"Please sit down, Mr Barratt." Her voice was soft, like her cousin's, but possessed a greater undertone of mischief, or irony. Barratt urgently wished not to appear ridiculous in front of this woman, not any more ridiculous at least, and this instinct was itself unsettling as typically he paid little attention to what others thought of him. He was not in any case a man who progressed through life in the free, graceful manner of the Rector, and the effect of this anxiety was to inhibit his movement still further so that when he attempted to comply with Mrs Walker's request he did so in an awkward and convoluted fashion, stretching a long arm behind his back to locate, eventually, the arm of the chair, before lowering himself into it in discrete stages.

"Would you like something to drink, Barratt?" the Rector asked. Mr Barratt had no idea whether he wanted a drink or not. He considered the matter for a moment.

"Sherry," he barked, before he could change his mind. "Any kind. Please."

"Of course." Reverend Archer disappeared in the direction of the kitchen. Barratt stared at his boots. They were very smart, he thought, with a good shine on them. The boots restored his spirits, he would have to remember to thank Johnson in some way. Thus buoyed he lifted his gaze to Mrs Walker and managed to smile.

"I'm not used to society," he said, as softly as he could. "You must excuse me if I forget my manners, or if they seem old-fashioned. I have only recently started going out again."

"John mentioned that you lived in London," Lucy said. "Surely you must have enjoyed the society there?" Mrs Walker took her daughter's wrist and pinched it lightly.

"When I was younger, perhaps. But I have kept myself to myself for a long time."

"I suppose that it is easier to go unnoticed in the city," Mrs Walker said. "Here in B_____ we are unwilling to leave anyone to their own devices." Barratt wilted somewhat beneath the sympathetic glance which accompanied this comment, but stared once more at the reflection of the fireplace on his boot, and this gave him courage.

"You live in B_____ then, Mrs Walker? I am surprised not to have seen you or Miss Lucy before. It is quite a small town, after all, and I have been here myself for a year now."

"I lived here until I was married," Mrs Walker explained. "And now Meadholme is let, that is the house of my late husband, Lucy and I have decided to return. We will be staying here with John until we find somewhere that suits us."

Reverend Archer reappeared with a bottle in one hand and three schooners in the other. For a moment Barratt was concerned that his host might essay an encore to his earlier performance, but the Rector placed the crystalware on the empty bookshelf without further legerdemain and poured two glasses.

"Will you join us, Susannah?" The two cousins then engaged in some badinage while Barratt replayed the sound of her name in his mind, as one might repeat a favourite phrase on the pianoforte. There was a pleasant musicality about it, he thought; it was a name which possessed both rhythm and emphasis.

"Mr Barratt is quite lost in a reverie." Her voice, warm and gently mocking, coaxed him back into the conversation.

"Excuse me," he said, "I was thinking about something else."

"I was telling Mrs Walker that you were renowned as a local Epicurus before, that is, you revealed yourself as Demosthenes," said Reverend Archer. "So if anyone could accurately assess the quality of my sherry it would be you. And you will be honest, terribly so I fear." He handed a glass to Barratt who sipped from it. The wine suffered from having spent too little time in the barrel and too long in the bottle, he thought, but it was drinkable.

"Not bad," he said, and he saw Archer and Mrs Walker laughing with what seemed like an affectionate amusement. Rather than feeling condescended to he felt included in a circle of private amity, and once more found himself moved by unfamiliar emotions.

"You are upset with us, Mr Barratt," said Mrs Walker, registering the strain on the older man's face.

"On the contrary, I am very pleased to be in such generous company," Barratt said, smiling at Mrs Walker. Reverend Archer was still chuckling to himself. "'Not bad,' he says. We'll make a diplomat of you yet, Mr Barratt."

"I fear it may be too late in the day for me to switch professions," Mr Barratt answered. Miss Lucy, who had begun to feel excluded, somewhat, from the conversation and who rarely allowed such a state of affairs to persist for very long, chose this moment to reinsert herself.

"You are not so very old, Mr Barratt, I shouldn't have thought. What are you, five and forty?" A firmer pinch was applied.

"You are very kind, my dear, but I might be your grandfather, almost," Barratt said. "I shall be one and fifty this year."

"Well," Miss Lucy began, feeling a threatening pressure on her arm, "you look very vigorous for it. And altogether too tall to be my grandfather." They laughed again, the four of them, and Mrs Walker undid the loving manacle she had placed on her only child and stroked her hand instead, with a small pout of pride and approval.

The Rector's cook was a temporary person of no great reputation, but was, however, relentless in her determination to never serve anything raw. The potatoes were blackened husks and the duck, prepared in honour of Mr Barratt, was desiccated. This latter dish was almost rescued by the gentleman guest's suggestion of squeezing the juice of Reverend Archer's juggling balls over the stringy flesh of the bird, but the meal was a disaster, which all four diners nevertheless greatly enjoyed. The Rector whispered apologies between each dire mouthful, and even Miss Lucy was allowed a glass of wine by way of recompense for the series of catastrophes that were presented as cuisine. Once a mysterious pudding was all but rejected Mr Barratt sent across the road for cheese and bread, as they had barely managed to eat half a meal amongst them. Reverend Archer offered profuse thanks to his makeshift staff nevertheless and sent them on their way a little richer, perhaps, than the quality of their service might have warranted. Lottie was reminded to return the following morning and Reverend Archer reminded himself never to allow the cook to cross his threshold again unless it was under some specific spiritual pretext.

Barratt feigned tiredness when it seemed polite to do so, and made a small joke about the Rector's responsibilities a few hours hence which was very well received. He might happily have stayed in their company until the bells of St Andrew's summoned them. Instead he crossed the road, feeling like he could sing almost, then he laid awake until two in the morning, thinking of the eyes of Susannah Walker, and hoping that he might see them again soon in daylight and at last determine their colour.

IV

HE ASKED JOHNSON to shave him again in the morning, to trim his hair and to singe his ears. The cook had been excused on an errand for her mother, so as the church bells sang into bright air just the two men crossed the road, the larger of them noticeably pink about the jaws and neck.

Faces turned towards Barratt as he entered the church and as ever he returned each smile and nod but did so on this particular Sunday with a deeper sense of pleasure, which in turn illuminated the faces of those who caught his gaze. We are all more disposed to like people who are happy and while the gentleman from the City had never been disliked, his personality had perhaps been misunderstood. The transformation in his mood and bearing encouraged the rest of the congregation to engage with him more fully, so that one or two of them mumbled "Morning, Mr Barratt," to him. Barratt was quite incapable of mumbling, of course, and reciprocated these greetings as if he were drilling infantrymen.

He ushered Johnson to the end of the second bench and stooped in alongside him, leaving a space to his left large enough to accommodate the petite Walker family. The two ladies had not arrived as Reverend Archer took to the pulpit. By the time that the Rector's sermon commenced Barratt had become resigned to the likelihood that they would not make an appearance. It was not a Sunday of any great liturgical significance, so he thought it possible that they chose not to attend on Ordinary days.

Mr Barratt himself went to church every Sunday only because it had been the habit of his late wife, Catherine. Any importance he might have attached to the service had been erased by her death, however, and while he might enjoy a particular hymn or well-argued sermon the words held no more profound meaning for him than a nursery rhyme or a riddle. The irony of his situation, which he did not fail to recognise, is that he persisted with his own superstitious ritual knowing that the dead could not stand in judgment against him any more than the God in whom he no longer believed. He was certain that Catherine could not perceive him, that they would never be reunited, that no other world existed, that death was not a gateway, unless what lay beyond the gate was absence and oblivion. Nevertheless he dressed himself for church every Sunday and had done so each week for the fifteen years since her passing, because it brought him comfort. It was dishonest, he recognised, but it was a dishonesty which injured no-one as far as he could tell. There was a surfeit of misery in the world, and if one were to make a ledger of it this small lie reduced the sum total. This had been the case at least, since Barratt had removed to B_____, and for many years before that, but as we shall see, in a world as imagined by Mr Barratt, governed only by chance, an omission or misrepresentation of this kind, once exposed, can have unfortunate consequences.

Mrs Walker and her daughter were unwell. Barratt did not linger after the service to obtain this information from the Rector directly, instead he sent Johnson across the street with a letter of thanks for the previous evening's hospitality and Lottie relayed what she knew. Both ladies were stricken with some gastric discomfort, Lottie suspected that the fish was the cause, as it was not of the freshest, a fact which the temporary cook had attempted to disguise with butter and strong herbs. Barratt's stomach performed a sudden somerset at the news. He dismissed Johnson, who had Sunday afternoons to himself, then sought out his sleeping powders, which he had learned were effective for all kinds of bodily pain. Having transferred some of the stuff into an empty vial he copied out Smith's instructions on dosage and took the bottle and accompanying recipe to the Rectory.

"For the ladies' comfort," he explained to Lottie.

"Would you like to come in, Sir?"

"No thank you," Barratt said. He walked back to the Red House and sat close to the parlour window, cleaning his long-neglected pipe without filling it, and looking back across the street from time to time, until it grew dark.

The next morning Barratt was obliged to travel to London to see his lawyer on a matter of conveyancing. He left early, so that his horses might be fed and rested midway. The day was fine but cold, even for November, and small clouds of steam came from the beasts as they stood waiting at the door of the Red House.

19

"They are fine creatures, Johnson, are they not?" Barratt said.

"Indeed, sir," the valet responded. "Are we ready?" Johnson was suspicious of any alteration in his master's spirits. For him change meant instability; he had been comfortably employed and generously rewarded for twenty years of service, had greatly enjoyed the food and wine that Barratt took no real pleasure in, and was thus opposed to anything which might disturb the monotony of the household's shared existence. Master Charles was not himself, and it wouldn't do.

Barratt's mood had darkened by the time the two men arrived in the city. The house on Whitecross Street stood empty, save for two rooms on the first floor. Johnson removed sailcloths from the furniture and lit a fire. They ate at a chophouse that evening, in a familiar, melancholic silence which was a balm to the valet's perturbed soul. On Tuesday morning they travelled first to Chancery Lane and then back to Finsbury and the churchyard where Catherine Barratt lay with the unnamed daughter who had survived her by just a day. Mr Barratt cleared leaves from the ledgerstone with the sleeve of his greatcoat then knelt beside the grave. His man remained with the carriage but from a distance of perhaps three chains he heard his master sobbing, and saw the heaving of his broad shoulders, and when Mr Barratt stood again after a quarter of an hour the knees of his breeches were smeared with mud.

They arrived back in B_____ just after sunset, having stopped again to rest the two mares and to endure another wordless repast. There was a note of thanks from the Rectory which Barratt read quickly then threw into the cold fireplace. Johnson offered to prepare something for supper, the cook was away until Wednesday morning, but Mr Barratt professed that he had no appetite and would take himself betimes to bed. He put on his nightclothes though it was barely evening and lay in bed, attempting to empty his mind of all thoughts. Then, as was his custom, he bade goodnight to his dead wife, and to their dear child and waited for sleep to come.

V

MRS WALKER AND Miss Lucy recovered quickly from whatever ailed them. They sat on the foremost bench in church the following Sunday, across the aisle from Barratt and his household. When the two ladies greeted their neighbour after the service they were confused to discover that he was once more awkward and formal with them, as if they were not already acquainted. Barratt, for his part, experienced an obscure sense of shame as he acknowledged Mrs Walker, and found that he could not look at her. Miss Lucy offered her thanks for the efficacious remedy that he had been kind enough to provide and Barratt nodded and smiled and reassured the young lady that it had caused him no inconvenience whatsoever and that he was sorry not have been of greater assistance to both Miss Lucy and her mother.

Mrs Walker saw the gentleman's smile fade as he made reference to her and wondered briefly what she might have said or done to provoke such a reaction. She was a woman of keen intelligence and discernment however, except in matters concerning her only child, whom she understandably overindulged, and in a very few moments she guessed the truth. It seemed that Mr Barratt had formed a slight attachment to her and had some reason to regret these feelings. Mrs Walker was amused rather than flattered by this realisation but she determined at once that she should revise the teasing manner in which, during their briefest of acquaintanceships, she had come to address Mr Barratt. To mock him, however gently or affectionately, would be to apply a kind of small torture. She regarded Barratt with an unaccustomed froideur which Miss Lucy, still dwelling under the misconception that it was her youthful pulchritude which had agitated the old man, found rather baffling.

"We must bid you farewell, Mr Barratt," her mother said. "We have already imposed upon you unnecessarily." Barratt and Mrs Walker then nodded to each other like the very worst of sworn enemies, their eyes never quite meeting, and Miss Lucy was dragged somewhat along the aisle and out into the crisp, November air.

Relations between the two households deteriorated detectably as Christmas approached. Reverend Archer and his young cousin were as puzzled by this trajectory as Johnson, across the street, was gratified. This latter person, it should be noted, would never have sabotaged any chance that his master might have at happiness, no *billet-doux* would have been misplaced had any been sent, nor any kind of Shakespearean miscommunication allowed to persist, but while Johnson recognised and enjoyed the pleasures of an uncomplicated existence with his employer he also admired him, and wished to protect him from the kind of all-encompassing despair from which Barratt, he felt, was still recovering.

Miss Lucy wondered if perhaps Mr Barratt had confessed the affectionate feelings he had for her to her mother, and that this was the cause of their falling out, but she was far too frightened of Mrs Walker to ask. Reverend Archer, who was a degree more sensible observed that Barratt's manner was not so greatly altered towards Miss Lucy and himself as it was towards Mrs Walker. One evening, after Miss Lucy had retired, the Rector sat reading by candlelight while Mrs Walker petted a cat on the sofa. He closed his book, and looked at her.

"Susannah, may I ask you something?"

"Of course you may."

"Has some disagreement arisen between you and Charles Barratt?" Mrs Walker laughed briefly.

"Not at all," she said, "but I appreciate how one might reach that conclusion." Reverend Archer, who listened more purposefully than he spoke, waited for further explanation. "He likes me, John, but for some reason it distresses him."

"He likes you?"

"Yes," she answered. It seems improbable, after spending so little time in each other's company, but I am sure he has developed feelings for me."

"He wishes to romance you, then?"

"Don't be cruel, John, the man is in difficulty."

"I fail to see what the difficulty is," Reverend Archer said. "He need only declare his intentions, and then see how the die lands."

"He is not like you, and you know it. Half the pretty girls in England have rejected you."

"Aye," said the Rector, "and some of the less pretty ones too." They laughed together and then were silent for a moment, looking not at each other but at the chair in which Barratt had sat a few weeks before.

"What do you know about him, John?"

"Oh, very little. He is wealthy, so you need have no concerns on that front. They say he has a small fleet of ships which sail in convoy to India and back, but that may just be gossip. He is a widower. Rather a sad man, I think, and shy."

"Anything else?" she asked.

"He is quite tall," Reverend Archer said. "And unusually broad."

"Thank you, cousin. That is very helpful." She shooed the cat from her lap and stood, then crossed the room to her cousin and kissed his cheek. "Good night, John," she said. "Save your eyes, go to bed soon yourself."

"I shall," he said, but opened his book again. "One further question, Susannah." She turned and put down her candlestick. "If you are so concerned about our poor neighbour why have you allowed him to believe that you are hostile towards him?"

"I did not wish to encourage him," she said, "if doing so caused him discomfort. I do not believe I have been impolite to Mr Barratt, rather I have been a looking-glass to his own formality. And it seems that his own feelings are not so strong that they can overcome whatever scruple prevents him from admitting his infatuation."

"You are insulted, then, because he does not declare his affection, though you admit that you have offered him nothing but discouragement, is that correct?" Reverend Archer looked at Mrs Walker with the same kind of satirical smile that she commonly employed with her younger cousin.

"Good night, John," she said again.

Mrs Walker knocked on the front door of the Red House just before eight the next morning. Johnson opened the door and raised an impertinent eyebrow.

"Mr Barratt is eating his breakfast," he said.

"Who's there, Johnson?" his master bellowed from within.

"It is Mrs Walker, sir." She heard a crashing of cutlery and then Barratt appeared, shoeless, in the vestibule. He raced forward, bowing as he came, in the cadence of an angry bull.

"Mrs Walker," he said with his customary ferocity, "an honour! An honour! Do come in, excuse me, I slept late and am just now having my breakfast. On Market Day! It is unforgivable, come in, come in." Mrs Walker had meant to adjust her demeanour gradually but found that she was unable to contain her amusement. "How kind of you to smile," he went on. "Yes, we're not usually in such a mess as this." His voice rang around the marble hallway and Mrs Walker followed him through to the dining room. "Would you mind terribly if I finished my breakfast?"

Barratt sat in front of a plate of bread and poached eggs and Mrs Walker sat beside him, across the corner of the table, still wearing her coat.

"I wanted to talk to you, Charles," she said. Barratt lifted his eyes from the food, panicked rather, by the sound of his own name. Mrs Walker said nothing further, she was looking at the portrait of the young woman, suspended in air behind Mr Barratt like some saintly protector. He put down his knife and wiped his mouth. In his left hand a fork remained, pointing at the ceiling.

"My wife, Catherine," he said. "It has been very difficult to live without her." He dropped the fork on to the table cloth and Mrs Walker reached across and placed her hand on his. Barratt looked at his guest and saw that her eyes were bright with tears.

VI

THE SEASON OF peace and goodwill came to B_____ and its blessings fell like the first snow on the Red House and the Rectory. Reverend Archer was absent a good deal more than usual, visiting parishioners or directing the beautification of St Andrew's, but when he did arrive home Mr Barratt frequently accompanied him, and the two men would disappear into the Rector's study to talk and smoke their pipes (Barratt having resumed the habit.) Reverend Archer had some Whiggish tendencies which Barratt thought naive and much of their conversation was taken up with his attempts to make his young friend see sense on one point or another. Barratt was not especially a political creature, and saw most problems through the eyeglass of pragmatism.

"I have seen a good deal of the world, John, and there is a darkness to it which for you is somehow imperceptible." This, after a third glass of wine, was the beginning of one such lecture, delivered with a comparable energy to that with which he had embodied the Rector's own words, back in the autumn. "This is a prosperous town," he continued, as the study door rattled in its frame, "and may grow more so. Yet there are people in the south end who see nothing of this prosperity, or rather they see it, as it rolls past in its carriage, but do not partake of it."

"The parish of St Jude provides for those people. I know that you have sent flour in sackfuls to Reverend Halliwell."

"What I do, what the parish does is immaterial. There are people, not you John, but people like you, who say that the poor must be put to work. They are not living but surviving, as it is, and you Whigs would enslave them. So yes, they must work, but they must be paid well enough that can sustain themselves, paid well enough that they can be taxed, paid enough that they don't slip into apathy and vice."

"You cannot make work where there is none, Barratt. And even if you could, it would be abstract labour, or the kind of cruel work that convicts are set to. How can that be rewarded?"

"First, you think about what people, what the society needs. Then you employ these people in the fulfilment of that need. Better still you get them to employ each other in some small enterprise. The parish, or some other benefactor, provides capital at a fair rate of interest, and may even see some return. What happens now? The money drains away from the parish in one direction, or is spent in greater sums on the construction and maintenance of houses of misery."

The ladies of the Rectory heard only half of these exchanges and were not invited to offer their own perspectives as all discussion of such matters ceased when Barratt and Reverend Archer emerged, smelling of pipesmoke, ruddy with the vigour of their dispute, and also perhaps as a result of the wine they had consumed, into the library. In the company of their gentler counterparts the two men assumed an aspect of dull politesse and they spoke about the weather, or whichever book Mrs Walker happened to be reading, until Barratt took his leave. He and Mrs Walker had reached no firm understanding since her morning visit, but this expedition had proven beneficial to them both. She now knew that while Mr Barratt admired her, he remained so attached to his late wife that it was improbable that he would ever profess his affection or passion for another woman, even if he managed wholly to acknowledge those feelings. Barratt, for his part, was reassured that Mrs Walker did not find him either ridiculous or despicable. From time to time he would recall the sensation of Mrs Walker placing her hand on his, and remember how he felt looking into her shining eyes (they were a very light brown, he had eventually established) and his face would burn as if it were a warm day and Johnson had neglected to sharpen the razor.

Mrs Walker and Miss Lucy were not blind to the plight of the poor, of course, and it was not unusual for the older lady to excuse herself from the Rectory on some pretext, even in the worst of weather, and traipse in her heaviest boots to the south end to distribute alms. If Mr Barratt happened to notice Mrs Walker leaving, from his vantage point in the parlour window of the Red House, he would send Johnson, armed with swordstick and billy club, to follow her at a discreet distance. Since Barratt spent a great deal of his time looking across the street at the Rectory, his eyes lifting from whatever he was reading between each sentence, or at any sign of movement at the periphery of his vision, Mrs Walker was rarely unaccompanied on these charitable sorties.

It was a long winter. The year turned and three months of bare trees and hard frosts ensued. Mr Barratt occasionally entertained one or other of his more intrepid acquaintances. Mr Cunningham, who was quite elderly, dined at the Red House on a bitterly cold Saturday evening in January, and the carriage of Sir Clifford Foulke, erstwhile mayor of B_____ appeared more than once at Barratt's door in the weeks which followed. Though it was not the return to his employer's hermitic London lifestyle which Johnson might have preferred, he was untroubled nevertheless by the visits of these senior gentlemen, who ate and drank in moderation, played leisurely games of chess, and talked about matters which may have engaged the attention of Mr Barratt, but were of no interest at all to his valet. Across the street Mrs Walker and Miss Lucy put off their house-hunting until the Spring and the cook came from Meadholme, somewhat to the chagrin of the thrifty Rector.

Easter was early that year and the children of St Andrew's, bundled up in hats, scarves, gloves and thick overcoats, hunted for eggs amongst stubborn patches of snow in the churchyard. The cold prevented any lingering in church and Barratt remained at an amicable distance from the woman he admired, even in the milder climate of the Rectory library. Miss Lucy was gratified that despite the thawing of relations between her mother and Mr Barratt she was still very much his favourite, greeted always with the broadest of smiles and the deepest of bows.

April arrived, bringing rain showers and warmer days, daffodils stood in sudden arrays amongst the graves and along the narrow verge beside the church wall, and Mrs Walker, in consultation with her daughter, decided to drop any pretence at looking for alternative accommodation, instead offering her cousin a monthly stipend, for which Reverend Archer was tremendously grateful, as the sum offered for the three ladies' upkeep (the cook now having taken the Rectory's last remaining room, on the understanding that she might, at any point, be obliged to remove to The Bull, were any further family members to be accommodated) was a good dealmore than any contribution he might have dared to request.

"Cousin John," said Lucy, one sweet-scented morning, "it is a pity, is it not, that there are no assembly rooms here in B_____?"

"It is indeed a grave oversight," the Rector replied. "Was there anyone in particular with whom you wished to assemble?" Miss Lucy ignored this exploratory thrust.

"There is the corn exchange, I suppose, but in such a place one would be rather fearful of dust."

"Our corn exchange is less dusty than many assembly rooms, I'll wager," the Rector said.

"And you have visited many assembly rooms," Mrs Walker said, laughing. "An unusual number, perhaps, for a clergyman." Lucy attempted to rescue Reverend Archer.

"Mama says that you are a wonderful dancer."

"He has had a great deal of practice," Mrs Walker observed.

"Your mother has been known to shake a leg too, dear Lucy," the Rector said."Her own skills and experience in this area are not as limited as she might have led you to believe." The young woman squealed at this information.

"Is it true, Mama?"

"Your cousin is too young altogether to remember my dancing days, Lucy, but yes, of course I have danced. There is no shame in it, even for a Rector."

"And yet you tease me, Susannah, without remorse."

Lottie announced Mr Charles Barratt and he loomed momentarily in the doorway. "We do not often see you in the morning, Charles," the Rector said. "Welcome!" Barratt entered the dining room and attempted a general bow.

"The roads are dry and I am heading into London. I wondered..." He was interrupted by Miss Lucy, who pulled him by the arm into a dining chair. "I wondered if I might obtain anything on your behalf." He looked at Mrs Walker and released a silent sigh. "For any of you."

"You must lavish gifts upon us," Miss Lucy said.

"Ignore her," instructed Mrs Walker. "We are all quite content."

"Yes, yes," said the Rector. "You have been far too generous, Charles. We could not possibly allow ourselves to become further indebted to you."

"It's really no trouble."

"When shall you return, Mr Barratt?" asked Mrs Walker.

"I will only be away two nights," he said.

"Mother and I are planning a dance," Miss Lucy said. "A benefit dance, for Mr Nicholson's Trust. You know him, I believe?"

"Mr Nicholson? No, we haven't met. I know of him, of course, my friends speak of him."

What Mr Barratt had heard of this gentleman was not encouraging, and he realised that he would have to find some way to dissuade the ladies of the Rectory from associating with Mr Nicholson. It was not the moment. Reverend Archer and his cousins wished Barratt a safe journey. Mr Barratt stood and collected his hat from Lottie. He bowed once more before speaking.

"Miss Lucy, would you consider keeping your plans secret until I return? It would be an honour to assist you and your mother in arranging the dance, and as you know I am so little employed over there in the Red House." Miss Lucy nodded and blushed somewhat and Mr Barratt ducked out of the front door, put on his hat, crossed to his carriage and rolled away northwards without once looking behind him.

VII

IT WAS TRUE that Mr Barratt and Mr Nicholson were not acquainted, but they had seen one another, and Barratt had made it his business to learn more about the other man.

On a warm afternoon midway through the previous August Barratt had stepped out from the Red House to smell the air. He walked towards the centre of town hatless, and in his shirtsleeves. Across the high street, outside The Bull was an open carriage, a beautiful low thing, which seemed to be balanced on air above its wheels. Its paintwork, framed by delicate lines of gilt, reflected the street scene like a dark mirror. A pair of black geldings with feathered headdresses kicked at the ground between the shafts. There was no coachman present, but a small boy stood holding the reins. Barratt was a man of plain tastes, for the most part, but he appreciated fine workmanship so he crossed the street to look more closely at this conveyance. The boy watched him as crouched to examine the springs. Barratt stroked the back of the nearside horse and felt in his pocket for a coin, which he handed to the child before walking a short distance on. He stopped again to wipe his brow with his kerchief and heard the boy shouting behind him.

"You said sixpence!" For a moment Barratt imagined that the child had some plot in mind against his own person. Turning to rebuke the young ruffian for his cheek he saw the boy pulling at the coattails of a long-haired gentleman, who, it seemed, had just emerged from the inn. The man carried a stick of some dark wood with a bright silver head like a billiard ball. He was a tall, angular fellow, and his eyes exhibited an alarming wildness, Barratt thought. The man raised his stick to swing at the child, but sensed the approach of a large figure, a person whom he did not recognise but who seemed to possess a certain authority, who carried himself with the air of someone who would not hesitate to disarm him and beat him with his own weapon. The man lowered his stick and shook his coat from the boy's hand before throwing some coins at his feet. He then appeared to dismiss Barratt and the boy from his consciousness, calmly mounting the box of his carriage before twitching the reins and proceeding southwards along the high street.

"What is that man's name?" Barratt asked the boy.

"Don't know," the child replied, appending his opinion of the gentleman in question, using a specific vocabulary the like of which Mr Barratt had not heard since leaving London many months earlier. Barratt frowned at the violent emphasis of the boy's language but gave him another coin. As he walked on towards the empty marketplace the frown, which was only a confection of moral duty in the first place, turned into a broad smile.

A few days later, over plates of a light mutton stew, he recalled the incident to his guest, the aged Mr Cunningham. It was a very warm evening, but Cunningham sat at the dining table in a crimson velvet frockcoat, which, Barratt suspected, was very nearly as ancient as the venerable gentleman himself. The old man was rather hard of hearing which allowed Barratt to express himself at his natural volume, and Cunningham appreciated the company of a gentleman whose voice he did not have to strain his ears to make out.

"I thought it strange," Mr Barratt concluded, "that a fellow might maintain such a grand carriage, with such fine horses and yet drive it himself." He waited while Mr Cunningham chewed, sipped at his claret, then chewed again, before swallowing and gathering himself to speak.

"I have no doubt that the person you encountered was Mr Henry Nicholson, and that his coachman has resigned temporarily because of some abuse, remunerative or otherwise, which he has suffered at the hands of that gentleman."

"Temporarily, you say? What's that?"

"Mr Nicholson and his coachman are dependent on one another," Cunningham explained, "to the extent that the latter fellow, Buller is his name I believe, is too rough to be employed by anyone other than Mr Nicholson. Nicholson cannot afford anyone better, meanwhile, and no sensible man would work for such a person."

"I suspected that he was no gallant," Barratt said. "Who is he?"

"He is a person of no importance, really. An idler, a gambler. I knew his grandfather, he was the First member for Bletchingley, though a good man with it. His father and I were close friends, like thieves at a fair, and his mother was a kindly woman. But as the Bard reminds us, good wombs have borne bad sons. Henry has lost everything, the house and stables are mortgaged, and I suspect the only income he has is from the Trust."

"He is not quite penniless, then," said Barratt. "I shall withhold my sympathy."

"You should do well to do so," Cunningham answered, suddenly and untypically angry. "The wicked thing is not that he has squandered his inheritance and stained the name of his parents, any foolish young man might do the same. The Trust I speak of is a Charitable Trust, Mr Barratt, established for the relief of the poor. My suspicion is that Mr Nicholson is stealing from the mouths of hungry children." Barratt savoured these words for a moment.

"How is that possible, he cannot be the sole trustee, surely? And if you have these suspicions so must others, how can the Trust survive in an atmosphere of mistrust?"

"Henry Nicholson is a man of weak character," Cunningham said, "but he is not unintelligent. He chairs the board and is indebted to all the other trustees. They are prepared to behave as Lord Nelson at Copenhagen, if there remains some hope of recompense. Who is to say that all of these men, most of them apparently respectable citizens, are not complicit or acting as Nicholson does? He has secured their positions as trustees after all. As for the Trust, it is my experience that very often the wealthy wish only to relieve their consciences where the poor are concerned, rather than to relieve any actual suffering. By contributing to Nicholson's Trust they fulfil their own needs, and are scarcely interested in the needs of those whom the Trust purports to assist." Barratt stood up from the table at this point, and walked back and forth across the dining room, beneath the cool gaze of his late wife.

"How certain of your case are you, Cunningham? Should you not expose him?"

"I know no way of proving it, Mr Barratt, but I am certain enough."

"There is always a way," Barratt said. "Sometimes unpleasant means are required to reveal the path, but it is always there."

Barratt had not seen Mr Nicholson since, and had not thought of him until Miss Lucy had mentioned his name. As he rolled towards the city, oblivious to the glorious rebirth of the Surrey countryside at each side of the carriage, his mind focused on a man he had seen for just a few seconds, several months before. He had formed no positive impression of Henry Nicholson during that encounter. By nature Barratt was reluctant to rely on hearsay to determine his opinion of any man, though Cunningham was scarcely a gossip. Mr Barratt recognised that what he had already seen and heard would tend to prejudice any interview between him and Mr Nicholson, so the utility of such a meeting was itself obscure. Nevertheless a certainty grew within him that they were on converging paths, and that a collision was inevitable; some kind of reckoning awaited Nicholson, and he, Barratt, would be involved in bringing it about.

VIII

MR BARRATT RETURNED from London with gifts for all at the Rectory. Lottie and Mrs Walker's cook were particularly pleased to be remembered. Reverend Archer received a copy of Ricardo's *Principles*, Miss Lucy was given a silver card case with the initial letters of her name engraved upon it and for Mrs Walker, a person whose beauty, he insisted, needed no adornment, Barratt had brought a piece of carved amber, the colour of her eyes, shaped into a swag or volution, and attached to a slender gold chain.

"You must go to London every week," said Miss Lucy. "What a pity that there is no printer here in B_____"

"No assembly rooms, no printer," the Rector remarked. "What a backwards spot you poor ladies have removed to! However have we managed, eh, Charles?" Mr Barratt had omitted to listen to this last interjection and only acknowledged Reverend Archer when he heard his own name pronounced.

"I'm sorry, John, what was that?" Reverend Archer turned to Barratt, expecting to see his friend gazing distractedly at Mrs Walker, as was his habit, but instead perceived that Mr Barratt was staring out of the library window, with a look of great concentration, like a cat stalking a bird. "I must go," Barratt said, before the Rector could repeat himself. "John, ladies, I bid you good day."

"What I have in mind is a stationery shop," Barratt explained, barely half an hour later, "which might also serve as a lending library. And a printworks."

"Why not also offer blacksmithing?" said Sir Clifford, in whose drawing room the two men sat. "You could reshoe the customer's horses while they browsed your wares."

"There are already two forges in B_____, and it would be imprudent, I think, to juxtapose fire and paper." Barratt looked at Sir Clifford, a round, ruddy man of similar age, who was smiling at him with a faintly paternal air. "You are joking, I see. This is no castle in Spain, my dear friend, nor is it an enterprise by which I expect to amass a fortune."

"If anyone has the wherewithal to make this emporium a success then it is you, Charles, I am sure of it. I would be happy to contribute, of course." Barratt raised a hand.

"Sir Clifford, your generosity is overwhelming, but I came here for advice." Mr Barratt stood and walked the length of the drawing and back. "Cunningham seems to think that you were offered a seat on the board of the Old B_____ Charitable Trust, but declined the honour, is that true?"

"It's true, yes."

"Our friend also informed me of his suspicions that the board was made up of gentlemen to whom Henry Nicholson, the chair, was personally indebted."

"Cunningham is a cute old fellow, is he not? He cannot know this for certain."

"No," Barratt replied, "he admitted as much."

"Well, then."

"I do not mean any offence, sir," said Barratt. "It is my wish that I may proceed in a certain course of action without causing any injury, albeit inadvertent, to those who have been most welcoming to me in this town. I am conscious that I may be regarded by some as a sort of parvenu, and so I am. I have occupied the Red House for a little under two years and there are decent people of our age whose families have lived here since the time of Alfred, and who scarcely travel more than five miles from St Andrew's." Sir Clifford laughed.

"Well, I suspect my lot were Norman," he said. "Not that that means much nowadays. Lady Foulke maintains that my nose bleeds if I have to go beyond Godalming."

"Does Henry Nicholson owe you money, Sir Clifford?"

"No, he does not, Charles. What is this about? Have you taken up the law since I saw you last?" Barratt was relieved by the untroubled manner in which his friend responded, and contemplated the possibility that he might embark upon the course he had set without further testing the limits of Sir Clifford's forbearance, and might have done so had the risk inherent to his plan fallen only upon his, Mr Barratt's shoulders, but he could not yet be certain that this was the case.

"Not quite a lawyer yet, Sir Clifford, though with the reassurance that I mean only to protect you, rather than prosecute you, will you allow me to ask two more lawyer's questions?"

"Please do."

"At the time when you were offered a position on the board of the Trust were you owed money by Henry Nicholson?"

"I was," Sir Clifford said, "but the debt was repaid in full shortly thereafter."

"Did you never question where the money came from?" Barratt stood above his friend and beyond the drawing room windows the clouds parted so that sunlight filled the room. Sir Clifford squinted up at Barratt, visibly discomfited. He did not answer. "This is what I propose. I will approach the board of trustees and tell them the truth, that I wish to invest a significant sum to relieve the suffering of the poor in B_____. I will stress that I require the money to be prudently distributed and that accordingly I wish to see their ledgers to establish whether I am better advised to place a sum with them or to establish a Trust of my own."

"Your presumption is that they will not agree to this, Barratt. What happens if they do?"

"I will examine the accounts. If I find nothing out of place I will make my donation, Miss Lucy will have her dance and I will denounce Cunningham as the most foolish and interfering gossipmonger who ever wore red. I shall return here, with a begging bowl, and we will still build our shop. Perhaps the Trust may be persuaded to invest in our project, who can say?" The idea pleased Sir Clifford. He was a good man, though one in whom a distaste for agitation of any sort had bred a complacency which was not altogether to be commended. His smile faded, however, when he considered the improbability of this outcome.

"Cunningham is neither a fool, nor a gossip," said Sir Clifford.

"No, he is not. I suspect that the very best we can hope for is that he has exaggerated the degree to which the Trust is corrupt, and that the fault lies with Nicholson alone, though it is difficult to see how that might be the case."

"It is your intention to expose him then?"

"I do not wish to ruin him, particularly," said Barratt, "but if there is such a thing as natural justice he must be obliged to desist and to give back what he has embezzled. I would grant him the opportunity for reparation before I turned to the High Court."

"The Trust's refusal to accept your donation on these terms would not be enough, in terms of proof, to involve the Sheriff though."

"No," Barratt admitted. "It would merely confirm what Cunningham suspects: that there is something false about the Trust. I would discover the rest." Sir Clifford pulled his pipe from his pocket and filled it. He took a match from a box on a side table, struck it and sucked the tobacco into life. Barratt watched his friend's cheeks expand and empty like the throat of a bullfrog. Satisfied that his pipe was lit Sir Clifford gestured at the window with the mouthpiece, indicating their mutual friend at some indistinct point beyond the glass.

"Cunningham, when did he tell you about this?"

"Towards the end of August, I think," said Barratt.

"The two of you have not discussed the matter since, I imagine?"

"No, actually. I confess that I have been distracted by other things."

"I quite understand," Sir Clifford said, "it seems unlikely, however, that the attention of our dear old friend was similarly diverted, though I imagine there are a number of plump widows whose sincerest wish is to make his last few years more comfortable." Barratt missed Sir Clifford's thrust altogether. "There is a reason, perhaps, why Mr Cunningham has not spoken of Nicholson since your first discussion."

"I myself had not thought of the man until three mornings ago," said Barratt. "I told you my news when I arrived."

"It seems probable that Cunningham thinks of him every day. Henry Nicholson is busy besmirching the name of a man he admired above all others, loved even. We have dined together, the three of us, half a dozen times since August, and I am sure that you have visited with Cunningham and he with you many times in my absence, so it is unusual that the subject of this young scoundrel has not been raised, is it not?"

"I feel as if you are circling around a conclusion without reaching it," Barratt said. "Please speak more plainly, you are certainly no lawyer."

"Very well," said Sir Clifford. "Cunningham has noted, as have I, how close you have become to the current occupants of the

Rectory of St Andrew's. He is also aware of what an upright and determined person you are, Charles, and may have imagined that you might conjure some scheme to reveal the iniquities of Henry Nicholson. Any such scheme inevitably risks damaging anyone closely associated with his person." Sir Clifford paused and sucked on his pipe. "It seems that we know something you do not. At the beginning of September a fellow called Piers Brandon, a gentleman farmer, breathed his last while chasing poachers off his land. He sat on the board of the Old B_____ Charitable Trust. A short time thereafter a new trustee was appointed to replace Mr Brandon, and as ever they tend to swap old wood for new." Barratt nodded, already certain of what Sir Clifford was about to say. "They chose the most respectable young man they could find, Reverend John Archer."

IX

AS HE BADE farewell to Sir Clifford the certainty of purpose which Barratt had enjoyed earlier that morning, setting off briskly for Foulke House with the zeal of a crusader, had all but dissolved. He had been ready to act, to engage surveyors and conveyancers, to withdraw monies and invest them, to inveigle and entrap (he was most unhappy about this last area of his syncretised strategy, since some moral compromise was inevitably required) but now he was deflated. As he walked back to the Red House, at a more gentle, melancholic pace, he considered why he had allowed himself to become so emotionally preoccupied with the success of a scheme which he had only finalised earlier in the day, in a moment, in response to an offhand remark. He calculated and recalculated, muttering to himself as he went, sending a menagerie of small creatures scurrying deeper into the hedgerows.

He realised that establishing the shop, which did not yet exist, and restoring the integrity of the Trust, in which until very recently he had failed to take an interest, could not be ends in and of themselves, and were instead means of achieving a different purpose, which might be generally insignificant but was of the greatest importance to Barratt himself. He wished to relieve the poor and to provide them with employment away from the workhouse, and he wished to ensure that whatever funds had been swindled from the Trust were restored but it was critical, he sensed, that he, Mr Charles Barratt of the Red House, was known to be the agent of these good deeds, not because he cared whether the citizens of B_____ held him in great esteem but rather because he wanted just one of them, Susannah Walker, to admire him. He hoped that she might experience some pleasure, or pride even, in their association. This, he acknowledged, was pure vanity. The idea of the printshop had arisen from conversations in Reverend Archer's study and on reflection Barratt had only minor qualms about this project; the intent was noble in the first instance, though such intentions were no guarantee of success. The matter of the Trust was more complex, particularly when the information recently imparted by Sir Clifford was taken into account. The instinct which lay behind Mr Barratt's quest to resolve this matter, however, was almost brutal. What he wanted was what any male creature might want, that is, to demonstrate his puissance by defeating another male. "You are no better than some rutting stag, Barratt," he said to himself, more amused than shamed, at first, by this characterisation. His self-examination was not concluded, however. "In fact you are a great deal worse," he continued, "since the aggression of the stag is part of its true nature. It is a performance, but it is an instinctive one, whereas as you, sir, are playing a role which is beyond the scope of your habitual manner or behaviour. The stag ruts in good faith, whereas you are behaving like some pandering courtier."

The tower of St Andrew's grew visible and Barratt turned south on to the London Road, which widened and grew more uneven as it became the high street. Some difficult interviews loomed ahead of Barratt, like high escarpments, and they could not be got around but required instead to be climbed. He considered knocking on the Rectory door for the second time that morning, but felt that such ascents, begun severally or at once, needed to be properly provisioned, and he was conscious that his cook had prepared sausages for his luncheon. He crossed to the west side of the high street and into Mill Lane and entered his own property from the rear garden.

Johnson sat on the kitchen step, reading *The Times* from the day before. A gardener, whom he had employed to tidy the borders, stood to attention with his hoe upright as Barratt appeared through the gate. Johnson got to his feet and offered the subtlest of bows to his master. "It is curious," he said, walking into the house behind Mr Barratt, "that these scribes rattle on about any and every topic as if they are experts, whereas the truth is they've never done a thing, only written about it."

"I am sure you are right, Johnson," said Barratt. "Tell me, what was the name of Mr Cunningham's nephew, who dined here in January?"

"I think you mean Mr Richards, sir. Mr Harvey Richards. But he is the grandson of Mr Cunningham's late sister, Lady Richards."

"That's the fellow," Mr Barratt said. "What did you make of him?"

"He seemed like a very presentable young man, I'm sure."

"Not too coltish, was he?"

"No indeed," said Johnson, "more sensible than most, considering his age." He waited for Mr Barratt to continue, prompting him, eventually, by taking up his newspaper again.

"Never been hungry, though," said Barratt. Johnson put down *The Times* once more.

"I'm sorry, sir?"

"I got the impression that young Mr Richards had never known a moment's need, never had his stomach tied in knots for want of a meal."

"Unlike you and I, you mean," Johnson said.

"Yes, I suppose that is what I mean. We appreciate our comforts, do we not, because we have known life without them."

"I'm sure you're correct, sir."

"On which subject, let us eat," said Mr Barratt. "Will you join me, Johnson?" The valet understood that this was more an instruction than a request and he followed Barratt into the dining room. Johnson turned his chair slightly so that he was not looking directly at Mrs Catherine, though her gaze fell on everyone, really, other than her husband who always sat with his back to her. The cook appeared with the sausages, mashed potatoes, a thick sauce and a faint scowl at her colleague, when he asked for Norfolk mustard. The two men ate in their wonted silence at first, but Johnson could not suppress his curiosity.

"What is your interest in Mr Richards?" he asked between mouthfuls. With a marked absence of enthusiasm Barratt once more outlined the plans he had presented earlier to Sir Clifford. The explanation took longer, being punctuated by sausage and Riesling, and there was of course an addendum: Mr Barratt's thoughts on how he might broach the subject of the Trust with Reverend Archer. He was inclined to approach the matter directly, to tell the Rector what he had heard about the Trust and to ask the extent of the clergyman's involvement.

"There is more than one way to catch a cat," advised Johnson. "I would congratulate the good Reverend first, then attempt to discover why he has made no reference to the Trust in any of your conversations. He may well volunteer the information you require without you seeming to pry. I would wager that he is not aware of any misappropriation, anyway, sir."

"Of course he is not, Johnson. He certainly does not have a penny to lend to Henry Nicholson, nor would he be inclined to do so. I would like to be reassured of the fact by the man himself, that is all."

"You will excuse me, sir, but I still do not understand how young Mr Richards is involved."

"Ah, yes," said Barratt, "I am easily distracted these days, it seems. I had originally intended to approach the Trust myself, and also to oversee the establishment of the printshop directly, but I have considered the matter and now think it may be better if I involve an intermediary. I would entrust these things to you, Johnson, but I fear you are too closely associated with me."

"Quite so," said Johnson. "I think it is important that you let the young fellow know precisely what it is you're putting him in for, though."

"I would not put the gentleman in a position where he has to tell an outright lie, if that is your concern. If anyone is misled it will be because of their greed, not because of any equivocation on our part."

"In which case I think he may do very well," said Johnson. He swallowed the last of his wine then laughed to himself. "I confess, sir, that I thought you had something else in mind for Mr Richards."

"What is that?"

"I thought perhaps you meant to introduce him to Miss Lucy. They would make a handsome couple."

"She is but a child," said Barratt, and Johnson was sensible enough to make no further comment on the matter.

Mr Barratt retired to his study to write a letter to Mr Cunningham and to allow his luncheon to settle. He sent the letter with Johnson then prepared to visit the Rectory, putting on his best jacket and the boots which his man had polished the previous evening upon their return from the city. He stood in the hallway and looked at his reflection in the tall looking glass. His was a hard face to love, he thought. He did not appear to be kind and forgiving, as the Rector did, nor good-humoured like Sir Clifford, but he was not a plain man. His ears were neat, his teeth strong and almost all of his hair remained, though there was as much white as brown at the temples. He did not know what he wished to say to

Mrs Walker exactly, he only wanted to be truthful with her. It was by no means certain that he would have an opportunity to talk to her, as he had resolved to speak with Reverend Archer about the Trust first. He was glad that he had taken some wine with his meal to strengthen his nerve. He shouted that he was leaving to no-one in particular, and each chandelier in the house tinkled a response. He opened the door and started. Across the street, outside the Rectory, a man sat in crumpled livery on the box of a open carriage. A terrible scar ran from his left ear to within half an inch of the corner of his mouth. Barratt had not seen the man before, but he recognised the sleek black carriage and its giltwork, and the two black horses waiting to draw it.

X

A STUDY MIGHT be made of Mr Henry Nicholson, thought
Barratt, physicians and philosophers might bring their knowledge
to bear and offer their opinions but none, he suspected, would be
able to truthfully identify what it was about the man which was
unusual. Mr Barratt was not a doctor of any kind but he was a keen
student of human behaviour; it was quickly obvious to him that
Nicholson was an oddity. There was something automatic about
his outward bearing which reminded Barratt of a clockwork toy.
When stimulated Nicholson was superficially charming, but this
was each time an effortful undertaking, and after each foray into
the conversation his anima would dissipate entirely and he would
sit motionless in his chair, his face a blank, as if waiting for his
creator to turn the key in his back. Barratt wondered if some new
science might not be necessary to explain such a person.

What was perhaps more extraordinary was that Reverend
Archer and his cousins seemed not to heed the strangeness of their
guest's manner. When Mrs Walker enquired after the health of his
family Nicholson mustered a wan smile and rather than politely
explaining that he had no close living relatives he instead assured
her that they were all very well. Miss Lucy seemed entirely
delighted with the newcomer, though he demonstrated no great
celerity of wit, Barratt thought, and his character was as slender
and benighted as his appearance. An atmosphere of well-wishing
nevertheless pervaded the Rectory library, such that Barratt felt the
need to excuse himself, beneath the implausible cloak of a dry
throat - sherry was offered and declined - in order to seek out
Lottie and thereby to calibrate his prejudice towards Mr Nicholson.
He found her in the scullery chewing on a piece of liquorice root.

"Help you, Mister Barratt, sir?"

"My dear Lottie," he said, "would you be kind enough to give
me your opinion of Mr Nicholson?" She beckoned, and Barratt
moved close enough to see that the inside of the maid's left ear
was not as clean as he might have wished.

"If I must be honest, sir, I do not like him," Lottie said. "There
is something about him which makes my skin turn cold. I have

heard some things about him that you wouldn't want to hear. I don't appreciate the way he stares at Miss Lucy, neither. And his eyes are black, like a dead fish!" Barratt, reassured, squeezed Lottie's elbow a trifle more firmly than he perhaps intended or she might have desired, but he dug out three pence from the pocket of his waistcoat and gave it to her so any injury was promptly forgotten. He turned in the narrow passageway which led from the kitchen to the main hall.

"Lottie," he hissed. The young woman's head appeared at the scullery door. "Has he been here often, this Nicholson fellow?"

"No sir, not to my knowledge. The first time I saw him here was back before Christmas. Haven't seen him since." Barratt thanked her and returned to the library, uncertain how best to proceed. There seemed little point in making any reference to the incident outside The Bull, he was certain that Nicholson would claim not to remember the event, and perhaps truthfully; no flicker of recognition had passed across his face when Reverend Archer had introduced Mr Barratt, our dearest friend, to him.

Mr Nicholson and the Rector had repaired to the latter's study, having some business to discuss, Mrs Walker explained. Barratt received this information with a slow nod. He looked at Mrs Walker and remembered that when he had set out from the Red House a few minutes earlier his aims had been twofold and now it appeared that he would conclude his visit doubly thwarted. Mrs Walker could hardly be expected to leave Miss Lucy, as resourceful a young person as she undoubtedly was, to entertain herself in the library while she wandered about the small garden of the Rectory being wooed by Mr Barratt.

"You have barely spoken since you arrived, Mr Barratt," said Mrs Walker. "Was there something you wished to say?" There were certain of her sex, Mr Barratt had observed, who were almost supernaturally sensitive to the moods, wishes and intentions of their fellow beings. Catherine had been such a woman, able to read his thoughts and those of others with whom she had only briefly been acquainted as if they were notes from a daybook. He doubted whether Mrs Walker possessed this faculty in any general sense, her nature tended more towards self-regard than his late wife's had, but was it possible, Barratt wondered, that she might enjoy some specific perspicacity of this kind when another's thoughts or feelings pertained to her? There was something challenging about the half-smile that lingered on her face after she had spoken which made the idea difficult to dismiss.

"I am conscious that my departure this morning was hurried, hurried enough as to seem impolite, perhaps, so I wished to apologise." Mrs Walker's smile remained. "And I had rather hoped, Susannah, that I might have a private conversation with you, about a matter of some importance." Still she smiled, though some faint evidence of strain may have been visible at the corners of her mouth. Miss Lucy looked intently at her mother, and then at Mr Barratt, but found that any meaning which might have inhered to the exchange of glances between them was beyond her grasp. She concluded, therefore, that whatever Barratt wished to discuss must relate in some way or another to her, Lucy, otherwise the old fellow could just come out and say his piece without this baffling desire for privacy.

"Is it truly so urgent, Charles?" Mrs Walker said. Barratt lowered his chin and looked at the floor.

"No," he admitted, "I suppose it can wait." He turned to Miss Lucy, but for once found no relief there. The child's usual complacent smile was absent and there was a hint of accusation in her expression. "Have you spoken with Mr Nicholson about your dance yet, Miss Lucy?"

"Cousin John has not allowed me to say a thing about it," she said. "And I was honouring your wishes too, Mr Barratt."

"I'm afraid I must ask you to honour them for a little while longer. I promise you that there will be no resultant delay and you shall dance at midsummer with every fine young man in the county." Miss Lucy seemed satisfied with this response, her mother less so. Barratt decided that he preferred not to spend any more time in the company of Henry Nicholson than was absolutely necessary, and he was in any case quite reduced by the walk to Foulke House and the strain which Nicholson's unexpected appearance had placed him under. Without waiting to speak to the Rector he bade farewell to the ladies, rather more gently than he had earlier in the day, and with a nod to Buller, the coachman, and a sense of general unease he crossed back to the Red House, shouting for tea as he walked through the door.

Barratt slept poorly and woke in the middle of the night. He had dreamed of Catherine, and as ever she stood in the doorway of the house in Whitecross Street, calling down the steps to him, pleading with him not to leave. It was she who had left, of course, and he remained. The sorrow he felt, whether sleeping or awake, was like a strong sea current, threatening to overwhelm him, to suck him under. He knew what she had never had to learn, that their child would die too, and provide no comfort to her husband but instead multiply his anguish. He sat up in bed and took a handkerchief from the cupboard of his nightstand and dried his face before rubbing the cloth over his hair. "She comes to me when I am stalled," he said to himself. "I must move forward." His breathing slowed and he tried not to think of his late wife, but she stood across the high street as he struck Henry Nicholson with the back of his hand, and looked from an upstairs window as he showed Susannah Walker around the newly manicured garden of the Red House. He smiled, understanding that his dream at last made sense. Mrs Charles Barratt had died, but she would never leave him. The ghost of her was in his mind only, he was certain, but its presence was nevertheless undeniable, and it did not wish him to escape. Looked at like this it was almost soothing to be haunted, Barratt felt. He turned his pillow over so that his head rested on the cool side and eventually fell back into a shallow, fitful sleep.

In the morning a letter arrived from Cunningham, which confirmed that young Mr Richards could be summoned as soon as the following day, since he was only in Milton, little more than an hour's ride away.

"Johnson, we are moving forward," said Barratt. The letter included, as a footnote, an invitation to dine with Mr Cunningham and his great-nephew on Saturday evening. Under normal circumstances this would have been a source of some small rejoicing for Mr Barratt, since Cunningham, if he was not inclined to eat alone, preferred to venture abroad for his supper rather than entertaining, his considerable age and the excellence of his staff notwithstanding. However, Barratt had hoped to secure an invitation to the Rectory on the following evening, and to have an opportunity then to quiz Reverend Archer on the scope and depth of his involvement with Nicholson and the Trust. The Rector would not be available in the interim, since Fridays and Saturdays were given over to visiting parishioners and sermon writing. It was not always possible, or even strategically advisable to advance on all fronts, Barratt reflected, and besides he was always keen to explore Cunningham's cellar, which was narrower than his own, but more ancient, rather like the man himself. Barratt chuckled and sat down to write his reply. As he dipped his quill the bell rang in the hallway.

"See who that is please," said Barratt. He heard Johnson's footsteps on the marble and then his voice, echoing around the empty vestibule, as he announced Mr Henry Nicholson.

XI

THE RED HOUSE was a good deal taller and more grand than the Rectory, but these qualities did not always benefit its occupants. It took a greater effort to keep the newer building warm, for instance, and the large windows required frequent cleaning, particularly those which faced the high street. There were no intimate spaces, where one might speak in confidence, and Mr Barratt keenly envied the Rector's small study. He worked, when necessary, in the library, at a mahogany bureau, a bulky object which he had been meaning to replace. He had a habit of placing crumbs from his breakfast on the window sill and would allow himself to become distracted from his correspondence by the birds which would land and feed beyond the glass. There were no birds to be seen on the morning that Henry Nicholson rang the bell of the Red House, and as he rose to greet his visitor Barratt wondered if it was this gentleman's appearance, which even his most fervent admirer would be obliged to concede had something of the well-dressed scarecrow about it, that had caused the skies to empty.

"Mr Nicholson, good morning Sir," said Barratt, bowing. "How kind of you to call!"

"I was visiting the Rectory, but they are all out," said Nicholson, affronted apparently by this inconvenient absence. He moved his weight from foot to foot and fiddled with the loosely wrapped parcel he was carrying.

"Reverend Archer has some parochial responsibilities, of course," Barratt noted smoothly. "The ladies, one assumes, are taking advantage of this fine weather."

"Yes, yes," Nicholson said, though his tone implied disagreement rather than concord. He ran the sleeve of his coat across his top lip. "It is unusually warm." Barratt observed a marked change in his guest from the person he had seen, at leisure, in the Rectory library the previous afternoon. There he had seemed languorous, inertalmost, when he was not speaking. Now his eyes flitted around the vestibule and he seemed to tremble as he caught his reflection in the large looking glass which hung on the south wall. He continued to perspire and Barratt wondered if

Cunningham's information was incomplete and that cards were not Mr Nicholson's most destructive vice.

"Did you walk to the Rectory, Sir? That must be above five miles. Join me for coffee and water." Nicholson greeted this invitation with a candid relief which was almost childlike, thanking his host repeatedly for kindness, and for accepting a near stranger into his home and Barratt, for the first time, saw how he might be considered charming, if one chose to ignore his mercurial manner. It would have to be so, Mr Barratt thought, since the gentleman's purported misdeeds could not have been achieved without some aptitude for persuasion or evasion, either of which required a quantum of personal charisma.

"My man, Buller, has taken my carriage," Nicholson explained. "Some urgent business." Barratt led him into the dining room and called for the cook to bring another cup and glass.

"What line of business are you in, Mr Nicholson?"

"Oh, not much really. There's the estate, of course, and I am the chair of a charitable trust." Barratt poured a coffee for his guest and a glass of water and pushed a small silver basket filled with sugar lumps across the table. Mr Nicholson popped one in his mouth then sipped the coffee, and nodded his approval.

"It was a long winter," Barratt remarked. "How are things on the estate, much improved, I hope, with the better weather?"

"Yes," said Nicholson, "quite so." Mr Barratt waited for him to offer some further explanation, but his guest had noticed the painting on the wall, which was less obvious on a bright morning, and was staring at it intently. "That is an extraordinary portrait, may I ask, who is the subject?"

"That is my wife, Catherine," said Barratt.

"I did not know you were married, Sir. She is very beautiful, and you are a fortunate fellow!"

"She died, a few months after the painting was completed. So perhaps not so fortunate." Barratt felt that this was unfair, and rebuked himself internally. Nicholson sat with his mouth open. "I apologise, Mr Nicholson, you were not to know. Thank you, she was a person of great beauty, not just in her appearance but in her manner and voice, in every way, in fact. I was indeed blessed to marry her and to be her companion for two years. But my good fortune was not inexhaustible."

"A terrible shame, yes." The two men sat in silence for a moment. "What is your business, Mr Barratt? Reverend Archer tells me that you have a fleet of ships which sail about the globe."

"I have an interest in a trading house, Mr Nicholson. I was a clerk there as a boy, and I have done some sailing too, on the company's behalf, but I have never owned a ship, I can assure you."

"So, buying and selling?"

"That is the essence of it," said Barratt. Nicholson pursed his lips and produced a dry whistle.

"You must have an aptitude for it." The younger man stood, fortified by the coffee.

"I live comfortably enough, Mr Nicholson, though my carriage is no match for yours. It is at your disposal, however. Johnson will take you home."

"That is very kind, though I will need to make a short diversion," said Nicholson.

"As long as Johnson is back for his luncheon you will hear no complaints," said Barratt, laughing. Mr Nicholson managed to summon a joyless smile at this apparent witticism. "I'm sorry, was there anything else you wished to ask, Sir? I realise that I have not enquired as to the purpose of your visit."

"Nothing," said Nicholson. "I merely hoped to further our acquaintance. Reverend Archer sings your praises, as do his charming cousins."

"Those ladies, I fear, are starved of better company," Barratt said. "It was very kind of you to call. I will ask Johnson to bring the carriage around." He escorted Mr Nicholson to the door and opened it, bowed his farewell then disappeared towards the back of the house. He delivered a short series of instructions to Johnson then went up to his bedroom via the back stairs. From the window he saw Mr Nicholson climb into the carriage and speak to Johnson, who turned the horses around. Barratt watched the carriage roll southwards along the high street until it was out of sight, then he went downstairs, took some coins from the lowboy in the hallway, put on his hat and coat and crossed the street to the Rectory.

Lottie was pleased, as ever, to see him.

"Mr Barratt, sir, how lovely. But I'm afraid they're all out."

"Never mind, Lottie, it was you I wanted to speak to. About

our friend Mr Nicholson."

"No friend of mine," she said, "and I don't care who hears it! He was here this morning, you know."

"So I understand. Did he ask you any questions, my dear?" Lottie considered this.

"No, Sir. He asked to be announced, but I told him there was no-one in."

"What happened then?"

"Well, he said he had mislaid something, and he thought he had left it in Reverend Archer's study."

"Did you let him in?" asked Barratt.

"I could scarcely prevent him, Sir. I am not paid to fight off young men with a duster."

"Of course not, Lottie. Where did he go?"

"He went into the library, and I presume, from there, into the study."

"You didn't follow him?" Lottie attempted a look of disdain but found that she was too fond of the noisy old gentleman for any ill-feeling to persist. "No, why would you? Tell me something, my dearest Lottie, do you remember if Mr Nicholson was carrying anything when he arrived?"

"He was not, Sir."

"You're sure of it?"

"Absolutely, not even a hat."

"And when the gentleman departed," Barratt continued, "did he have anything then?" Lottie set her mind to thinking and Barratt saw her small, snubbed nose twitch.

"He might have," she said. "Not in his hands, but as he was leaving he had one arm across his chest, as if he'd been shot, and he was sweating."

"Lottie, you are a marvel," he said, handing her a coin. "Should you ever consider making espionage your profession His Majesty's Government would be lucky to have you."

"What's that?"

"A spy, Lottie. You'd make a wonderful spy."

"Like your friend, Mr Cunningham, you mean? They say he brought down Bonaparte."

"You should not believe the gossip in the market square, Lottie. Besides, if Cunningham really were a spy then no-one would know about it, would they?" Lottie nodded, as if accepting the wisdom of Barratt's remark. Her eyes widened as she noticed Mrs Walker standing in the open doorway. Mr Barratt turned and started.

"If you must conspire with my cousin's maid, Charles, you would do well to be more discreet about it," Mrs Walker said, accompanying this remark with a mordant smile. Lottie helped the lady with her shawl then disappeared towards the kitchen. "I am all yours," she went on. "What is it that you wished to discuss? Come out with it, I will not allow you to leave until you have spoken."

XII

THE GARDEN OF the Rectory was not designed for communion between mortals, but rather as a space in which a man of God might seek inspiration from the dazzling variety of his maker's works. The paths were crowded by dense borders planted with flowers and grasses of every kind, and were narrow in any case, so it was inconceivable that two persons might walk side by side without being soaked by dew, dusted with pollen or clawed at by thorns. Until Miss Lucy had arrived in the autumn, accompanied by a mother and a cat, an abundance of animal life, airborne and earthbound, made its home amongst the shoots and branches, so that the Reverend Archer was obliged to tread carefully with his eyes fixed on the path ahead, in the manner of certain Hindoos, to avoid crushing an overly adventurous frog or vole. Since that time, however, the latter of the young lady's companions, his skills honed in the expansive pastures of Meadholme, had either exterminated or driven off almost all of the indigenous fauna, cats having very little notion of husbandry, such that only the faster flying insects survived (no butterflies outlived the spring cull enacted by this dread beast) and Mittens was obliged to travel further afield in search of prey.

Mrs Walker and Mr Barratt stepped out into the garden nevertheless, since Lottie's hearing was as acute as her curiosity about the affairs of others. They moved in procession to the north-east corner and Mrs Walker turned and stood in dappled spring sunlight, revealing those marks of age which, Barratt felt, only enhanced her beauty.

"Susannah," he began, "you must know that if I were ten years younger, if we both were, I would have spoken much sooner of my feelings."

"That is untrue, Charles, though I understand that you do not mean to mislead me. Ten years ago I would have been invisible to you. Even now I see that you struggle to admit your feelings to yourself."

"That is no longer the case, my dear. It was a struggle, I must own, but my misgivings have been overcome by the great strength of feeling I have towards you."

"I am less than captivated by this talk of misgivings," said Mrs Walker. "Do you mean to persuade me of your affections or to warn me off?" Barratt had been staring at his own hands as he spoke but he lifted his gaze and was greatly relieved to see that Mrs Walker was smiling at him.

"When I speak of misgivings I should be clear that they relate only to myself. I would be offering to share with you the end of my life, rather than its greener years. I have settled into a number of habits which may prove disagreeable to you. My general vigour is naturally diminished."

"I am sure that you are vigorous enough for me, Charles," said Mrs Walker, "and I am not a young woman, indeed I wonder that you have not fixed your eye upon a more youthful prospect."

"It was not my intention to love again, or to consider remarrying, my dear woman. I could not conceive that such a thing might happen. You are aware that my attachment to Catherine has persisted these many years and that other women have been, as you suggest, invisible to me. When I met you it was if a blindfold was pulled from my eyes, and I could see not only your own conspicuous beauty but that of everything around me."

"And yet you grew cold towards me, Charles, as if you did not wish to be troubled by the difficult emotions associated with the happier ones. I wonder if you have forgiven yourself completely for these feelings."Barratt considered this.

"I knew that there was nothing improper about feeling an attraction to someone after so much time spent alone," he said. "It is one thing to know something and quite another to feel it. I know that the Earth is a sphere and that it travels around the sun, but I do not feel these things in my heart."

"I am again perplexed," said Mrs Walker. "Are you saying that you cannot love me because the Earth is flat?"

"I mean only to explain why I may have appeared to vacillate. The truth, as you have surely discerned, is that I do love you, Susannah, and I have loved you from the earliest days of our association. I do not love you in contradiction to my instincts, as you seem to believe, but because of them, because you possess those qualities, warmth and wit and beauty, which any man must treasure, and most of all because my admiration for you has grown with prolonged acquaintance rather than diminishing. I am certain, quite certain that a life lived without you at my side would be a life wasted. I cannot forget Catherine, it is true, nor would I expect you to forget Mr Walker. It is also true, however, that I cannot imagine a future without you." Mr Barratt felt that he had said all he could say, and had not blundered too greatly. Mrs Walker's eyes were not aglow, as he had hoped they might be, but seemed darkened by melancholy.

"Not all marriages are as felicitous as was yours, Charles. I cannot regret mine, since Lucy was the fruit of it, but it would not greatly pain me if I never thought of Mr Walker again. He was not a kind man." Barratt paced backwards and forwards on the damp path, then kicked himself firmly in the back of the ankle.

"I am sorry, Susannah, please pardon my ignorance," he said.

"How could you possibly have known, Charles? Society may have grown more permissive but we have not yet reached a point where one can safely enquire about another's matrimonial happiness, not even in France."

"You are altogether too forgiving," Barratt said. "Had I been familiar with your history I would not have dared to speak. Let us return to the house, Lottie will be beside herself already."

"So that is it, Charles? One might almost believe that you were hoping for some pretext for an honourable retreat." Mrs Walker spoke these words without her usual wry tone. She seemed genuinely dismayed, Barratt thought.

"What do you mean, Susannah?"

"I was a headstrong child," said Mrs Walker, "my mother used to complain of the fact. I first rode in a carriage when I was two years old and I was terribly sick, so my parents avoided taking me anywhere until I was considerably older, but if I disappeared from the nursery, as I did from time to time, I could always be found in the stables, having climbed up into my parent's vis-à-vis." She looked at Mr Barratt, whose face wore an expression of tender puzzlement. "I was not dissuaded, Charles, by that first unpleasant experience, and I paid no heed to what others thought was best for me. I do not believe that my character has greatly altered in the succeeding years." She watched as her meaning became clear to Barratt. He looked, she thought, like someone who has stepped into sunlight on a cold morning. He approached her, bowed as deeply as his heavy frame would allow, and kissed her hand.

"Susannah, would you do me the greatest honour and consent to be my wife?"

"How could I possibly refuse you, Charles? You are the most decent and handsome man I know." Barratt took Mrs Walker in his arms and a whooping sound which issued from the tall windows of the library indicated that Lottie, at least, was very happy with this arrangement.

They went inside and Mrs Walker threatened to pinch Lottie's ears if she breathed a word to anyone about what had passed in the Rectory garden. Mr Barratt, meanwhile, sat in his usual chair smiling broadly, though in truth he was as exhausted as he was relieved. He took his watch from his pocket and was surprised to see that it was still an hour before noon. Mrs Walker, who had stepped out to speak with her cook, returned and stood beside Barratt. She placed a hand upon his shoulder and for a few moments they gazed together at the corner of the garden where their momentous conversation had taken place, each of them remembering the words the other had spoken, and their own responses, as if they were rehearsing a play.

"I must speak with Johnson," said Barratt eventually, and he stood and kissed his fiancée just above her forehead. "I will see you soon. I love you with all my being." Mrs Walker looked up at him, her eyes filled with tears, and found that she could not speak. She nodded and touched his face lightly and he left. Once he had gone she felt his absence for the first time, a looming absence in proportion to the man himself, and thought that she might find some comfort in this, in having someone to wait for.

XIII

JOHNSON AND MR BARRATT had first met in India, a quarter of a century earlier. Their arrangement had been an informal one at first. Johnson was engaged occasionally as a fixer for the trading house which also employed Barratt, and had been in Bombay for five years prior to Barratt's arrival. Johnson had acted as counsellor and guide around that distant city and they returned to England a few months later having already assumed the relative positions which were to persist to the morning of Mr Barratt's proposal to Mrs Walker. Nor would any significant immediate alteration occur even once Johnson learned of the betrothal, since the patterns of the two men's behaviour were very deeply worn in, like cart tracks on an unpaved road. Sometimes weeks would pass during which their routines would not vary at all and then some small upheaval would take place, the removal to B_____ being the most recent of these disturbances, and after the household had settled a new period of equilibrium would be established.

Mr Barratt's talk of 'moving forward' had not unduly alarmed his valet. Johnson presumed that Barratt was speaking of some new project relating to his visitor, Henry Nicholson. Certainly this gentleman was the subject of discussionin the dining room ofthe Red House when Mr Barratt returned from the Rectory.

"What is the general condition of the estate?" asked Barratt.

"As you expected Nicholson asked to be put down a good distance from the house, perhaps a quarter mile off, but I had my long glass with me. I turned the cart around and went back past a turn in the road and from there I could see the state of the place well enough. Fences are down, the outbuildings are dilapidated, the roof of the main house is in need of repair. Had I not known otherwise I would have thought the place blighted and abandoned."

"What of the land itself, Bill, does it seem unfit for any use?"

"I am no farmer," said Johnson, "but the weeds seemed to grow well enough. The ground's not steep or low."

"And there are no tenants thereabouts?"

"There are some plots but they are all gone to seed."

"Then it is as we feared," said Barratt. "Mr Nicholson has no income, or no legitimate income at least."

"One wonders why he does not sell up," said Johnson. "Land is land, after all."

"Yes, it is interesting. My suspicion is that there is some covenant which prevents him from doing so. Cunningham will doubtless have some idea." Mr Barratt pushed himself up from the dining table. "I think we should rest this afternoon, eh, what do you think? It has been a busy day already and there is more to come."

"It will be a pleasure to see young Mr Richards again, Sir."

"Indeed," said Barratt. "And I believe you also enjoy the company of Mrs Flannery, Cunningham's woman, is that not so?" Johnson waved this remark away, as if it were a fly. "I shall retire with the question unanswered, it seems. Allow me to ask you something else, where did Mr Nicholson deposit the package he was carrying?"

"He left it at the haberdashers, on the high street. They carry out repairs and so forth." Mr Barratt nodded at this information, offered a gesture of farewell, and climbed the stairs to his bedroom. He kicked off his boots and laid on the counterpane and in a few moments fell into a deep sleep.

Lottie kept her promise. When Reverend Archer returned to the Rectory with Miss Lucy, she having accompanied him on his parochial calls, no mention was made of transactions in moist corners of the garden, though Mr Nicholson's brief visit was spoken of and its purpose speculated upon. The maid's eyes flashed at Mrs Walker when Mr Barratt's name was mentioned in passing, but she received by way of reply a look of such fierce disapprobation and implied threat that she fled from the library, as the teacups on the tray she carried rattled in their saucers.

"I wish Mr Barratt would explain himself," said Miss Lucy. "I am sure he must have some good reason for prohibiting me from speaking with Mr Nicholson but it is most vexing to be kept in the dark, like..." For the moment the young lady was doubly vexed, as she could not think of a single living creature which was thus sequestered. "Like a bat!" she said eventually.

"Every day spent with you is an education, my dear Lucy," said the Rector. "I had always mistakenly assumed that a tenebrous existence was the natural preference of the bat, and I am not a little alarmed to learn otherwise." He turned to see if Mrs Walker would deplore his cruelty in some inventive fashion but it was clear that she was not listening. A light rain was falling and she stood by the garden window watching the drops bounce from the leaves outside. "Are you well, Susannah?" he asked.

"Quite well, thank you." Mrs Walker turned and smiled at her daughter. "What were you saying, Lucy darling?"

"I wish that Mr Barratt would tell me why I can't talk to Mr Nicholson about the dance."

"Have you asked him?"

"I did not wish to appear impertinent, Mama."

"Our friend Barratt is something of a non-conformist, you know," said Reverend Archer. "It is possible that he disagrees with the whole idea of dancing." Miss Lucy was noticeably upset by this remark and her mother sought to reassure her.

"Mr Barratt is not some kind of Puritan, I am sure of it. Besides, he has given you his word that your dance will take place, and there is no cause to doubt him."

"Thank you, Mama," Miss Lucy said. "May I then ask him?"

"By all means," her mother replied. Mrs Walker's mind was still elsewhere, though it had shifted from a spot a few yards beyond the library windows, and a happy reverie related to those coordinates, to another place which was altogether less agreeable, somewhere dark and chaotic. Something about her cousin identifying Mr Barratt as a non-conformist, light-hearted or ironic though this characterisation surely was, had aggravated her considerably. She wondered what Reverend Archer meant by it, and felt certain that while he aimed only to amuse himself he had struck upon a seam of truth. Mrs Walker, it might be recalled, had not been in St Andrew's on that Sunday in September when Mr Barratt had thundered away and held the congregation rapt. She had only noticed the way that her fiancé stared without interest at the back of the foremost bench during Sunday Service, stirring only for hymns, or smiling briefly at some conceit in the Rector's sermon. It appeared that Barratt did not care for the trappings of the established church, though he never failed to attend, nor did he short-change the collection. She was alarmed, momentarily, by the thought of being dragged to some half-constructed, malarial outpost in the name of religious liberty, though it was impossible to imagine Lucy in such a place. Mrs Walker yearned to see Mr Barratt's face. A strong, kindly face, his, the mere sight of which, she felt sure, would assuage her irrational fears.

"I have never known you so distracted, Susannah," the Rector said. "Did something happen this morning on your walk?"

"No," Mrs Walker replied. "Nothing ever happens to me, as well you know."

The evenings were already lengthening and the sun had not long set into a westward sky of saffron hue when Mr Barratt's cart arrived at Steddon Hall, the home of Mr Cunningham. The old man appeared below the portico to greet his guests, dressed in a long black coat which appeared to be of an unusually recent vintage. Behind him, showing two rows of strong teeth, bright as pearls despite the fading light, Mr Harvey Richards appeared. The younger gentleman was closer in stature to Mr Barratt than to his elderly relative, though less stout, and his features were more well-proportioned still than his frame, so that an artist of some accomplishment might wish to paint him or sculpt a bust, but an Old Master would see nothing of interest in his face. His beauty was a forgettable kind of perfection, and it seemed, indeed, that the gentleman himself was oblivious to the gifts bestowed upon him by nature. He raised a hand of greeting to Mr Cunningham's guests, and then pushed the same hand through his hair, in a rather diffident fashion.

"Will you dine with us, Mr Johnson?" the old man asked. "Or do you prefer to take your supper in the kitchen? I believe Mrs Flannery may have kept something warm for you." Mr Cunningham laughed heartily at his own comedic panache while Johnson nodded and climbed down from the box. He bowed and handed the reins to a groom who had emerged from behind the house. Mr Barratt embraced Cunningham and shook Mr Richards' hand and the four men proceeded into the hallway.

"We have a great deal to discuss," said Mr Barratt.

"Yes, yes," his host replied, "but let us first enjoy a glass of wine."

XIV

"IF THE BUSINESS thrives the burden on the parish is relieved, and families are kept from the workhouse. If it fails then there will still be assets to sell and certain of our poorer residents will have acquired some useful skills. I need someone with energy who will get the thing up and running, and do his best to ensure that the project succeeds."Barratt concluded this explanation at the same time as he completed the filling of his pipe.

"Your expectation is that the Trust will provide some capital?" Mr Richards asked.

"We shall sound them out," said Barratt. "My expectation, frankly, is that the Trust has no funds to support an investment. Which is why we must first dangle the carrot."

"I'm still not sure I quite grasp the idea," said Mr Richards.

"Harvey, my dear boy, perhaps it is better if you remain innocent of Mr Barratt's schemes," said Cunningham. "If the Trust can demonstrate that it operates legitimately we shall make our donation. That should be our expectation."

"Quite right," said Mr Barratt. "It is essential that we carry on without prejudice and within the law."

"At the same time, forgive me," said Mr Richards, clearing his throat, "this donation is a trap, is it not?" Barratt sucked on his pipe and thought about what the young man had said. The question one had to answer, he calculated, was an old one: was the righting of a wrong cause enough for a deception of this kind? Did the end justify the means? He suspected that Mr Nicholson was not any more wicked, really, than the majority of men. He was merely incapable of overcoming whatever vices afflicted him. Barratt then turned his thoughts to the children of the South End and a familiar anger rose within him. A person who would deprive the hungry of food in order to keep a fine carriage did not deserve the pity of any man.

"I doubt that you are uncomfortable with the idea of helping those most in need of help, Mr Richards," said Barratt.

"No indeed."

"If the Trust has acted unlawfully, and if we expose these activities, this may deter others from behaving as we believe Mr

Nicholson and his associates have done, thus benefiting the disadvantaged generally, not solely those living in B_____."
Cunningham chose this moment to intervene.

"There is also a danger, one might suppose, that some degree of disrepute may adhere to these types of institution as a result of this kind of exposure," the old man said. This was not a consequence that Barratt, in his zeal to correct the current impropriety, had considered.

"I am sure that the charitable instinct is like water, and would find a way. It is in any case my preference to have Mr Nicholson return what he has borrowed."

"How can he possibly do so, Sir?" Cunningham demanded. "He has a coach and pair which seem to have disappeared, and two suits of clothes. This is the great flaw in your scheme, I fear. Nothing will accrue to the Trust with Nicholson in the Marshalsea."

"What about Hope Hall?"

"You would deprive a man of his ancestral home, Barratt? Remind me never to cross you myself." Cunningham laughed, but a note of reprimand was implicit in this laughter. "How fierce you are, Charles. No matter, he cannot sell the place, it is a condition of his father's will."

"I suspected as much," said Barratt. "I have some other ideas as to how the estate might afford the gentleman some solvency."

"I believe I mentioned to you previously that the place is already mortgaged."

"There is more than one way to kill a cat, as my man is fond of saying."

Summoned by this allusion to her most ardent admirer, Mrs Flannery, a middle-aged woman of rather high complexion, appeared with the cheeseboard, its pungent combination of odours preceding her by a few feet. Curls of hair, still golden, escaped from her cap in various directions and she had a gently epicurean air about her which made the fascination she held for Johnson, and it seemed for her employer too, rather more comprehensible to Barratt. She bent to cut the cheese and made several charming yet meaningless exclamations as she did so, moistening her lips and smiling as she bowed her farewell, so that the three gentlemen forgot their business momentarily, then Mr Cunningham raised his glass and said with a wink "To pretty widows!" and they stood and emptied their schooners.

The lack of a profession and any associated income was Harvey Richards' sole disadvantage in life; he was a handsome young man, of good family and a sensible and discreet nature, and he demonstrated this last quality by retiring immediately after supper so that his dining companions might converse with absolute candour. Cunningham and Barratt refilled their pipes and ordered their thoughts while doing so.

"It is the prerogative of our Creator, and Him alone, to determine the direction of other's lives," said Cunningham.

"I am less interested in God than you are, my friend, I make no secret of it."

"If He wills it my meeting with Him is a good deal more proximate than yours, Barratt."

"I do not believe in such things," Barratt said. "Nor am I comfortable joking about them. I understand and accept your reservations. I would only observe that every day in Whitehall decisions are made by mortal men which directly affect the well-being of the nation, particularly its poorest citizens. Besides I am scarcely about to erase the cities of the plain, I mean only to do what I think is right, according to my own conscience."

"I am correct in surmising then that you mean to replace Mr Nicholson, to usurp him?"

"Since we cannot simply borrow against the estate we must make it work for us. Mr Nicholson lacks both the skill and the inclination to do this. The title of Hope Hall will remain with him, but the Trust will take over the estate. Once the debt is expunged the income will also revert to Nicholson."

"What of the gentleman's pride?" asked Cunningham. "The simplest farmhand wishes to direct the affairs of his own household. What is he to live on?"

"What is he to live on once we have prevented him from stealing from the poor, you mean? I understand your squeamishness, good Cunningham, he is the son of your closest friend, but it is you who brought his supposed misconduct to my attention. As for Nicholson's pride, well, as a gentleman it is his birthright I suppose. I myself was always proud, even as a child, when I survived in reduced circumstances. Once a person succumbs to vice and criminality then pride becomes a luxury they can ill afford."

"I never thought you a hard man, Charles," said Cunningham. "Not before this evening at any rate."

"My goal is to improve the lives of a few folk, and to save one person in particular from himself. Whether I am successful depends not on my actions, hard as they may be, but on those of this latter soul." Barratt stood and went to Mr Cunningham. He took the older man's hand and bowed deeply. "I promise you that my scheme is not informed by malice, quite the opposite," he said. "Have Mr Richards call on me in the morning."

Mr Barratt called for Johnson, who brought the cart around. Both had enjoyed their evenings and Barratt climbed up and sat alongside his valet on the box as they travelled homewards. The night was cool and clear, the moon almost new, and the sky a blanket of stars beneath which the two men bumped shoulders and sang songs they remembered from their youth.

Mr Richards had been more circumspect in his intake that evening and appeared at the Red House very early on Sunday, so early in fact that Johnson and Mr Barratt were still abed, respectively one floor beneath and above the violent clanging in the hallway initiated by their young visitor. Johnson, fortuitously, had fallen asleep in his clothes so had only to slide into his boots before hurrying upstairs to answer the door. He guided Mr Richards through to the dining room where the young man sat terrified by the spectre of a woman who closely resembled his own sister, now married to a gentleman in Ireland. Richards heard some contretemps from a distant upstairs space and the familiar voice of Mr Barratt, noisily expressing his sincere hope, by gad, that he did not smell as ill as his valet. A large woman appeared from the bowels of the house and wordlessly placed a pot of coffee, a plate of cakes and toasted bread, and a small serving tray of preserves in front of the young man. She reappeared moments later with more plates, cutlery and a covered dish from which steam and the scent of strong spices emanated. Mr Barratt stepped in from the hallway, acknowledging Mr Richards and encouraging him to eat with a single gesture, before opening a small cabinet which stood on top of the sideboard. Barratt took out a bottle of powders and measured half a teaspoon of the substance into an empty cup which he filled with the coffee and drank off, flinching but slightly at the temperature of the beverage.

"Good morning Mr Richards," he said hoarsely. "Good to have you on board." Mr Richards prepared some courtesy equal to the occasion but Mr Barratt raised a hand and said "Eat first, speak later," and the young man, who was after all quite hungry, could only comply.

XV

ONCE BREAKFAST was done with Mr Barratt began to brief Mr Richards more fully on the details of his scheme, a briefing which continued while the older gentleman bathed, was shaved, and dressed and only concluded at the wych-gate of St Andrew's, fully an hour after it had commenced. The powders and pampering had proven effective and Barratt entered the church in an amiable mood, offering nods and acknowledgements to his fellow worshippers. Mrs Walker turned and looked at him as if he were some army captain returned uninjured from battle, a look of relief and strong affection accompanied by a heave of her handsome shoulders, which puzzled her fiancé almost as greatly as it pleased him. Miss Lucy barely registered his presence at all, having eyes only for the fine young person entering the pew alongside Mr Barratt. Mr Richards sat down with his knees to one side, a manoeuvre necessitated by his height, and Mr Barratt did the same, so that the two gentlemen, viewed from the perspective of Reverend Archer, entering at that moment from the vestry, appeared to be riding sidesaddle, two abreast, on a pair of invisible ponies. The Rector laughed quietly at the sight and his congregation took this as an intimation that this Sunday's sermon would be one of the Reverend's briefer, more light-hearted and at least partially audible meditations on a topic that was comprehensible, if not precisely relevant to their own modest existences. Such auguries are often ambiguous, however; one ancient gentleman might state that a gathering of three crows had a specific meaning, and another, equally qualified to pronounce on such matters, might insist on a different or even contradictory interpretation. So it was, alas, on that cool, spring Sunday morning. The Rector took as his text the thirteenth chapter of Leviticus, on the Discernment of Leprosy by the Priest, and spoke at some length, almost to himself it seemed, about the function of the clergy and its relationship with greater society, weaving a cloak of words that a fisherman in the German Sea might have worn, so remarkable was its density and imperviousness. Poor Mr Richards, who had lately been subjected to another prolonged monologue, could not stay the course. His chin fell to his chest and he slept. Mr

Barratt took a few moments to perceive his companion's somnolent condition then applied a powerful elbow to the young man's ribs. Mr Richards started awake, mouthing a silent apology to no-one in particular. Miss Lucy, who had taken in this pantomime from across the nave, giggled delightedly and received a pinch on the knee from Mrs Walker.

The homily approached its conclusion in a leisurely and indirect fashion, but end it did, eventually, and even its author seemed relieved. There were some prayers, some singing, coins jangled on plates or rattled in bags and a general sense of liberation spread over the devout. Miss Lucy stood on the tips of her toes as her mother invited Mr Harvey Richards, whose acquaintance the two ladies has just made, to call upon them at the Rectory that afternoon, and Mr Barratt wondered how long the young lady meant to maintain the pretence of being a little taller than she truly was. With Miss Lucy's comfort in mind he attempted to usher Mr Richards towards the font.

"You will join Mr Richards, I hope, Charles?" said Mrs Walker, and as previously the sound of his given name on her lips caused a shiver to pass through Barratt. He turned and lifted his hat and the two men, who might have been mistaken for father and son had the features of one not been so much more finely drawn than the other, disappeared into a pool of sunlight.

"Mr Richards seems like a very pleasant person," said Miss Lucy.

"Yes," agreed her mother, "and rather less foolish than one might expect someone of his appearance to be." Mrs Walker had noticed that Mr Richards was not only pleasant but unusually pleasant-looking, but she had taken little interest in the young man beyond the registration of these qualities. For the greater part of their conversation she was barely conscious of what was being said, as she was overwhelmed by the sensation of being looked at by Mr Barratt, whose gaze she experienced as a kind of enhancing glow. If he looked at her face, her face felt more beautiful, if he looked at her hands they seemed more shapely, her fingers more slender. When he looked away, however, the sensation lingered only briefly, so that when he conversed with Miss Lucy, who was herself distracted by the other gentleman at Barratt's shoulder, Mrs Walker grew anxious to have him look at her again. She marvelled at the absurdity of this, following her daughter from the church and around the low wall which separated the dead from the high street. She had anticipated Mr Barratt's declaration and had known what her response would be. Her expectation had been that her feelings would not alter greatly and that at worst she might experience that sense of anticlimax which typically inheres to such moments, but instead her feelings had grown in intensity. She had spent much of her waking time since their conversation in the garden the previous day imagining reasons for Mr Barratt to change his mind, having never previously doubted the strength or sincerity of his affections. More surprising still, perhaps, was this yearning for his company and his attention. Mrs Walker was an unusually self-possessed woman, who enjoyed the autonomy, or the appearance thereof, which her wealth afforded. She had spent five years of widowhood honing this independence as if it were the edge of a blade, and it seemed unimaginable that she would surrender it, like a defeated sea captain, so readily. She had foresworn the isolation she enjoyed for Lucy's sake. Meadholme was too remote a spot in which to spend one's best years, a young woman needed society and the promise of romance, but instead it was she, Susannah, whose heart had been stirred, by this terrible monolith of a man.

They were too old. His voice was too loud. He might inadvertently squash her at some point. She smiled each of these arguments away as she rehearsed them, summoning to mind his long, restless visage above those broad shoulders.

"What are you thinking of, Mama?" asked Miss Lucy as they stepped into the cramped hall of the Rectory. "Your face is a picture." Lottie smirked, then raised both eyebrows as she took her mistress's cape. Mrs Walker bared her teeth.

"I was wondering what we might give the gentlemen for tea," she said. Lottie coughed meaningfully and disappeared towards the kitchen.

"I'm sure cook will have some ideas," said Miss Lucy, following the maid along the passage. Mrs Walker, conscious that the Rector would not return for a while and not wishing to be alone, scooped up Mittens and took him into the library. The cat protested in an insincere fashion but allowed himself to be placed in Mrs Walker's lap as she half-reclined on the velvet chaise. She petted him until they both began to find the activity tiresome. She let go of the creature and he made his escape.

"Run away too, why don't you?" she said, as the cat's tail disappeared around the edge of the door. Mittens did not reply.

XVI

MISS LUCY HAD countless questions to ask Mr Richards, about his family, and his future plans and his preference in dogs. Mrs Walker interrupted from time to time so that the young man might have a moment to breathe and to take a bite of cake. Reverend 0Archer and Mr Barratt found themselves superfluous to the central business of the hour and having sought the kind consent of Mrs Walker with a triangular exchange of glances the two gentlemen slipped into the Rector's study.

"What a pleasure this is, Charles! It's seems an age, does it not, since we have had an opportunity to converse man to man."

"It has been too long, yes," said Mr Barratt. "You know how highly I value your opinion and enjoy your company. You have been very busy, and no-one likes an indolent priest."

"You are referring to my sermon, I see. Yes, some difficult ideas there, I hope some of them came across."

"An amount of attentive listening was required, certainly," Barratt said, "but your meaning was not, I feel, beyond the comprehension of a thoughtful parishioner."

"You are very kind," said the Rector. "I fear I must answer your kindness with a regrettable confession. The book that you gave me, Ricardo's *Political Economy*, I seem to have lost it. It was here on my reading table, I'm sure, but it has disappeared, like a puff of pipe smoke."

"What a mystery," said Barratt, though no trace of surprise was evident on his face.

"A mystery indeed," said the Rector. "I have ransacked the library, suspecting that I might have shelved the thing in an unguarded moment, but to no avail."

"The binding was unusual, was it not?"

"Quite right, blonde calfskin, with speckled endpapers."

"I am sure it will turn up," said Barratt. "Have you asked the ladies of the house if they know of its whereabouts?"

"Susannah says I have misplaced it somewhere in here, and I should tidy the place completely. Miss Lucy has no recollection of any such book and Lottie swears, with considerable vehemence incidentally, that she has not touched it, not even to clean underneath."

"Lottie offered no other observations?" asked Mr Barratt.

"Ought she told have done so, Charles? Do you mean to implicate the poor creature?"

"I am convinced as you are of Lottie's innocence, Reverend. I would only observe that she is a remarkably keen-eyed and curious young woman, and is more likely to know the comings and goings of this household than anyone else."

Mrs Walker had taken a turn about the room, meanwhile, stopping at the chair which Mr Barratt generally occupied, that was closest to the study. Her fiancé had left a substantial hollow in the upholstery into which she lowered herself, like the first pea in the bowl. Miss Lucy's interrogation of Mr Richards continued, but Mrs Walker would nevertheless have expected to be able to hear Mr Barratt's voice through the thick oak of the study door. The fact that she was unable to discern anything other than a low, rumbling sound seemed to indicate that a conversation of the greatest confidentiality was taking place, and there was but a single topic about which the two gentlemen would converse in this muffled fashion.Mrs Walker was mistaken, for the time being at least. Mr Barratt had yet to make any reference to his recent engagement to Mrs Walker but was instead attempting to determine the nature of Reverend Archer's involvement with the Trust.

"What do you make of Mr Nicholson?"

"He is an unusual fellow, certainly," said the Rector. "Though I suppose the same might be said of you or I, Charles." A smile of happy kinship passed between the two men. "Nicholson is perhaps a stranger fish altogether. I have met him now on half a dozen occasions and each time it is as if I encounter a different individual. As if, in fact, there are several Henry Nicholsons walking the Earth, all possessed of discrete personalities."

"May I ask what business you have with the gentleman?"

"I don't believe I have discussed it with you, Charles, have I? A thousand apologies, I am generally so preoccupied with parochial affairs that I forget about it myself. Mr Nicholson's Trust, as dear Lucy calls it, is properly the Old B_____ Charitable Trust."

"And you are a trustee, John? How do you find the time?"

"You have guessed it," said the Rector. "My impression thus far is that it is a kind of honorary position, and that very little is demanded of me. The Trust needs but one helmsman, it seems, and Nicholson is at the wheel." Barratt was pleased, in fact, by this response since it appeared to absolve his friend of any culpability relating to the operation of the Trust, but he summoned a convincing expression of concern, pouting rather, and pointing his eyebrows down towards an alarmed Reverend Archer. "Is that an unusual state of affairs, Charles? It seems that you disapprove."

"Every court has a king," Barratt said. "I am sure that there are other organisations which are similarly arranged. I do wonder though, what the purpose of a board of trustees is really, if it does not participate in the management of the Trust. It seems that you have some misgivings about Mr Nicholson too, John, so if I were you I might also question the wisdom of granting this petty monarch unchecked power over his realm." The two gentlemen lit their pipes then, and Mr Barratt's observation seemed to mingle with the smoke beneath the low ceiling of the study.

"Is it a curse or a blessing to view the world with such clarity, Charles? To see what needs to be done and then to set about doing it."

"I feel neither cursed, nor blessed," said Barratt.

"What is that you want me to do?"

"If I wished you to take action I would have said as much, John. I do not mean to manipulate you; I mean only to ensure that you are insulated from harm."

"I take it that you suspect Mr Nicholson of some malpractice," said the Rector, "and that is why you asked Miss Lucy to refrain from speaking to him about the dance."

"It is only a suspicion, but one which I felt you, my dear friend, should be aware of."

"Thank you," Reverend Archer said, sighing. "I know you, Charles, you could not allow such a situation to persist once you became aware of it. What would you have done if I had offered a more admiring assessment of Henry Nicholson?"

"You are too kind, actually. I first heard of the Trust, and of the possibility that our acquaintance might be exploiting his position many months ago, and the matter slipped from my mind."

"We cannot combat all of the devil's doings at once," said the Rector, and the laughter which followed this remark restored the two friends to their customary sense of fellowship.

"I was greatly relieved, I admit, that you did not think too highly of Mr Nicholson. I would still have sought to protect you from him, of course, assuming that he has acted as I believe him to have done."

"Do I need to be protected, then? What on Earth are you planning, Charles?"

"Nothing revolutionary," said Barratt. "I mean only to restore the probity of the Trust, and for Mr Nicholson to reimburse what he has taken. As for you needing protection, perhaps I misspoke. It is the reputation of your household which I seek to preserve, and I have a particular interest, which is related to but lies beyond the limits of our close friendship, in doing so."

"My dear Barratt, even your riddles are transparent," the Rector said. "If your interest is in someone to whom I am related, and who is beyond this door then I can only advise you to announce that interest without delay. This is the other matter you wished to discuss with me, is it not?"

"I sought to provide information, Sir, rather than to enter into a discussion, since it is a *fait accompli*. Mrs Walker has accepted my proposal of marriage." Reverend Archer emitted a type of delighted squawk which was not dissimilar in timbre to that which had issued from his maid the previous morning, and he embraced his friend, who stooped considerably to facilitate the gesture. In the library Mrs Walker heard the Rector's momentary outburst, a sound familiar to her from her cousin's childhood, and she exhaled, and with an expression of great satisfaction rose from Barratt's chair, just as the door to the study opened. Reverend Archer emerged smiling broadly, followed by Mr Barratt and the eyes of the betrothed met briefly before Mrs Walker turned and spoke to her youthful companions.

"Mr Richards, you will be devastated to learn, I'm sure, that I must tear my daughter away from you for a few moments. Will you survive?"

"Oh, I think I may manage," the young man said, and Miss Lucy, who did not possess the most brilliant of minds but was nevertheless sensitive to gentle slights of this kind, particularly those of maternal origin, offered a surly look at her mother and Mr Richards in turn, but she allowed Mrs Walker to usher her into the garden.

"A drink, gentleman!" the Rector said, grabbing a bottle from a cabinet beneath the largest bookcase. "To the happy couple." Mr Richards repeated the toast and sipped his sherry then politely sought to learn the identity of the couple in question, before declaring Mr Barratt a very fortunate gentleman indeed, an observation which carried with it a certain degree of risk, but one which the considerable personal charm of Mr Richards ensured was not misinterpreted, and no offence was taken any more than it was intended. The two ladies reappeared from the garden, their cheeks fetchingly doused with tears, and Miss Lucy complained in the quietest way that she must now look utterly blotchy, and was reassured by the gentlemen that on the contrary she had never looked prettier and the young lady chose to ignore the fact that the person whose opinion on such matters was of the greatest importance to her was by some distance the least qualified to make such a comment, having set eyes on her for the first time just a few hours previously. Mrs Walker explained that the tears she had shed were those of joy and relief, and she crossed the room to stand beside her husband-to-be and placed her hand in his.

Volume the Second

XVII

ONCE THERE WAS only a river, which rose in the Downs and flowed along a serpentine path of its own creation towards the Thames and thence to the sea. The river altered along its length, widening in one location, flowing more quickly in another. There was a place a little less than a day's ride from the great city where the river was neither very broad nor deep. Here it was possible to cross on horseback or even on foot if absolutely necessary. This place was useful for the washing of clothes and in the warmer months, we may assume, for washing one's person. Boats might be readily loaded or unloaded there, however until the river was dredged during the reign of the second King Charles only those of an unusually shallow draught could pass the spot. Before that a bridge was built so that no-one need get his boots wet and an inn appeared and a scattering of houses and at a distance, a church. This was the south end of B_____, and for many yearsit was all the town there was. St Andrew's and the Rectory stood isolated a half-mile north north-east of The Bull (the south end being informally and approximately named) and the pious endured an unpleasant trudge to and from the church on wet Sunday mornings.

This separation persisted for centuries until a longer, wider and altogether more sturdy bridge was constructed by masons and engineers from His Majesty's Navy, it having been determined by some brilliant young men from the Royal Observatory that the town stood on the very shortest path between Whitehall and Portsmouth. Traffic increased, and some fraction of those who passed through liked the look of the place, with its willow trees, and thick hedgerows and the noble old church out beyond the town's end, and some smaller fraction of those admirers returned and settled in B_____, buying land and putting up grand new houses on either side of the London Road.

The grandest of these properties was the Red House, built for Admiral Jephcott and leased by a descendant of that venerable mariner to Mr Charles Barratt, himself no stranger to the high seas. Barratt had travelled to both the East and West Indies as a young man though in a mercantile rather than a martial capacity and the sum of these experiences, by his reckoning, was that dry land was generally to be preferred. Had anyone called upon this singular gentleman early on the Friday before Whitsun, they would have found only his cook at home, an enormous yet taciturn woman who would offer no clue to her master's whereabouts. Barratt and Johnson, his valet, were abroad that morning, back where our tale recommenced, beside the banks of the river.

It was a warm morning and Johnson carried Barratt's coat and his own as the two men passed over the bridge. On the other side of the river the land was low and flat and a great many insects seemed to drift in the air. A collection of buildings stood to the west of the Portsmouth road, but barely stood, it seemed, so bowed and ramshackle was their condition. A few of these edifices had foundations of brick or stone but all seemed to be constructed otherwise from whatever timber lay at hand. The buildings were arranged along four sides of an open space, like a farmyard, or some parody of a grand city square. This was Butcher's Green, though again we might note that the nomenclature of B_____ was not always to be relied upon. No grass grew there, nor had any butcher ever prospered on the wrong side of the bridge. One might have thought these structures too mean to house livestock so neglected and inhospitable they seemed but in fact they were human dwellings, in which bread was made and children slept and prayers were offered. Mr Barratt had seen worse places to live, in foreign cities and in that of his birth. Nevertheless he experienced a confusion of emotions and memories as he considered the prospect of life in Butcher's Green, a few furlongs from his own home, just as he might have when confronted by the destitution of Calcutta or Aldgate. He grew angry, and kicked at the barren ground with the toe of his boot, but this anger was alloyed with guilt, and the sense that removing oneself from poverty did not amount to an escape. It could not be left behind; the knot of hunger in one's stomach never fully unravelled, and any comfort seemed fragile or provisional.

Barratt approached the first building on the left, which must once have stabled horses, and knocked gently at the door. He heard a woman whispering and hushing beyond the ragged portal.

"I mean you no harm, Madam," he said. "I bring relief, I hope, and alms at the very least." An eye appeared at a knothole. Despite his stature no-one could have mistaken Mr Barratt for a bailiff. A bolt slipped within and the door opened, scraping a crescent of dust and stone aside. Barratt's chest tightened and he felt afflicted by the contrast between the brightness of the morning and the darkness of the hovel's interior. The woman leant on the ledge of the door, considering her visitors with a calm expression. Her eyes were a very bright blue, though her skin and hair were dark, like some Mediterranean beauty, and a beauty she was, or might have been. Her clothes were shabby and sat very tightly on her, since she was heavy with child. Barratt would not have put her age above four and twenty.

"Are you quite well, Sir?" Mr Barratt collected himself and handed the woman some coins.

"Quite well, yes, thank you," he said. The woman registered the weight of the coins and the volume of the generous gentleman's voice with equal surprise. "My name is Charles Barratt, may I speak with you?" The woman gestured for him to enter. As Barratt's eyes adjusted to the gloom he became aware of a rectangular space, and a low bed in a corner with two very small children sat upon it. There was a small table and two chairs and a stove. Aside from a small bundle of blankets at the foot of the pallet and the clothes they wore the family seemed to have no possessions at all.

"Rebekah Broady," the woman said, sitting. "You are welcome." Barratt bowed deeply and having sought permission with a glance at his host he sat in the other chair. Johnson pushed the door to from outside.

"This may not be of interest to you, Mrs Broady, but I am considering an investment in the south end, and I will need persons to come and work for me. I know that many of your neighbours, and your husband perhaps, will be engaged in the fields until the autumn, but it is my understanding that winter can be a struggle."

"We borrow in the winter, Mr Barratt, or depend on the parish."

"There is no dishonour in that," said Barratt. "I may seem a fat old fellow but my family once relied upon the church."

"I congratulate you, Sir, on your present happiness." Mrs Broady offered these words without a trace of bitterness and Mr Barratt felt a strong admiration for the young woman. "What kind of business is it?"

"Printing, stationery, other related items." Mrs Broady smiled.

"It will have to be some kind of investment, then, if your aim is to employ the folks of Butcher's Green," she said, "since not one of them can count higher than the fingers on their hands."

"I'm sure that cannot be true," said Barratt.

"It is absolutely true," Mrs Broady said. "I know because I have tried to teach them. And if you want fellows for printing they will have to be able to read backwards, will they not? There is not another person this side of the river who can read a word in any direction. Before you teach them to read you must first teach them not to drink and not to fight each other over the slightest thing."

"You seem to have an advantage over your neighbours," said Barratt.

"I have a little education, Sir, though I have other disadvantages." Mrs Broady noted the gentleman's disappointment. "What about a forge? The men here are strong enough to swing a hammer, and the fire would keep them warm."

"There is already a forge, Mrs Broady, and half a dozen more between here and Milton, I dare say." Barratt stood and looked at the two small boys wrestling on the bed. "You are hoping that the third child will be a girl?"

"This baby will be my fifth, Mr Barratt. The Lord in his wisdom took Matthew and Mary from me." Mrs Broady's eyes filled with tears and she began to sob. "Excuse me," she said, "it is my condition."

"There is no need to apologise," said Barratt. "I too have lost a child and the pain is with me every day."

"I recall their names, Mr Barratt, but I begin to forget their faces. Isn't that a terrible thing?"

"My own daughter is but an idea," he said. "Our minds are not made to contain all the grief we know. Perhaps feeling the absence of a loved one is less injurious than feeling their presence, and being unable to hold them or speak with them."

"The Lord knows best," said Mrs Broady.

"So our friends in the church tell us." Mr Barratt handed three more coins to Mrs Broady. "For the midwife," he said. She held Mr Barratt by the wrist for a moment and thanked him, and assured the gentleman of his kindness, but Barratt could not disguise the sense of deflation he felt. "Thank you, Mrs Broady, you have been most helpful. I will think again."

"I am sure you will find a way, Sir."

"I will be sure to call on you when I do," said Mr Barratt. He bowed again, waved a disapproving finger at the ruffians on the bed who jeered in response, and then left. Barratt and Johnson walked back across the bridge.

"The situation there is worse than I imagined," Mr Barratt remarked.

"It usually is, Sir," said Johnson.

XVIII

IT WAS TRUE,certainly, that the death of Catherine Barratt had cast a pall of sadness over her husband which had taken many years to lift, but in general he was not a person who dwelled on setbacks or reversals, preferring instead to pursue a different course with undimmed energy, and by the time Barratt arrived at the Red House, having walked back from the south end in silence for the most part, with Johnson beside him, his spirits were largely restored. The cook had accepted a letter while the two men were out.

> *Harvey Richards Esq.*
> *The Martyrs*
> *Milton*
> *SURREY*

23rd May 18__

Dear Mr Barratt,

You will be pleased to learn that I kept an appointment with Nicholson at The Bull yesterday evening. He is a strange fellow, as you have described him, and he appeared not to be listening to much of what I had to say. He did ask the very same questions that we thought he likely might, but I managed to parry these without misleading the gentleman entirely. He says he is not in possession of the Trust's ledgers, and that they have gone away, he did not specify whereto, for auditing. I told him that it would be impossible for us to proceed withoutseeing them and he implied that there would be costs involved in their retrieval. I advanced him the sum you authorised and have added this figure to the gentleman's account.

I hope that your plans for the printshop are proceeding apace and I await further instruction. Meanwhile I remain

Yours etc.

Harvey Richards

Barratt handed the letter to Johnson who read it then put it in his pocket for disposal at some later moment.

"You did not expect him to take the bait so easily, I presume," said Johnson.

"No, of course. For now it is enough that he has sniffed it."

"Do you suppose he will ever surrender the ledgers?"

"I cannot say with any confidence that the ledgers exist," Barratt admitted. "The bank will have a record of the Trust's deposits and withdrawals, but that will not be enough to condemn Mr Nicholson. It is also possible that the Trust's accounts have been falsified so carefully that we cannot demonstrate where or how funds have been misplaced. Cunningham says that the young man has many flaws, but is capable of considerable ingenuity."

"Why then did you authorise Mr Richards to offer an advance to Nicholson?"

"I meant to tempt Mr Nicholson," said Barratt. "When you walk among the stalls at Spittle Fields the grocers offer you small pieces of fruit to taste, in the hope that you will buy a bushel. The advance works in a similar fashion. It is also a test of his conscience."

"How so?"

"You recall your visit to the haberdasher's with Nicholson?" Johnson nodded.

"He left a small bundle there, I assumed it was something he wished to have repaired."

"It was the book I purchased for Reverend Archer when we were last in London," said Barratt. "It seems that the haberdasher's also serves as a kind of pawnbroker, and that our friend Mr Nicholson, for whatever reason, found himself in urgent need of ready money. Now, if he retains any kind of gentlemanly instinct Nicholson will use the advance to retrieve the book and return it to the Rectory. Such a man might be persuaded that he may still redeem himself, in spite of his previous conduct. If Reverend Archer does not get his Ricardo back we can assume that Mr Nicholson will have to be removed from the chair of the Trust by stronger means than simple persuasion."

"It seems that the Rector has a better chance of clapping eyes on his book than we do ours," said Johnson.

"For now we have only to wait and see."

"There was a saying in India, do you recall? Go softly to catch the monkey. I suppose it means you have to have a bit of patience where these matters are concerned."

"Patience and stealth will be our watchwords, as ever," said Mr Barratt. There was a pause while the two men looked at each other, each attempting to suppress their laughter for longer than the other, a game they had played for a quarter of a century. Johnson turned quite pink with the effort, but gave way first, loosing a great peal of guffawing, which the cook mistook for choking, and it was the sudden reappearance of this estimable gentlewoman, her face a mask of panic, which finally unmanned Barratt, whose own hilarity then expressed itself with such force that the second best china rattled on the dresser. The two men reassumed their usual composure eventually, just long enough for Johnson to remark that Mr Barratt was indeed the stealthiest of gentlemen, and as such, had he ever turned his hand to the hunting of tigers the results would have been truly remarkable, the conclusion of which statement caused both parties to fall about the place in uproar once more. This second outburst proved too much for the cook, who had remained concerned, to this point, for the health of the household. She threw her teacloth over her shoulder and her hands in the air and shaking her head and muttering unintelligibly she retreated to the kitchen.

"What about a school?" said Barratt, wiping his eyes on a handkerchief.

"A school? I thought it improbable that you'd turn a profit from a printshop, but with a school it's an impossibility. And the idea is to provide employment for these people, or so I thought. Mrs Broady says they can't sell wrapping paper, let alone teach arithmetic."

"I was not thinking of a Sunday school, Johnson, or a

Charterhouse. We ought first to teach the adults to read and write, no?"

"They are unwilling to learn," Johnson said. "You were told so not an hour ago."

"My word, you are just like Lottie, nothing escapes your attention." Barratt leaned on the back of a dining chair and looked up at his late wife, like a man seeking divine inspiration. "What if we offered them an incentive?"

"You would need to give classes in the alehouse, Mr Barratt, if you wished the gentlemen of Butcher's Green to attend."

"Perhaps you are right," said Barratt, checking his watch. "I am late for Mrs Walker. Excuse me, Johnson." He considered himself in the hallway mirror and made some corrections then left by the tall front door. Johnson flinched as the door slammed then made his way to kitchen. He picked up a teacloth and opened the stove then took the letter from his pocket and threw it in. He crouched to make sure the paper caught and watched for a few moments as the letter flared, Mr Richards' elegant hand still visible, and disappeared.

Mrs Walker was unhappy. A week had passed since she had agreed to marry Mr Barratt and nothing had changed. In fact, she had seen less of him these past few days than she might have expected to in her previous, unaffianced state, since Barratt had spent a great deal of the intervening period in conference with young Mr Richards, whose company her husband-to-be seemed to delight in almost as he did her own, and even after the young gentleman had travelled back to Milton his Mentor had seemed thoroughly distracted. She had decided to give voice to her unhappiness, even if it meant that she and Charles would have their first disagreement, and now he was late, and Mrs Walker had grown extremely agitated, since she feared that Lottie might return before she had had the opportunity to convey her feelings, and felt furthermore that in this anxious condition she ought not to be held responsible for anything she might say or do.

Mr Barratt knocked at the Rectory door, causing small bonbons of moss to tumble down from the building's ancient roof. Mrs Walker answered the door and Barratt stooped to enter. Without straightening himself he placed an arm around Mrs

Walker's waist and kissed her. Mrs Walker had endured some years without any physical attention of this kind and found that for the moment her knees could not support her weight. It was no matter, since Mr Barratt was able to carry her into the library on his hip, with her feet floating a few inches above the floor, as he continued to kiss her. He placed her carefully upon the chaise then retreated to his own favourite chair saying, "Susannah, my own love, I have no words to express how much I have missed you!" He sat down and looked across the room at his fiancée, whose face had coloured deeply, and Mrs Walker found that it was not at present necessary to communicate the disappointment she had felt just a few moments earlier, which seemed somehow already a distant, half forgotten sensation. She sat silently instead, enjoying the joy in Mr Barratt's face, and the excitement in his eyes as he regarded her.

XIX

REVEREND ARCHER did his very best to appear blasé about the dance which his young cousin meant to organise but in fact he was looking forward to it greatly. He was delighted, therefore, when Miss Lucy asked him to invite Mr Nicholson to tea so that she might apprise him of her plans. Mr Barratt had lifted his embargo on discussion of the matter, though privately he assured the Rector that the best course to follow was one which kept as great a distance between oneself and Henry Nicholson as possible.

It was no simple thing to reconcile Mr Barratt's abject portrait of Nicholson with the gentleman himself, particularly that incarnation who called at the Rectory on a bright afternoon in the first week of June, and cut a dazzling figure, so much so that Miss Lucy forgot all about Harvey Richards for at least half an hour, unless it were generally accepted that any person of a mutable, mercurial nature is inherently untrustworthy. This was yet another new Nicholson: polite, attentive and suave. His hair had been cut and his jacket cleaned and the slight wildness of his gaze was almost entirely suppressed. It should be noted, in fairness to this gentleman that his offers of assistance to Miss Lucy were genuine and his enthusiasm for the project sincere and heartfelt. Whether that enthusiasm had its root in a sense of civic duty or in the barren soil of self-interest will have to remain, for the moment, to be seen.

Mr Barratt had been in the garden of the Red House when Mr Nicholson arrived, worrying at his sweet peas, but he spied the gentleman's carriage when he went up to his bedroom to find his best boots. Barratt sat at the edge of the bed watching the street below, and once Nicholson's carriage had rolled away he skipped downstairs, put on his hat and a light wool jacket and crossed to the Rectory.

Miss Lucy answered his knock, as Lottie was preoccupied with the tea things. Some young women might have adopted a tone of heightened reverence towards a gentleman recently betrothed to their mother, but Lucy Walker was not of this number, and continued to giggle freely at Mr Barratt, even as the prospect of becoming the daughter of Mrs Barratt loomed.

"You will never guess who was just here," said Miss Lucy.

"Never?"

"Mr Henry Nicholson."

"I do feel as though I might have been given more of an opportunity to speculate, Miss Lucy," Barratt complained. "Was the subject of the dance raised at all?

"We spoke of nothing else," Miss Lucy said. "I would not allow it."

"So I can readily believe. Is your mother at home?"

"She is in the library with Reverend Archer. The two of them spend an uncommon amount of time in there, if you ask me. It cannot be good for their health."

"Your concern for your elders does you credit, my dear child," said Barratt. "Perhaps we should join them?"

Mrs Walker smiled and coloured slightly as her daughter and fiancé entered the library, though she blushed in delight, rather than in discomfort, imagining that she might listen to the two of them chattering in duet, soprano and baritone, for many years to come.

"Charles, welcome," said Reverend Archer. "The ladies will soon inter you beneath a pile of news but allow me to scatter the first handful. Ricardo is found!"

"Mr Nicholson had borrowed the book, I suppose, leaving a note that was somehow misplaced, is that about the tall and short of it?"

"My word, Charles," said the Rector, "you are the quite the cleverest person I know."

"My cousin's friends from Oxford are a truly exceptional group of young men," said Mrs Walker. "This is no mean compliment. They excel at all the noble arts: drinking, punting, gallivanting..." Reverend Archer acknowledged the accuracy of Mrs Walker's dart with a nod and a pout.

"It is true that I keep better company now than I once did," he said. "Even Mr Nicholson is not so dastardly a fellow as you would have us believe, Charles."

"What's that?" Miss Lucy was a picture of perplexity, as if she believed it improbable that anyone with the slightest stain on their character might be allowed to converse with her, and that even were such an exchange to take place the privilege of proximity to her own spotless nature would effect a kind of baptism, cleansing her sooty-souled interlocutor of their sins. "Is Mr Nicholson suspected of some misbehaviour?" Mr Barratt was vexed with his friend and made little attempt to disguise the fact. Reverend Archer returned his glare with a complacent smirk, resembling nothing so much in that moment, Barratt thought, as one of those defiant squirrels in the Rector's own churchyard, who would stop in their tracks, daring passers-by to fight them, before scurrying up the nearest yew. The thought amused Mr Barratt, then calmed his ire.

"There is still hope for Henry Nicholson," he conceded. "I will be keeping a close eye on him, however, since he is one of those young gentlemen whose personality is as yet unformed."

Mrs Walker had watched this exchange with acute interest, since it had revealed that the information which her fiancé had withheld from Miss Lucy and herself was no trifling thing, as she had previously assumed. The fact that Reverend Archer was privy to this intelligence and she was not caused a stirring of dissatisfaction which Mrs Walker struggled to control.

"Well," she said, her voice exhibiting the faintest note of strain, "it is only a pity that the gentleman is too old to study for the church; that would be just the spot for him." Mr Barratt had developed a new sensitivity to his beloved's moods, and registered the alteration in her tone. Their eyes met, and he attempted a look of reassurance. Mrs Walker frowned very slightly so Mr Barratt turned his eyes towards the window. Mrs Walker, almost indetectably, shook her head: the Rectory garden was now so overgrown as to be almost impassable.

"It is terribly stuffy in here," Mr Barratt said. "I wonder if Mrs Walker would care to join me for a turn about the church?"

"You are quite right, my dear Charles," said Mrs Walker, suddenly revived. "Lottie, do open the window more fully, how the poor Rector can think at all in these torrid conditions is beyond me." Lottie, who had only re-entered the library moments before grumbled something about it scarcely being her fault if the gentleman was incapable of opening a window but Mrs Walker, who had already placed her arm in Mr Barratt's and found a new serenity in having done so, elected not to upbraid her.

They strolled down Rectory Lane and once beyond the range of even Lottie's remarkable hearing Mrs Walker squeezed her lover's hand and spoke.

"I am not a naive person, Charles, I understand that there are parts of your life which you may wish to keep me separate from, for whatever reason. I know also that there are matters which men often seek to keep to themselves because they feel they are unfit for discussion in front of women, but I do not feel that is the case where Henry Nicholson is concerned. I should be grateful, therefore, if you would tell me at least as much as my cousin knows about that gentleman. If my daughter and I are to involve ourselves in the raising of funds for the Trust we should know the character of the man on whose behalf we are making those efforts."

"Susannah, you are the most wise and perspicacious of you sex, for you have hit the nail square on its head. I mean only to ensure that the proceeds from the dance benefit the Trust, and not Henry Nicholson himself."

They turned in to the Backs, a path which ran between the boundary of the church and the rolling fields beyond. Mr Barratt explained what he had learned from Cunningham, and the condition of Nicholson's estate, and why and how he had involved young Harvey Richards in the affair. As he spoke he watched Mrs Walker's face from the corner of his eye, wary of any hint of displeasure at his conduct. None appeared, however, and by the time he had concluded his account his betrothed was smiling.

"I am relieved, Charles, that I agreed to marry you so readily. Only the Lord knows what lengths you might otherwise have gone to in order to ensnare me." Mr Barratt laughed. "I would have travelled to the ends of the Earth and back, I assure you," he said. "I would not have ceased until I found the tenderest of traps in which you might be captured. Quilted silk, scented with rose..."

"And gold bars to peer out from, no doubt." Mr Barratt held his fiancée's hand more tightly for a moment, so that she paused and turned to him. They kissed, and each felt the years slip away, so in that instant, as a light breeze moved the grass in the meadow, they were the youngest of lovers once more, with a lifetime together to look forward to.

They walked on, eventually, enraptured by the beauty of the afternoon.

"There is something else that I ought to tell you which I have yet to tell Reverend Archer," said Barratt. Mrs Walker was already awash with pleasant sensations, but the idea of having an advantage over her cousin brought more pleasure still.

"Go on," she said.

"I told Harvey Richards to advance Mr Nicholson a sum of money, I felt sure he would ask for it. I wanted him to feel what it might be like to be free from financial obligation for a while. There was a chance that he might fritter it away, but it seems that he is not so abased. Almost the first thing he did was to retrieve the good Rector's book from the haberdasher's..."

"The haberdasher's? What on Earth was it doing there?" Mr Barratt smiled at Mrs Walker. "No matter, I can guess."

"And now it is returned. It is a hopeful signal, I think." They walked around the north end of St Andrew's in a joyous silence, looking at each other from time to time, and choosing to disregard the knowledge which they shared, that such moments of perfect happiness are evanescent by their very nature. Everything else which life consisted of, its imperfections, sorrows and finitude would afflict them once more, soon enough, but for the moment they were able to pretend otherwise.

XX

THEY RODE IN the cart, since there were some items which Mr Barratt required for the garden which were not readily available in B_____ but which might be obtained en route to or from Milton, or in that town. Their first stop was at Butcher's Green, where, they were pleased to learn, Mrs Broady had given birth to a little girl. Both mother and baby were healthy, and the child asserted this status at length and at considerable volume.

"She has lungs like yours, Sir," observed Johnson.

"I wanted to name her for your wife, perhaps," said Mrs Broady. "Would you mind? What is her name?"

"I have no wife," said Mr Barratt. "I was married once, when I was a good deal younger. She died and is much missed. Her name was Catherine." Mrs Broady was mortified.

"Forgive me, Sir, when we spoke before of your loss I thought it was a little one that God had taken."

"My loss was twofold, unfortunately. No matter, it was a long time ago. Catherine is a fine name for a child. She is very bonny, is she not, Johnson?"

"She is certainly very pink, Sir." At this point one of Mrs Broady's boys, jealous of the attention lavished on his newly minted sister, attempted to climb Mr Barratt, as if he were some sort of fruit tree.

"I wondered if Mr Broady would be here," said Mr Barratt.

"He has been back in the fields these past two days," Mrs Broady replied. "I am glad of it, we must feed the children."

"Indeed. Would you object to us calling again on our return from Milton? I am anxious to speak with your husband, as I may have some additional employment to offer him, and I wish to consult him about another matter."

"Not at all, you are always welcome, Mr Barratt. Too few show us any kindness, though those that do are held in high esteem. There is a lady from the north end who visits, she is a very fine woman, I think, but you would not know so from her manner. And Reverend Halliwell darkens our door from time to time."

"You are a Methodist then, Madame, I take it?"

"I will accept alms from whichever church offers them, Sir," said Mrs Broady, smiling. Her eldest son had climbed as far as Mr Barratt's waist and was attempting to grab a sleeve in order to further his ascent. His brother, who was surely no more than a year younger, had decided that the activity seemed to be of a kind best enjoyed in tandem and was exploring the lower extent of Barratt's breeches for a foothold. "Leave the gentleman now, boys." Johnson removed the elder child from his master's trunk and placed him on the bed. The younger boy abandoned his own escalation and threw himself on his brother and the two of them resumed what appeared to be a near perpetual wrestling match."They will be pleased to see you again, anyway," Mrs Broady added.

The gentlemen bowed and left. The sun was higher and the horses sweated between the staves. There was little shade: what woods there were stood to the west of the road, and the journey seemed longer than either man remembered, though their shared stoicism prevented any open acknowledgment of this impression. They arrived in Milton half an hour before noon, a little hot and travel-sore. While Johnson attended to the horses Mr Barratt took a stiff, cautious stroll along the main street of the town. Milton was somewhat smaller than B_____ and its buildings generally newer and more homogeneous. As Barratt passed the George, an inn named for the first Hanoverian monarch, he espied a familiar frame approaching. Young Mr Richards spotted his Mentor at the same moment and waved, quickening his pace. A strong affection had developed between the two gentlemen, in spite of the fact that each envied the other's situation in life. Harvey Richards could only imagine the satisfaction that Mr Barratt felt, in having amassed a sizable fortune, and in his betrothal to a charming, handsome widow whose own wealth was almost equal to his own. Barratt, meanwhile, might have surrendered every penny of that fortune, and perhaps even Mrs Walker, to be a young man once more, with the gifts which Mr Richardspossessed.

They shook hands and Mr Barratt expressed his delight at seeing his young friend again.

"I pray you are well, Sir," said Richards. "It is unseasonably warm."

"Quite well, thank you, Harvey. It is indeed a little warm, for England."

"England is all I know, I'm afraid," Mr Richards said. "You have travelled a great deal beyond these shores, I recall."

"I am no Raleigh, not by any consideration, but I have lived in hotter climes. Johnson is the true adventurer. We should locate him, and he can tell you all about the Moluccas." Messrs Barratt and Richards walked side by side back to where the cart stood, exchanging further pleasantries. Johnson and the horses had disappeared and for a few moments confusion reigned before Mr Richards suggested that perhaps Johnson had found a shaded spot in which to rest and water the horses, though his reasons for leaving the cart remained opaque.

"Perhaps we should wait here for him," said Mr Barratt, and young Mr Richards agreed that this was certainly the best policy, although the sun was almost at its zenith and the prospect of a glass of small beer was hard to keep from one's mind. Johnson reappeared after a few minutes leading the two mares.

"It's good to give them a break from the harness," he said, as he retethered the horses, and the beasts did indeed seem refreshed, trotting back to the George with an elevated gait.

Mr Richards expressed his relief that he had run into Mr Barratt and thus spared his visitors a trip to The Martyrs, as if this were some happy accident, whereas in fact he had been patrolling the main street for an hour in the hope that just such a meeting would take place, so keen was he to avoid Mr Barratt seeing his obscure accommodation. Barratt had lived in some low places himself, of course, and would scarcely have judged his protégé for choosing to rest his head in some affordable spot, nor indeed were the young man's rooms so squalid as to create a negative impression. The Martyrs had been a monastery, and subsequently the home of a friend of Thomas Cranmer, but it retained its claustral atmosphere, having suffered little improvement during the intervening centuries.

It was decided that they would take luncheon in the George and Mr Richards secured a private room while Johnson made sure the horses were looked after. The innkeeper's daughter, captivated by the beauty of Harvey Richards' outward form, was still more impressed by his modest manner and stood staring at him from the doorway after she had brought beer and pies to the table.

"Thank you, Mademoiselle," said Mr Barratt, with his

accustomed emphasis, which was enough to bring the young woman to her senses. She stepped backwards, curtseying repeatedly, and Johnson stood and closed the door. "Where have we got to, Harvey? Tell us all." Mr Richards finished chewing on a particularly resistant piece of pastry, sipped his beer and cleared his throat.

"There is no sign of the ledgers. I have written to Mr Nicholson twice requesting that he inform me of his progress in securing their return, and offering to retrieve them on his behalf, but it is clear that he has no intention of allowing me to see them, if indeed they exist. If they do not I am unclear how we are to calculate the sum which Nicholson owes the trust."

"Let me concern myself with that," said Mr Barratt.

"The gentleman will pay," Johnson added, with a kind of leering expression which made young Mr Richards somewhat uncomfortable.

"I anticipated that access to the ledgers might be deferred, perhaps indefinitely, so I asked Mr Nicholson's permission to speak with the other board members, who would presumably vouch for the propriety of the Trust. I explained that I might then report back to the person whose interest I represent and ask him to authorise me to transfer the capital."

"I imagine Nicholson provided names and addresses by return," said Barratt.

"He did," Mr Richards replied. "In addition to Mr Nicholson and Reverend Archer there are five other Trustees. They all seem to be gentleman farmers and those I have already conversed with spoke very highly of Mr Nicholson's father, while admitting that they knew his son less well."

"You have been busy, Harvey," Mr Barratt said. "I applaud you." The young man nodded and took a bite from his pie.

"I explained my purpose in speaking with the gentlemen, but it was clear that none of them had any detailed knowledge of the operation of the Trust. The Board meets once a year, Mr Nicholson is elected as Chair and Treasurer, the general aims of the Trust are reaffirmed and they all go and have a jolly nice dinner." Johnson harrumphed at this and kicked the wainscoting.

"Were you able to discover if Nicholson is personally indebted to the other Trustees?" Barratt asked.

"I was unable to concoct a strategy for this. If I were to have simply asked it would have aroused suspicion, I fear. How might I have guessed such a thing? I thought it best that we did not risk Mr Nicholson learning that I was asking questions about his situation, rather than about the workings of the Trust."

"Never mind," said Barratt. "It may not prove to be important. You have done very well, Harvey. We can expect Mr Nicholson to approach you, I think. He will wish to know what you have relayed to the mysterious benefactor. Meanwhile, do you think that the Trustees, Reverend Archer aside, might be readily persuaded to remove Nicholson?"

"They seemed like decent men, and they must appreciate that Henry Nicholson is a different beast from his father. I think we would need to demonstrate his corruption in some indisputable way, but they will of course be embarrassed, so it would be best to be as confidential as possible."

"Your mind is as a mirror to mine own, Harvey," said Barratt.

"I did have one concern, however," Mr Richards said.

"Tell it."

"I presume the Trust will benefit a great deal from Miss Lucy's dance, if it is a success, and we have no reason to suspect it will not be. For the moment Mr Nicholson has money in his pocket, which we have provided..."

"The gentleman will pay," Johnson repeated.

"Of course," Mr Richards continued. "The gentleman will pay. I would only observe that the dance hampers our scheme somewhat, since it offers another route to fiscal security for Nicholson, and accordingly lessens the importance of our benefactor's contribution."

"Would you have me break my promise to Miss Lucy, that most admirable of young women? No, Sir, it will not do." Mr Barratt smiled at Mr Richards, who had failed to grasp that he was joking, and whose face wore an expression of mild alarm. "Trust me, Harvey. The dance is the thing, the device which lowers the drawbridge from without."

Two large pots, in the Hellenic style, rattled together in the back of the cart, along with bamboo canes, severally bundled, and a small sack of garlic bulbs, and having bade farewell to Mr Richards and exchanged a glance which served to silently communicate the degree to which each of the two older gentlemen admired the younger, and having visited the merchant from whom the items which filled the cart had been obtained, this being the reason, ostensibly at least, for their round trip to Milton, Mr Barratt and Johnson headed home. The sun was at their shoulder now, and the woods offered occasional shade, so their return journey was altogether more comfortable than their morning ordeal. They had enjoyed a few more glasses of the George's small beer, which intake necessitated a break in their ride home, the two old associates surveying the distant fields of rape like Cortez on his peak, and been delighted furthermore by the ministrations of Lizzie, the excitable daughter of the innkeeper, who had succeeded in making the blameless Mr Richards blush on two or three occasions, so ardent were the flames of her passion. They approached B_____ in good spirits, therefore, as the sight of the spire of St Jude's and the tower of St Andrew's therebeyond afforded to their no longer youthful souls a gratifying sense of homecoming. The bridge came into view and before it, to the west, Butcher's Green. Johnson pulled the horses off the Portsmouth Road and into the mean quadrangle.

There was a commotion outside Mrs Broady's home. An old woman was banging at the door and stretching her low frame to peer through the knothole.

"Bekah!" she shouted. "Bekah, are you living? Open the door!" A sound of sobbing came from within. Mr Barratt jumped down from the box.

"What has happened here, Madame?"

"It's none of your concern, I'm sure," the old woman said. Silver hair spread from beneath her scarf and her body was bent but she retained a certain hostile vitality, Barratt noted.

"I am a friend of Mrs Broady," he explained. "I wish only to be assured of her wellbeing."

"I heard her scream, then he run off and she has bolted the door against him." Barratt absorbed this information then lowered his voice to a degree that would have been unfamiliar to those closest to him, and spoke through the narrow gap in the door.

"Mrs Broady, this is Charles Barratt. I am sorry for whatever has happened, but I must know that you are safe." The sobbing ceased at the sound of his voice.

"We are quite well, Mr Barratt, the boys and Catherine and I. Leave us now, we are in no danger."

"I do not doubt you, Madame, but you must understand that I have to see you, and check your condition."

"We are unharmed, I assure you," said Mrs Broady. "I would not mislead you, not after the kindness you have shown me." The old woman seemed satisfied with this and retreated to her own mean lodgings. Mr Barratt's worst fears were not so easily subdued.

"Mrs Broady, I cannot leave without seeing you. Open the door or I will break it down." Barratt heard her footsteps approach and a faint groan as she pulled back the bolt. It was nearly midsummer and the sun would not set for another hour so a warm, slanting light fell on Mrs Broady's face as she opened the door, a light which might at another time have flattered her features. She wore a scarf about her face, like her neighbour, intended to disguise a crimson swelling on the left side of her face and a cut on the opposite cheek which was still bright with blood.

"My dear woman, what has happened?"

"I'm sure you can guess, Sir," Mrs Broady said.

XXI

MRS BROADY INSISTED that she was to blame. Her husband had returned from the fields half-drunk and exhausted; she should have let him collapse on the pallet and sleep it off, as he had on many previous evenings. The work was hard and thirsty and he was not to be begrudged these small measures of relief. Mr Barratt scoffed at this.

"Small measures? Not small enough, it seems."

"He is not like that, Mr Barratt. He has not laid a hand on me for a year or more." Barratt grumbled again, recognising however that much of the anger he felt was born of a sense of responsibility.

"Come with me, if you do not wish to see a physician my cook can help you with your injuries," he said.

"I cannot leave the children," said Mrs Broady.

"Bring them, I'm sure the boys will enjoy a ride in the cart."

"I will speak plainly, Mr Barratt. I would be ashamed to leave my home with you. It would make it seem as if my husband had good cause to strike me." Barratt recoiled at this, though he understood the reasoning. "It is unfortunate, Sir, but there is nothing to be done. My husband's pride and my lack of sense are no fault of yours. I'm sure you will find another gentleman to assist you."

"I apologise nevertheless, Madame," said Barratt. "Be sure to bolt the door behind me."

Johnson sat on the box of the cart smoking his pipe. He lifted the reins as Barratt emerged from the Broady home. Mr Barratt climbed into the back of cart and tapped at the lip of a pot with his wedding ring, which he wore then on his right hand. When they reached the Red House he had had time to think. "Find him and bring him here," he said to Johnson. "You may wish to arm yourself."

Barratt was still eating his supper when the front door opened. He heard two male voices, the familiar hectoring tones of Johnson and another he did not recognise. Mr Broady was attempting some kind of communication but only managing to broadcast a low wail of confusion.

"There is no point talking to him now," Johnson observed,

dragging Broady's limp carcass through the dining room. Mr Barratt shook his head and swallowed.

"Put him in the cellar," he said.

Mr Broady woke the next morning on a straw mattress, in a dark, cool space which smelled of coal dust. There was a chute of brickwork close to the ceiling which admitted a little light, enough for him to make out a door on the opposite side of the room. Broady found that the door was locked and almost immediately began banging upon it and demanding his release. Two or three minutes elapsed before he heard a voice on the other side of the door and a key in the lock, minutes during which Broady, now sober and somewhat afraid, attempted to reconstruct the events which had brought him to this place, but found he could recall very little beyond an argument with his wife and a hasty escape from his home in Butcher's Green.

An older man, of a similar height and build to Broady, opened the door. The man nodded towards another door.

"You can clean yourself up in there," he said, before handing Broady a small pile of clothes. "Put these on. Your old garb goes in the basket. It'll be washed and returned."

"Where am I?" Broady asked.

"You're at the Red House," replied the older man. "Mr Charles Barratt wishes to speak with you, so you will speak with him."

"What about?"

"You will discover what about. Meanwhile I recommend that you keep a civil tongue in your head and express your gratitude to Mr Barratt for his hospitality. If you'd have been left on the street, in the condition in which you were found, you'd have been robbed or worse." Broady's hands went instinctively to his pockets. Johnson, for it was he, lifted a finger and produced a small purse. "It's all there," he said, handing the purse to Broady. "What you hadn't already pissed away, that is."

The door opened into a cobbled washroom, with a bench, a trough for laundry and a mangle. A piece of olive oil soap sat on a stack of folded cloths on the bench. A large wooden bucket stood on the floor three-quarters filled with steaming water. Broady removed his clothes and threw them into the basket beside the trough. It had been a while since he had cleaned himself with hot water; the river sufficed, once a fortnight. He found that the process soothed somewhat the ill-feeling that the drink had caused. He dried himself and dressed. Johnson was waiting for him outside. He directed Broady into the kitchen and gestured towards a plate of food on the table.

"Do you drink coffee?" Broady shook his head. "I suggest you do on this occasion. It will clear your head."

"What I need is a hair of the dog that bit me," Broady said.

"You will have to wait for that," said Johnson, checking his watch. "Five minutes, then come upstairs."

Charles Barratt walked up and down along the edge of the carpet in the library, in an effort to remain calm ahead of his interview with Broady. Johnson coughed meaningfully in the kitchen passage and Mr Barratt sat at his bureau, but then turned his chair to face the room. Broady entered with Johnson behind him, and Barratt gestured towards another chair which he had placed in the centre of the room. The younger man was wearing Johnson's clothes and the two of them were of such similar height and build that the garments might have been tailored for Broady. Mr Barratt cleared his throat.

"We meant to call upon you yesterday afternoon, Mr Broady, but when we arrived you had already left."

"I had a disagreement with Rebekah, Mrs Broady, Sir. It does me no credit, I fear."

"No indeed, I have only met your wife on two occasions, three occasions if you include the aftermath of your sudden departure, but she has impressed me as the kind of woman that any man might consider himself fortunate to know, would you not agree?"

"She is a fine woman, Sir, yes," said Broady.

"I did not wish to speak with you simply so that we might extol the virtues of your spouse, however, as attractive and intelligent a young lady though she undoubtedly is. I wanted to offer you some work, Mr Broady, nothing too physically taxing, but something which might make the lives of your family more comfortable for a little while. It would not interfere with your current employment and it might keep you out of The Bull on a

Saturday evening, and thus prove a double benefit, do you follow me?"

"I do, Sir, you are very kind..." Mr Barratt raised a hand.

"The person who occupies this position would be working under the direction of Miss Lucy Walker, the daughter of my fiancée, and would have to be, therefore, someone of impeccable moral standing. Yesterday's events, taken as a whole, would seem to indicate that you are not a person who I should consider recommending for the job, Mr Broady. Yet your wife says that you are a good man, and that your behaviour was out of character."

"Sir, if I can explain..."

"I think that I will attempt my own explanation, Mr Broady, if I may. It was uncommonly hot yesterday, was it not? Johnson and I certainly suffered on our way to Milton so I can imagine it was hard, draining work in the fields. So you and your fellow workers relieved your thirst while turning the soil, in anticipation of the week's pay that was very nearly in your pocket. When you arrived home the children were screaming and your wife was telling you to clean yourself up because a gentleman was expected. 'What, am I not a gentleman?' you might have said. Mrs Broady then explained that this Mr Barratt had visited previously, and shown your family some kindness, and naturally your pride was dented, and your belly was full of ale and so a falling out was inevitable. Mrs Broady blames herself but in fact it is my fault, for not anticipating your reaction, which seems perfectly reasonable, considered in this light."

"I am very sorry, nonetheless, for what happened," said Broady.

"I'm sure you are," said Mr Barratt, "and because I believe you to be truly penitent I will tell Miss Lucy that I have found just the person to assist her." Mr Broady had been staring at the library carpet but looked up at this moment, as he attempted to muster a smile. Barratt was not smiling, Broady was surprised to discover, his face wore instead an expression that was in extreme contrast to the tone of his conversation, a look of anger, barely suppressed, which was enough to make the young father anxious once more. "I wish to tell you something about myself," Barratt continued, "something which only very few of my most trusted associates know." Mr Broady's head began to ache with renewed ferocity.

"I would be honoured to hear it, Sir."

Barratt leaned forward, rested his elbows on his knees and clasped his hands together, as if in prayer.

"I believe that God, the unseen entity that we go and sing praise to every Sunday, who we shall all go and worship later this morning, is nothing but a fantasy, an unnecessary invention. God does not exist, except in the minds of men, and even there he is no more real than Prince Hamlet or Robinson Crusoe. There is no Heaven, nor Hell either, though there are places on this Earth which closely resemble the latter. I do not fear the wrath of God, Mr Broady, or his divine judgment, why should I? I am not a child trembling at ghosts in the closet. I know that I may face the consequences of my actions in this mortal realm, but even here I am protected by wealth and the assumption that because I behave like a gentleman I am incapable of ungentlemanly behaviour. So in fact I have nothing to fear, and I live accordingly, do you understand me?" Broady nodded slowly.

"I am soon to be married, Mr Broady, save your congratulations, and my wife and I may wish to increase our household. Should we need a housekeeper I would prefer an educated woman, I think, a young respectable widow. A good-looking creature, who might be grateful to be taken in, someone to keep me comfortable should my wife need to travel, for instance. Again, who is God to judge me?" Mr Barratt stood and approached Broady, who slouched fearfully on his chair, so that the older man seemed three yards tall. "Would you be missed, Broady, if you were to disappear? Would anyone come to look for you?" Barratt stepped backwards and sighed. "Mark my words, Sir. If you ever strike Mrs Broady again, if you touch her in anger, or abuse her in any fashion and I learn of it, it will be your last living action. I will bury you too deep for your bones to ever be found and I will make your children my own. Is that understood?" Mr Barratt delivered these last words at such volume, and with such righteous emphasis that Broady struggled to remain in his chair. Barratt then repeated his final question in a more temperate tone and the young man nodded again. Beyond the library window the birds returned to the trees. "Go home," said Barratt. "Make peace with your wife, tend to her. I will see you here tomorrow afternoon." Broady got to his feet and Johnson led him to the front door.

"Does he mean it?" Broady asked.
"Every word," said Johnson.

XXII

IN ALMOST EVERY way Miss Lucy Walker more closely resembled her father, a gentleman she barely remembered, than her mother. She was unfortunate in this regard, since Susannah Walker, though no conventional beauty, had a presence which commanded the attention of everyone around her, and Miss Lucy was of course obliged to spend the great majority of her waking hours in her mother's company; a lively girl, almost pretty, though otherwise unremarkable. This is how the young lady thought of herself, at least. Mrs Walker could see no flaw in her child, and indulged her every whim. It is scarcely worth noting that young gentlemen, now as always, value vivacity and an encouraging manner over more classical qualities, so while Miss Lucy lacked height and was somewhat round-featured, it was inevitable that she would never lack admirers. There was also the matter of Meadholme, which was not entailed – in any case neither Mrs Walker nor her fiancé Mr Barratt had any close living relatives – and the young lady's own refusal to be ignored. These various factors, and the natural affection a child has for a single remaining parent notwithstanding, Miss Lucy was always glad to spend time beyond her mother's shadow.

The Corn Exchange was as dusty as she had feared. Certain of the windows had been painted shut and the first task which Miss Lucy allocated to Broady was to prise these open so that a greater amount of clean air might circulate within the building. It was a fine structure, built recently in high Hanoverian style, with a great upper gallery in the shape of a horseshoe and a floor of polished sandstone with a broad dais at the far end, but in truth it was something of a civic folly, which stood empty from month to month.Miss Lucy was disadvantaged by never having attended a ball, however she had read various accounts, factual and otherwise, of how such an affair might be managed, and as we have noted was not a person lacking in confidence. She was accustomed to having her instructions followed and had inherited a degree of shrewdness from her father, along with his nose. She had already asked the current tenants of the late Mr Walker's estate for access to those items which were used to decorate Meadholme during times of celebration and which were now stored there in the dry vaults, signing and sending the letter with no pang of regret for her former life.

Miss Lucy was impressed with her volunteer, Broady, who seemed so anxious to assist it was almost as if his life depended upon her good opinion.

"Windows are all open, Miss," he said, standing before her brandishing a besom like a musket. "Should I start the sweeping?"

"Begin at the far end of the gallery, Mr Broady, and sweep towards the stairs."

"Of course, Miss."

"Very good," she said, before stepping outside, into the warmth of the afternoon. In spite of his impassioned assurances Mr Nicholson had failed to appear. Miss Lucy was certain that she had informed him that she would be collecting the keys from the churchwarden on Monday. Had Harvey Richards given such an undertaking, she reflected, there was no doubting that he would have kept to it. Yes, Mr Richards was in every way superior to Mr Nicholson, even though he had no property. A face and bearing such as his was all the estate any man needed. His height was another cause for admiration, thought Miss Lucy, particularly since the Walkers were such small people, and yet he was not so solid and top-heavy as Mr Barratt.

This gentleman surprised Miss Lucy by emerging from her imaginings into plain sight, walking along the high street in shirtsleeves and breeches, as was his habit on warm days. As ever, when she cast eyes on Barratt, the young lady experienced a rush of affection intermixed with a small dose of pity, such as one might feel towards an old workhorse, relieved of the bridle and allowed to chomp at windfalls at the end of its life. Mr Barratt had in his hand a sheaf of bills which he waved towards Miss Lucy in the fashion of a radical politician at the stump.

"Fresh from my man in London," he said. "Not a word misspelled, my dear." Miss Lucy took one of the bills and read it quickly as a prickling sensation, which was not unpleasant, spread across her shoulders. She found her own name at the foot of the bill and smiled.

"I dare say we shall raise quite a sum," Miss Lucy said.

"So we must hope. Did my man Broady arrive promptly?"

"He was waiting for me when I arrived," she said. "He is a most conscientious fellow, Mr Barratt. He had the windows open in no time at all." Mr Barratt nodded and put his head around one door of the building. Broady was halfway down the stairs, pushing the broom into the corner of each tread. He appeared to be at the point of collapse. Barratt skipped up a few steps and pushed some coins into his hand.

"Finish up and then straight home, do you understand me?"

"Yes, Sir." Barratt went back outside.

"Broady is almost done with the galleries and stairs," he said. "Perhaps we should release him for the day. He has a young daughter he is missing."

"Oh, he made no mention of it," said Miss Lucy. "I had hoped to get the ground floor swept as well this afternoon."

"I am no stranger to the broom, my child," said Barratt. "Let the poor fellow go, I shall carry on in his stead." Broady bowed repeatedly to Miss Lucy then disappeared towards the bridge.

Mr Barratt's technique with the broom was rather more energetic than Broady's and might have proved less efficient had it not been for the open windows and a light, southerly breeze which ushered much of the dust which Barratt had unsettled out into the gentle air of B_____. By the time he was satisfied that the flags of the hall were clear Mr Barratt was perspiring freely, and was alarmingly red about the face. He struggled up to the gallery and closed the upper windows, then descended and pulled the lower sashes down. For a moment he considered walking down to the river for a swim, but it was now that hour of late afternoon when the insects which hovered there were most agitated and apt to bite. He loosened his collar, opened both doors to the building and pushed the pile of matter he had gathered with his broom into the gutter, then leant upon his implement, panting slightly.

"Since I have been good enough to agree to marry you, Sir, I should be grateful if you would endeavour to survive at least until such time as we are able to exchange vows." Mrs Walker stood beside her daughter, upwind of Mr Barratt, in a magnificent purple hat crested with feathers.

"New bonnet?" Barratt asked, grinning at the disparity of appearance between himself and his wife-to-be, she still more elegant than was her custom, and he looking like an Irish canal digger, even in his best breeches.

"Impossible man," said Mrs Walker, as her daughter giggled. "Where is your volunteer?"

"We sent Mr Broady home," he replied. "He had already worked a day in the fields before coming to Miss Lucy's aid. He will be back tomorrow."

"Oh, it is Broady then? I know his wife." Barratt smiled and nodded his head slowly.

"Yes, I thought it must be you she was speaking of, she admires you greatly." Mrs Walker turned to Miss Lucy.

"Perhaps you should lock the doors," she said to her daughter, pulling Mr Barratt homeward with one arm.

"How do you know Rebekah Broady?" Mrs Walker asked quietly.

"Hers is the first house on the left," said Barratt, before offering an outline of their brief acquaintance, which omitted Broady's mistreatment of his wife. Mrs Walker seemed satisfied.

"She is a very handsome young woman, is she not?"

"I could not say," Barratt answered. "Since I have known her she has either been heavy with child or exhausted, as I believe many nursing mothers are." The first part of Mr Barratt's statement was a falsehood, she sensed, though one employed diplomatically rather than for any sinister purpose, and the rest was likely true. "I do get the impression," Barratt continued, perhaps unnecessarily, "that the young woman's qualities are unsuited to her current station in life." He realised too late that such an observation might cause some displeasure to Mrs Walker and turned anxiously to measure her reaction, but she was placid.

"I agree, my darling, and I am so pleased that you seem to be helping them. Mr Broady is no volunteer, I take it?"

"No indeed," he admitted. Miss Lucy caught up with them then and they parted to their respective sides of the high street, as Mr Barratt thought it best that he have a bath before his supper and ought not to shame the two ladies further with his disreputable appearance. Mrs Walker insisted that Mr Barratt should visit the Rectory after he had eaten, since dear Lottie had previously indicated that she possessed some intelligence relating to the matter lately under discussion and had been told to still her gossiping tongue. At this point Miss Lucy observed that Lottie was a very oracle when it came to the goings-on of the town and her word should never be doubted.

"It had gone right out of my mind until you mentioned her name," Lottie said. She stood with Mrs Walker and Mr Barratt in the scullery yard. The moon was full and the night smelled of honeysuckle, until Barratt succeeded in lighting his pipe. "Mrs Broady, you see, five summers ago, she was the belle of the town. Mostly all the men were in love with her; boys, husbands, grandfathers." Mrs Walker scowled at Mr Barratt, who sucked on his briar and raised a complacent eyebrow. "I've never known someone so admired. So although she's not particularly high-born, the opposite almost, people thought she could have her pick of any fellow she chose to marry."

"In which case it is difficult to see why she chose Broady," said Mr Barratt.

"Well, by that point it wasn't a matter of choice," Lottie said. The shoulders of her audience sank, anticipating a familiar, sad tale. "I see you've guessed the rest of it. A clever girl like that should've known better. But she fell for the lies of a gentleman, like so many have done before her. He refused to marry her, of course, though a young man from his father's estate, the son of the land agent, took pity on her."

"Mr Broady," said Barratt.

"What a good soul," Mrs Walker said. Mr Barratt rubbed at his forehead with a thumb and forefinger.

"I think I know the rest of the story," he said. "The master died and the young gentleman dismissed Broady and his father, and insisted that none of the other local squires employed them, other than as labourers, am I correct, Lottie?"

"Quite correct, Sir. It was the most spiteful thing you ever heard of." Mr Barratt looked at Mrs Walker.

"Have you not guessed it yet, Susannah?" he said. "Old man Broady died in the fields, no doubt, being too old for heavy work. Where was God in this?"

"He did die too, Sir, just before his grandson, I mean his own grandson, was born."

"It is a horrible story," said Mrs Walker. "I wish I had never heard it. Who could behave in such a fashion?"

"Someone you know, Ma'am, and I can't say how surprised I

was to see him sat there in the library before Christmas, like some kind of Judas."

"Lottie!"

"Broady's father was the agent at Hope Hall," Lottie said, "and the young gentleman who cast him out was Henry Nicholson."

XXIII

A LETTER AWAITED Charles Barratt when he returned home that evening. He recognised the hand and seal of young Mr Richards, and the floury thumbprint of his cook into whose hands the missive was placed but he was still digesting the information which Lottie had provided and went straight to his bedroom without opening it. The moon remained bright and it was Mr Barratt's habit and preference to sleep in total darkness, accordingly he crossed to the windows to draw the curtains then started somewhat. Across the street, half in shadow beside the Rectory stood a man. The wide brim of his hat concealed most of his face but his mouth was fixed in a strange, sneering shape and it seemed certain that he was watching the Red House. Barratt gathered himself and drew the first pair of curtains. He did not fear anyone, nor however did he relish unpleasant surprises of this sort, and his heart thumped against his ribs for a moment. He approached the second window and stared upwards as he pulled the curtains together, though the man remained visible in the lower periphery of his vision, an indistinct shape, utterly still. Barratt left a small gap, narrower than a child's finger, between the last set of curtains and positioned himself a few feet back into his room so that he could observe his mysterious sentinel, the watcher thus became the watched. Mr Barratt's vigil was short-lived; satisfied, apparently, that his mark had retired for the night the man in the hat hurried away northwards just moments later, keeping his head down at all times. Barratt listened for the sound of horses and a carriage but heard nothing.

It was not Nicholson, that much was certain. The spy was of a different build entirely. It might have been his man, Buller, but Mr Barratt had only seen that fellow sat on a carriage and could not therefore gauge his shape. In any case there was no reason to suspect that Henry Nicholson meant to act against him, other than his own intention to act against Nicholson, who remained oblivious presumablyto Barratt's machinations. It was a conundrum, but would not remain so for very long, Mr Barratt suspected. He undressed, whistling quietly to himself as he did so, then took to his bed and fell asleep within a minute.

Barratt woke early and dressed himself in the clothes that Johnson had put out for him. He went downstairs and retrieved the letter and read it as the cook laid out his breakfast. The letter contained some disturbing news and he was glad that he had not opened it the previous evening, since Mr Richards' words might have succeeded where the shady 'sentinel had failed, and prevented Barratt from sleeping.

The Martyrs
Milton
SURREY

27th June 18___

Dear Mr Barratt,

It seems probable that Henry Nicholson is now aware of your intention to expose him. I met him today at the Trust's own premises in B_____ and while he was outwardly courteous, to start with at least, his behaviour was more erratic even than usual. He began by telling me that he had learned that I am related to Mr Cunningham, to which I replied that I was, that it was no secret, and that I had often heard Cunningham speak of Nicholson's father in terms of the highest praise and greatest affection. He then enquired why I had not availed him of this information myself, and I explained that since it scarcely pertained to the business between the gentleman I represent and the Trust I had not thought to mention it, it being nothing more than a trivial coincidence. He asked if Cunningham was the gentleman I represented and I told him that I was not at liberty to reveal that person's identity, but that I served Mr Cunningham solely as befitted his status as my familial elder, and in no specific capacity. Nicholson seemed satisfied at last, saying "I thought it unlikely that the old man would extend me any credit," and I corrected him, asserting that the small sum I had advanced was intended to secure the return of the ledgers and was not a loan for his personal use. He became very angry at this point and flung the doors to his bureau open, shouting that he would release the ledgers only on receipt of the sum which we had previously discussed, this being the full amount to be disbursed, since he had no faith that this secret benefactor had any intention of helping the Trust but meant only to undermine him, Nicholson, personally. I offered no response to this, partly because I felt that a denial would transgress the rules of engagement that you and I agreed upon, and partly because, as I gathered my own papers, I took the opportunity to study the contents of the bureau. The ledgers are there, I am sure, bound in gold and crimson, and Mr Nicholson meant for me to see them. I felt that this was trap best avoided, so made my excuses and left him there. I feel that perhaps I have not done justice to the extremity of emotion which afflicted Nicholson when I contradicted him, he seemed almost desperate, and if he were not so slight and ailing in appearance a man might almost fear him. As I departed I heard him shouting to himself in his office. Much of it was indistinct, though there is a possibility that at one point I heard "Run off to the Red House!" though I cannot be certain of it. I thought it best to return to Milton in any case and send this immediately.

I implore that you take care with Henry Nicholson, he seems truly wild with rage and may even be dangerous. Awaiting your further instruction I remain

Yours etc.

Harvey Richards

Barratt read the letter again before folding it. He had outmanoeuvred greater minds than that of Henry Nicholson in the past, of course, but in business the other party rarely acted out of malice and usually had a great deal to lose, so caution prevailed, as did Barratt, by being bolder than whoever he was dealing with. Mr Barratt had hoped to mitigate the ruin of Mr Nicholson, but this had come to seem more difficult to achieve precisely because the two of them had certain traits of personality in common. After Catherine's death her husband's daring had turned into something more like recklessness (he was more circumspect nowadays) as he ceased to care about outcomes, profitable or otherwise, and so was feared, and in turn respected. Had Barratt shared Mr Nicholson's destructive vices, whichever they were, he would have pursued them with a similar energy, he felt sure, and when cornered, as Nicholson then must have felt himself to be, Barratt too would have fought until surrender was the only option.

He called for Johnson, who walked into the dining room buffing the polish on a boot. Barratt outlined the contents of Mr Richards' letter and asked what his man made of it.

"Hard to know if it is a challenge or a trap, Sir. He is not the most predictable of souls, after all."

"Quite so," said Mr Barratt. "We can presume that he sent that fellow to watch the house last night, do you think?" Johnson nodded. "And yet there is no sign of him this morning. As if the likes of you and I only get our hands dirty after dark."

"An unfortunate misconception, certainly. Do you have a plan, Sir?"

"I usually do, don't I?" Mr Barratt said. "I think a show of strength is in order, Bill. We are not about to kill the cat, just yet, but we need the cat to know that we will not hesitate when the time is ripe. Go and fetch Mr Richards, will you, and bring him to the Rectory after lunch. I will send a note to Hope Hall, telling Mr Nicholson to expect us."

"Do you mean to place our trumps upwards, then?"

"Not all of them, no. I will explain later, but first I must pay my respects to my fiancée."

It was market day and Reverend Archer had elected to accompany Mrs Walker's cook on her weekly shopping expedition but the two ladies were at home and were delighted, as ever, to hear Mr Barratt's voice in the hallway.

"We have anxiously awaited your return!" declared Miss Lucy as Barratt entered the library. The young woman knelt in front of her mother while Mrs Walker fashioned her daughter's hair into an elaborate plait.

"I have not been gone much more than ten hours," said Mr Barratt, "and I imagine you were asleep for most of those."

"Nonsense," said Mrs Walker, laughing. "We cannot sleep in your absence, dear man, we lie awake fretting and biting our nails until you return. Is that not correct, Lucy?"

"Absolutely Mama, it is torture when he leaves us." A warm feeling settled over Mr Barratt, on a morning that was already balmy, and he might have sat quite contentedly in his usual chair and allowed himself to be teased until lunchtime. Such pleasures would have to wait, however, since there was a situation which needed to be resolved, and in his favour.

"I fear I must leave you again, and almost immediately. I wondered if I might borrow a horse?"

Narcissus, the Rector's gelding, was saddled and trotted off with a great and unfamiliar burden upon him. Mr Barratt rode first to Butcher's Green to call upon Mrs Broady. He tied the horse and knocked at the crooked door with unaccustomed care.

"It is Charles Barratt, Mrs Broady." The door opened after a few moments, and she appeared, still wearing a scarf and the marks of her husband's drunken temper. Barratt made a fist and pushed his fingernails into his palm to calm his own ire. "How are you, Madame?"

"Quite well, Mr Barratt, yes. My husband is appalled by his actions and is sincerely penitent. He has pledged that there will be no repeat of his behaviour." Mrs Broady's eldest child pulled at Barratt's breeches.

"Can I sit on the horse?" asked the boy. Mr Barratt sought Mrs Broady's consent with a glance. She nodded and he lifted the lad up onto the saddle. "It is very high," the boy said immediately. "I should like to come down now." The child flopped into Barratt's arms. As he set him down Barratt studied the boy's face. There was no obvious resemblance to Henry Nicholson and Mr Barratt wondered briefly how reliable Lottie's version of events was, but then the child's eyes grew wild and he shouted that it was a stupid horse, anyway, before running back into the family's meagre lodgings.

"Forgive the boys," said Mrs Broady, "they have grown jealous of my attention since Catherine was born."

"It is only natural," Barratt said. "Miss Lucy is very impressed with Mr Broady, by the way. She says he is very hard-working and capable." Mrs Broady seemed to blush, beneath the bruising and Barratt would not have made any further reference to her husband were that gentleman not central to the purpose of his visit. "I am sorry to enquire, but previously you advised me that your neighbours here are unlettered, I presume that is not the case with Mr Broady?"

"No, Matthew reads well enough, he was taught by his father. Last night he stayed up reading the bible, in fact, until he might have needed a candle."

"Thank you," said Barratt. "I need to speak to Mr Broady as a matter of some urgency, perhaps you could advise me where he might be found?" Mrs Broady named a farm just three miles distant and Barratt thanked her again, forgetting to modulate his voice and thus waking the baby. He raised a hand of apology and whispered a farewell. The horse lodged its own complaint as Mr Barratt remounted and gathered the reins. Mrs Broady reappeared in the doorway with Catherine in her arms. The infant's cries soon ceased as her mother stroked her head. Barratt looked down at the young woman and child and was reminded of a painting he had once owned, by some ancient Venetian, sold after his own Catherine had departed. A small cloud passed before the sun and cooled the day for a moment. Barratt bowed to Mrs Broady, gave the horse a kick and rode away.

XXIV

HARVEY RICHARDS had already arrived at the Rectory by the time Mr Barratt returned and was perched at the end of the chaise in the library with his knees almost level with his shoulders, the seat being somewhat sunken and he being an unusually long-legged young fellow. Miss Lucy had provided tea and a cup and saucer rattled in Mr Richards' hands as he rose to greet Barratt. The two men bowed to each other, their eyes alive with a peculiarly masculine excitement.

"I am grateful to you, Sir, for coming so swiftly," said Mr Barratt.

"It is nothing, Mr Barratt. I expected your summons rather sooner, in fact. Johnson is refreshing the horses and I am at your disposal."

"Drink your tea, my dear chap, and then we shall proceed." Mrs Walker, who had been battling with the precocious verdure of the Rectory garden appeared through the French windows at that moment, carrying a pair of hedging shears.

"*Quo vadis*, gentlemen?" she said, lifting the veil of her hat. "What exactly is afoot, Charles?"

"We are hunting rabbits, my love," said Barratt. "Mr Richards here has been working entirely too hard, so I thought it was time for some sport." Mrs Walker studied the face of her fiancé. She wondered if their life together might settle into a less picaresque pattern, or if instead Mr Barratt would move periodically from one enthusiasm to anotheruntil he ran out of energy altogether.

"When we are married I shall expect you to inform me of your movements and intentions several weeks in advance, is that understood?"

"Of course, my dear," Barratt replied. "My diary will be at your disposal at all times."

"Excellent," said Mrs Walker. "You know how I like to be prepared, Charles, and there have been rather too many surprising developments over these last months, not all of them of an agreeable nature." Mr Richards, who had been staring intently at the lees of his tea during this exchange, looked up at Mrs Walker and Miss Lucy in turn.

"Thank you for your perfect hospitality," he said. Miss Lucy, who had barely managed three words of conversation with Mr Richards after returning with tea, and who had hoped to monopolise his company while her mother was in the garden, made her displeasure known, emitting a short, somewhat undignified expression of her feelings. The two gentleman smiled and Mrs Walker turned an unforgiving eyebrow on her daughter.

"You are very kind, Mr Richards," said Mrs Walker. "Lucy, perhaps you will show the gentlemen out?" She bowed her head and disappeared through the library windows.

Reverend Archer arrived home from a parochial visit as Barratt and Mr Richards said their farewells to Miss Lucy. Mr Barratt explained that he had borrowed Narcissus, with Mrs Walker's consent, but that they had not gone much above a trot, and that the creature appeared to be in need of further exercise, accordingly, he presumed, the Rector would not mind extending the loan for the afternoon. Reverend Archer remarked that Mr Barratt had a peculiar skill for offering instruction under the guise of a polite request and the gentlemen laughed among themselves as Miss Lucy returned, sulking to the library. Barratt then explained, *sotto voce*, the true aim of their expedition and the turn of events which had necessitated it. The Rector urged caution, but made no attempt to dissuade Barratt, reasoning that to do so would amount only to a waste of breath.

The road which sloped down to Hope Hall was bone dry and a cloud of dust rose behind them as they approached the old house. They were but four men – Mr Richards, Barratt, Johnson and a stableman chosen by the latter for the breadth of his shoulders and the thickness of his beard – however, any soul who witnessed their advance might be forgiven for assuming they were far greater in number, such was the impression of strength and purpose created by two tall men on horseback and a wide cart full of rifles arrayed upright, resembling a Roman phalanx.

A figure was visible outside the house, who wore a wide-brimmed hat against the afternoon sun. This person ran inside as Barratt's party came into view. Moments later he reappeared with Henry Nicholson behind him and pointed towards the horsemen. Nicholson stood with legs apart and hands on hips staring towards the oncoming cataclysm in an attitude of defiance. Barratt quickened his horse into a trot and rode ahead, stopping in front of Nicholson and his man without dismounting.

"What do you say, Mr Nicholson, Sir?" Barratt began. "May we hunt on your land? The terms I have offered are very reasonable."

"I might have saved you the trouble, Mr Barratt, but I receive a great deal of correspondence, what with managing the Trust you understand, so I am sometimes unable to respond immediately to requests of this kind. I fear that no hunting lease is available for the estate." Mr Nicholson's voice was calm, but his eyes betrayed the degree to which he was agitated, an agitation which increased when Harvey Richards rode up and stopped his horse, a big chestnut mare, beside Mr Barratt. Nicholson nodded, his suspicions having been confirmed apparently.

"Now that is a pity," said Barratt, smiling. "I have also written to a Mr Newland Spraggs, a Noah Barnes..." Mr Nicholson flinched as Barratt named each of his fellow Trustees. "Every one of these gentlemen has indicated that they would be more than happy to accommodate my sporting instincts, as it were, but I thought I would give you first refusal, since we are already acquainted. Even our mutual friend, the Rector of St Andrew's, has given his blessing to the pursuit." Barratt's smile broadened as witnessed the growing discomfort of his interlocutor. "We will trouble you no further, Sir." Mr Barratt leaned towards Nicholson and said, in a kind of hiss, "I should be grateful if you would extend me the same courtesy, so that matters may be resolved in a spirit of mercy. None of us, I am sure, wish to discover what the opposing inclination would result in."

Barratt walked his horse forwards and took a wide turn in front of the house, followed by Mr Richards and the cart. Johnson offered an ironic salute to Nicholson and the groom laughed, displaying a set of teeth which would not have shamed one of his charges. They proceeded up the low hill away from Hope Hall, followed by a rolling cloud of dust. Once they had crested the slope Barratt put his horse into a gentle trot. Mr Richards assumed the same pace.

"I think that all went as well as might be expected," said Richards.

"He looked like his skull might go off, like a French bomb," Mr Barratt replied, chuckling.

"Are you not concerned that he may prove dangerous?"

"In my experience," Barratt said, "which is not inconsiderable, men like Nicholson are generally only a danger unto themselves. Yes, he is a vicious sort, but that viciousness exists to disguise other flaws, the most important of which, I suspect, is a profound and pernicious self-loathing. He is the weak son of a strong father, by all accounts. That situation is not his fault, yet he was still blessed with wealth whatever the limitations of his character, and was thus in a position to make choices about the kind of person he might become. Sadly he has surrendered to his worst instincts, which will lead to dissipation, and self-destruction."

"You speak with a surprising authority about a gentleman you know but scarcely, Mr Barratt."

"I was never quite so Apollonian as you, Harvey, even as a young man, but at first glance we might appear similarly constructed. The truth is that I am much more like our friend Mr Nicholson, or at least I was. Rather than succumbing to vice, as he has done, I turned my loathing outwards, towards God and all his creatures. Rage and misanthropy once consumed me, even as I sat in St Luke's on a Sunday morning." Mr Richards, wide-eyed though speechless, bumped up and down on his saddle. "Fear not, Sir," Barratt continued, "I am no longer enraged. Grief subsides, time smoothes the waters. I strive to be better. That does not alter the fact that there is some seed of wickedness in my soul, which might expand at any moment and take over the whole."

"I do not suppose that you were ever quite so mercurial as Mr Nicholson," said Richards.

"No, he is genuinely peculiar in that regard. One wonders if perhaps he fell out of a tree as a young man and landed on his head."

Back at the Red House the two gentlemen each refreshed their toilet while Johnson and the groom stowed the horses and weaponry, then all four shared a bottle of Barratt's second best port, saluting the success of their entirely bloodless hunting expedition. The midsummer sun had dipped behind the roofs on the west side of the high street and the day begun to cool when Messrs Richards and Barratt crossed to the Rectory for their supper. Lottie greeted them in her best attire, "Here they are, Gog and Magog," and candles were already lit in the dining room, though the garden remained bright beyond the sashes. Miss Lucy and Mrs Walker had also gone to some lengths to enhance their appearance, with hair and dress arranged to display as much skin as might be appropriately looked upon within the walls of a clergy house. Mr Barratt admitted himself dazzled by his fiancée and stared at her lovingly throughout each course of the meal, even as she chewed her meat. Mr Richards encouraged Reverend Archer to relate some stories of his time at Oxford and the Rector duly obliged, though one or two of these yarns were suddenly truncated, as the narrator realised that their dénouements were not fit to be heard by the ladies. Miss Lucy's gaze fell on Mr Richards rather as Barratt's fell on her mother, that is intently, and almost without interruption. This ceased to discomfit the young gentleman after the first half hour and indeed the young lady managed to ask some questions of him which did not invite altogether trivial responses, nevertheless he was somewhat relieved when he and his elder counterparts were allowed to excuse themselves to smoke beneath a sky of surpassing crimson brilliance in the Rectory garden. Mr Richards' face continued to glow as a result of the attention - as if he had fallen asleep in a sunny field - and also perhaps because of the wine he had consumed.

Shortly after the gentlemen returned inside the fiddler arrived. This was an acquaintance of Lottie's, a person whose body seemed made up of lumps and bumps, since no garment he wore seemed proximate to his size. There was an amount of straw in his hair and the particular odour of The Bull, where he generally plied his trade, clung to him as loosely as his clothes. Lottie had given her assurances that the musician, whom she knew only by his nom dethéâtre, Odd Jake, was a veritable repository of lively airs which he could reproduce with an unerring accuracy of rhythm. If one were to judge from the fellow's appearance alone then Lottie's claim would have seemed a rank overstatement, but as we have previously remarked, the Rector's maid was rarely, if ever, mistaken in her assertions. So it proved with Odd Jake, who, once the library furniture was pushed back against the bookshelves, demonstrated his skill so convincingly that Mr Barratt himself was tapping a toe and nodding along after no more than a dozen bars. Mrs Walker crossed the library carpet with a solemn expression and stood before Mr Barratt. He laughed and picked her up under the arms and span her around so that her shoes almost came off.

"John, you will have to teach me step by step, as I have not danced for twenty years, near enough," said Mr Barratt. Reverend Archer, to the enormous relief of Miss Lucy, had presented himself to Lottie.

"Just follow us Charles, it's jolly straightforward, really." The dance which the Rector led was anything but straightforward, of course, but Mrs Walker was a nimble and encouraging partner, and Mr Barratt did not disgrace himself altogether. His fiancé had evidently expected far worse and as the fiddler ended his first tune she looked up at her hulking lover with a kind of astonished pride.

"Your dancing, my dear, is rather like my cousin's sherry," she whispered. "Not bad!" Barratt greeted this compliment with a small bow and kissed Mrs Walker's head at the parting of her hair.

"Some vigour remains," he said. Mrs Walker pursed her lips at him and Barratt experienced a tightening in his chest which was not caused by his recent exertions.

Mr Richards had fared less well. He was an inch taller than Barratt and Miss Lucy was somewhat shorter than her mother, and the discrepancy, which a more capable dancer might easily have overcome, proved insuperable to one as limited as Harvey Richards. Miss Lucy might at any point have lost a toe or an eye, so erratic were the young man's movements, indeed the young lady was greatly relieved when the fiddler's next melody was interrupted by a loud, urgent knocking at the Rectory door.

XXV

LOTTIE WENT TO answer the door. The fiddler began his air once more but was instructed to desist. There was something about the knocking which would brook no distraction. Mr Barratt followed Lottie out of the library. The Rectory door was opened to reveal Henry Nicholson in a state of partial dishevelment, as if he had been tearing at his own clothes.

"What ails you, Sir?" Lottie said, as Nicholson shifted his weight from foot to foot. "Would you like to come in?"

"Where is Barratt? It is him I wish to see." Mr Barratt stepped from the passage into the low vestibule and stooped in front of Lottie.

"What is it, Nicholson? I thought we understood one another."

"Burglar!" Nicholson shouted. "Larcenist!" Barratt stepped outside and placed himself a short distance from Mr Nicholson. Mr Barratt was no taller than Nicholson but he was altogether larger. Nicholson raised his stick but Mr Barratt pulled it from him then threw it some distance over the churchyard wall.

"You forget yourself, Sir," Barratt said, looming over his adversary. "I suggest that you regulate your emotions, say your piece, then retrieve your property."

"I have paid a boy to watch the Trust," Nicholson began, struggling to contain his agitation. "He reports that he saw a man, dressed like your valet, and of that size and manner, leaving the Trust this afternoon, and yet I locked and left the place yesterday evening and did not return before an hour ago."

"At what time this afternoon was this person seen?"

"The boy thinks it was around three."

"You will recall, Sir," Barratt said, "that Mr Johnson and I were at Hope Hall at three o' clock, is that not correct?" Nicholson made no sound or gesture of acknowledgment. "We are none of us supernatural beings, I assure you, capable of being in more than one place at a time. Was the door locked when you arrived at the Trust this evening, Mr Nicholson? Was anything missing? Had anything been disturbed? Or was all as you left it?"

"It was some agent of yours, I am sure of it," said Nicholson.

"Otherwise this is all a fiction, Nicholson, a dagger of the mind. The product of a quixotic reading of Mrs Radcliffe, mayhap. Whatever the case, you have made a public accusation, at the home of my friend, and thus doubly impugned my honour. You have named me a base criminal. And what is this crime of which I am accused? You cannot say precisely, yet you are certain that I am responsible. What you do know is that my associates and I were on your property, some miles distant from the location of the purported transgression, at the time it is supposed to have taken place. You, Nicholson, are my alibi for an outrage which seems to have occurred only in your head." Lottie tittered audibly in the vestibule but a look from Mr Barratt silenced her. "It is fortunate that I am neither an excessively proud gentleman, Sir, nor of a hasty, vengeful temperament. If I were then I might feel obliged to put a bullet between your eyes. As it is I shall put this outburst down to intoxication. My man will take you home if required, you know which door to knock at. Good night."

Henry Nicholson was a thin man, who appeared thinner still as he made his way, weak-kneed, from the Rectory door. He clambered over the low churchyard wall and spent some moments searching for his stick. There was a little light left in the sky and Carter, the sexton, had recently run his scythe between the graves; Mr Nicholson's quest would otherwise have proved impossible. He discovered the stick eventually by tripping over it, and cursed his ill fortune aloud and in the most unpleasant terms before climbing back over the wall. "To Hell with all of you!" he shouted, waving the recovered staff in the air like some primitive being. Then he walked away, in an indirect fashion, towards Hope Hall. Mr Barratt waited until he was out of sight and went back inside.

"I fear your position at the Trust may be under review

come the next meeting, John," Barratt said, stepping into the library.

"Was it Nicholson shouting then?" the Rector asked.

"Indeed, and he has damned us all to Hell."

"That is not his prerogative, I think. He damned all of us, Charles?"

"Perhaps not the ladies," said Barratt, "though I suspect you are included in his reprobation." Reverend Archer chuckled.

"I, a humble country pastor?"

"He has seen through your disguise, cousin," said Mrs Walker. "Tell me, Charles, how have you managed to implicate the dear Reverend in your scheming?"

"My implication was very general in nature," said Barratt. "I merely suggested to Mr Nicholson that should an investigation take place into his activities he would do well not to depend upon the partiality of his fellow trustees."

"You did not think to consult us?" Mrs Walker asked. "We are not family yet."

"You are not involved, my dear, and I thought that I might safely presume that a servant of God would want to see justice done and probity restored."

"If some enmity exists between the man I am to marry and some other person who seems half mad then of course I am involved, particularly when it seems that you are the principal agent of that ill-feeling. You may think yourself impregnable, Charles, but am I? Is Miss Lucy?"

"You need not fear Henry Nicholson. I have gauged his personality."

"What if you are mistaken? What if you are wrong, about everything? What is all this posturing for, to demonstrate that you are a better man than someone you believe to be barely a man at all?" Mr Barratt was surprised to find that he was himself enraged. He was unused to having his actions and motivations questioned. That Mrs Walker, who ought to have demonstrated some appreciation of or deference to the intentions of her fiancé was instead interrogating them proved almost too much for him to calmly accept. Barratt studied the tip of his boot until his anger subsided.

"I find that I am too tired for any further dancing," he said.

"Please excuse me." He walked briskly from the library before any farewells were bade and returned immediately to the Red House, where his word was law and his strong instincts valued.

Lucy Walker acted as peacemaker the next morning. Word had arrived at the Rectory that the decorations had been retrieved intact from the dry vaults at Meadholme, but that no conveyance was presently available to transport them to B_____. Miss Lucy rang the bell of the Red House a little after nine o'clock. There was some minor commotion within and when the door was opened the fine, long form of Harvey Richards stood above the young lady. Miss Lucy had never travelled out of Surrey; had she been fortunate enough to venture as far as Florence and to stand before the David of Michelangelo in the Piazza della Signoria, she might hardly have been more impressed by that edifice of male nobility than she was by the young gentleman who stood before her, his skin brightened by a June sun that was already well elevated and shone full in his face, one cheek of which retained a streak of shaving soap.

"Miss Lucy, what a pleasure," said Mr Richards. He had grown accustomed to the young lady's habit of gazing at him like Miranda.

"I need to borrow your cart," Miss Lucy said. Mr Richards leant against the open door and gestured for her to enter.

"Do come in, we are all decent." As she stepped into the vestibule Mr Barratt appeared from the dining room.

"My dear Miss Lucy, welcome! Do excuse my disappearance yesterday evening. I had spent a while in the sun, you see, during the hottest part of the day. As did Mr Richards, of course, but he is a great deal younger than me, and thus immune to the sudden losses of vigour that I occasionally experience." Miss Lucy blushed at this and Mr Richards looked at his stockinged feet. "Anyhow, what can we do for you?"

"I wondered if you might make your cart available to me, Sir. I need to bring back the decorations from Meadholme. And your horses."

"Of course, Miss Lucy. Everything which is mine is as much yours, and since the Reverend was kind enough to lend me Narcissus how could I refuse?"

"You are very kind, sir."

"It is nothing. We shall accompany you on your mission, yes? As long as that will not inconvenience you, Miss Lucy."

"Not at all, Mr Barratt," she said. "Reverend Archer has volunteered to drive me, but he is very busy."

"It is settled then, we will be at your disposal in twenty minutes." Barratt made to return to his breakfast but turned again, smiling. "If I may offer one small morsel of advice, Miss Lucy?"

"Please, Sir."

"In future I would counsel against borrowing the cart before the horses, ha ha!" With this Barratt disappeared into the dining room, his laughter continuing sporadically for some moments afterwards. Miss Lucy and Mr Richards smiled at one another in the hallway, which seemed very empty following Mr Barratt's departure.

"It is hard to credit, is it not, that this is the same gentleman we saw stomping off into the night a few hours ago," said Mr Richards.

"His spirits are quite restored," Miss Lucy said.

"It is not a failure of temperament, I think, nor has he forgotten whatever upset him. He talks often about the importance of moving forward, you see, rather than dwelling on reversals. *Quaeest altera* might be his motto."

"Is that Latin?" Miss Lucy asked. "I do not know Latin."

"Nor I," admitted Mr Richards. "Or rather I have forgotten most of what I ever did know. It means 'What is the next thing' or something to that effect."

"I see," she said, though she reflected privately that knowing what the next thing was would prove more useful, in many situations, than simply asking about it. "You admire Mr Barratt a great deal then?"

"I do. He has no family or connections to rely upon and is respected on the basis of his intellect alone."

"And his wealth."

"What, are you a cynic, Miss Lucy?" said Richards, laughing. "Has his intellect not enabled him to acquire that wealth?" She smiled up at the young gentleman, then gestured for him to bend towards her, as if she wished to whisper a confidence. Mr Richards, who was unsure of the propriety of such an undertaking,

0angled himself halfways. This was enough for Miss Lucy's purpose. She took her handkerchief and wetted one corner of it, a quick triangle of pink tongue disappearing as quickly as it had emerged. She put one small hand on Mr Richard's right cheek to keep his head still, making a shushing noise as one might with a nervous colt. With the other hand she wiped away the dried lather from the opposite cheek, employing a brisk, maternal technique. She showed the foam, which contained a number of his own blonde bristles, to Mr Richards, then crumpled the handkerchief and passed it to him.

"I have plenty more," she said. The young gentleman, somewhat amazed, watched her cross the high street, his eyes never leaving the small, bustling figure until she disappeared behind the Rectory door.

XXVI

MR BARRATT STOOD with Lottie outside the Rectory door.

"She is indisposed," said the maid.

"In what sense? Is she unwell?"

"In the sense that she is not well enough to see visitors."

"Lottie, you and I are friends, are we not?" Mr Barratt said. "It is just me that Mrs Walker is not well enough to see?"

"I couldn't say, Mr Barratt, Sir. My instructions only extend as far as you. For all I know, if King George himself were to turn up here he might be turned away." Barratt sighed and Lottie offered a consolatory smile. Across the street Mr Richards was explaining the function of each part of the horses' tack to a rapt Miss Lucy. "It is a curious thing," Lottie remarked, "that a fine young gentleman like that should be such an unaccomplished dancer." Mr Barratt laughed. "The Reverend, meanwhile, well, I never saw a fellow so light on his feet. It is almost as much of a puzzle how he has never found a young lady to keep him honest." Lottie's face fell into an expression of heartsickness and Barratt squeezed her shoulder.

"My poor Malvolio," he said.

"I do not know to what you are referring," Lottie said, suddenly recovering herself. She gestured towards the Red House, where the cart stood, by lifting her chin. "Do you suppose that Mr Richards has feelings for Miss Lucy?"

"If he has," said Barratt, "I imagine they are fraternal in nature. Miss Lucy is very young."

"So you are fond of saying, Mr Barratt, but the fact that you consider Miss Lucy a child does not guarantee that everyone feels the same. She will be eighteen next month." Barratt was somewhat alarmed by this information.

"Can that be so, Lottie?"

"I'm afraid it is so, Mr Barratt. I will admit that she seems younger, because of her manner, and her being so little, but she is very much a young woman."

"In which case she is a woman of property; she need not rush into marriage. For what it is worth, my dearest Lottie, Mr Richards has never hinted of any particular affection towards the young lady, I presume that is the information you seek."

"I just wondered if he liked her," Lottie replied. "If he doesn't then he may change his mind once he sees Meadholme. They say it is the prettiest house for ten leagues in any direction."

Mr Barratt was not a young man and had spent more time in the saddle or on the box recently than was his preference. He bade Lottie a warm farewell then crossed to the Red House, entering and retrieving two large cushions from the parlour. These he tossed into the back of the cart before climbing up and arranging the cushions into a type of settle onto which he lowered himself. Lottie appeared from the Rectory a few moments later with a parasol which she handed to Miss Lucy, already sat next to Mr Richards on the box. Harvey Richards was no dancer, but he was a decent horseman and the two mares responded immediately to a flick of the reins and a clicking noise from the back of the young man's throat.

Meadholme lay to the west and a little to the south so that it was equidistant from Milton and B_____. Mr Barratt, lulled by the motion of the cart on the quiet road and still rather worn out by the previous day's exertions, fell asleep with the sun on his face. He snored at a conspicuous volume and woke himself from time to time, on each occasion remarking on the freshness and beauty of the morning, before quickly resuming his slumber. Any person who stumbled across this rolling, bucolic tableau might have taken the two young people giggling on the box for newlyweds, and the fellow in the back for a drunken uncle, or perhaps an overdressed and unusually tame bear.

After an hour Miss Lucy began to recognise the landscapes which surrounded her old home and clapped her hands in delight. This caused the horses to accelerate into a canter andBarratt was thrown from his impromptu couch before Mr Richards could reassume complete control of the vehicle. Mr Barratt possessed some natural cushioning of his own and was able to avoid any serious injury, however. Miss Lucy soon pointed out the entrance to the estate. A young man stepped from the gatehouse and bowed deeply at the approaching cart before running ahead of the horses and up the drive.

Charles Barratt was not generally the kind of person who would allow himself to get caught up in another's excitement, but as someone affianced to the estate, in effect, he experienced a sense of anticipation as the cart rounded each turn in the path. He stood, leaning on the back of the box, and bent towards Miss Lucy's ear.

"It is a fine house, I understand," said Barratt.

"Yes, truly beautiful, I think," Miss Lucy answered, "but at its very best in the spring, when the lawns are surrounded with thousands of daffodils." Meadholme then came into view. Its situation was impressive, since it sat on a broad, grassy plateau, with shallow terraces sloping away at each side. Sheep grazed indifferently before the house, the front of which was nobly proportioned and faced in a light stone. Mr Richards stopped the cart in front of the house and Mr Barratt climbed down from the tailgate. The boy who had run ahead of them emerged from the grand portal at the centre of house, somewhat breathless from his efforts.

"I told 'em you was come, Miss Lucy," the lad said.

"Can that be you, Arthur?" she replied. "My goodness, you must have grown a full foot!"

"And you 'aven't grown one bit, Miss. Anyhow, the new master'll be out in a moment." Without any further farewell the boy made his way back down the drive, at a more measured pace than that at which he had raced up it moments earlier. Captain Billings appeared then, a sailor who seemed remarkably intact, given his profession, with but one visible scar, no more than two inches long and neat as anything, on his left cheek.Billings greeted them with a series of short declarative sentences, the cadence of which were familiar to Mr Barratt from his own time at sea, decades earlier. Mrs Billings, a plump, well-dressed woman, came and stood beside her husband as he encouraged the visitors to enter the house and a different boy, taller, and with something of a maritime stamp to his dress and bearing, skipped down the steps and took the reins from Mr Richards.

"One of my midshipmen," Captain Billings explained to Barratt as they stepped inside. "Fifth son of Lord Someone-or-other. At a loose end so I said I'd have him here. Five sons, can you imagine such a thing? The endless racket? Mrs Billings and I only seem to make girls. A new one appeared every time I sailed back from Mahon. They are a superb crop of things, though." These young women made themselves visible as the visitors entered the hallway. Miss Lucy's eyes filled with joyous tears as she looked over her childhood home. A year had passed, almost, since she had last seen it. Mr Barratt, meanwhile, knew a moment of agonising sadness as each of Captain Billings' daughters bowed in turn to their guests. They ranged in age from about twelve to twenty and were all prettily turned out in different colours, in order to avoid them being confused for one another. They all had their father's small, anxious eyes and narrow nose and were rather plain, in truth, despite their gay attire. Sometimes grief attacked Barratt unexpectedly, and without obvious cause. In this case the antecedent was as clear as the smiles of the four girls. Captain Billings was rich where his new acquaintance was poor, and knew abundance where Mr Barratt had known only loss, but since the sailor's good fortune could not be resented, so clear was the affection and esteem in which he held his children, Barratt could only rage secretly and inwardly at the great chasm in his soul.

"You are truly blessed," he said hoarsely.

"That I am," said the Captain.

"Are you quite well, Sir?" Mrs Billings asked. "There is always rum about the place, should you require some."She took Mr Barratt by the arm, as if they had been long acquainted and slowed his pace. Mr Richards and the rest of the Billings household proceeded ahead of them, along with Miss Lucy, who pointed out various sites of childhood mischief to the party.

"Quite well, Mrs Billings, yes," said Barratt, rallying. "I have lost the naval habit, I'm afraid."

"Were you in the service then, Mr Barratt?"

"No Madame, though I did sail with the Company in my youth. I can attest to the restorative powers of grog, therefore, but none is required I assure you. The young people sat me in full sun on the way here, wishing to gossip to one another, it is perhaps this which has affected me, but I am fully recovered."

"Here is some wickedness, indeed," said Mrs Billings. "I cannot fault the young lady though, Mr Richards is a handsome fellow."

"Really, Mrs Billings?" Barratt said. "It is almost never remarked upon."

"You are teasing me, Sir. Recall that most of the young gentlemen I encountered when I was young wore the marks of battle, for I am a Pompey lass. What manner of fellow is yon Mr Richards, what is his family?"

"He is a good soul, I think," Barratt replied. "Uncorrupted by wealth or influence, having neither. His grandmother was a friend of Queen Charlotte, but Lady Richards' brother, Mr Cunningham, is a spy, or so it is widely supposed. Young Harvey might marry well, but it seems more probable that he will fall in love with some penniless beauty and have to work for the rest of his life."

"There is no dishonour in that," said Mrs Billings, smiling.

"No indeed," said Mr Barratt. "In fact it is the happiest fate that can befall a gentleman."

There was rabbit for luncheon and after a second glass of wine and a couple of broad facial gestures aimed at his young associate Barratt mentioned that he and Mr Richards had gone hunting rabbits the previous afternoon.

"Did you bag many?" Captain Billings asked.

"Not a one," said Mr Barratt. "These Surrey rabbits were altogether too sly for us. We trotted home in shame and disappointment."

"You were on horseback, then?"

"Aye, Captain Billings," said Barratt. "Is that not the custom?"

"I am no expert, Sir. The coney is a notoriously nervous creature, I believe. Perhaps they are rattled by the clip-clopping."

"In which case," Mr Richards interjected with a grin, "they would certainly have been sent to ground by our artillery carriage, Mr Barratt, what say you?" Captain Billings guffawed at this, and sincerely, since he understood that some boyish sport was afoot. Mrs Billings, whose devotion to her husband was somewhat transcendent in character, soon followed his cue and the Billings girls, save the youngest who was playing with a kitten beneath the tablecloth, responded with delight to their mother's amusement. The kitten grew uncomfortable with the crescendo of noise and fled, which vexed the little girl, who endeavoured politely, nevertheless,to disguise her irritation. Only Miss Lucy remained unmoved, recognising something unworthy,though harmless, in the gentlemen's *bavarderie*.

"It is quite possible," said Barratt, "that like St Patrick we have driven the beasts from the land altogether!" A great chorus of male jollity succeeded this comment and such was the esteem in which the distaff element of the gathering held their male counterparts, and so infectious the rhythm and volume of their laughter that napkins were soon dabbing away hilarious tears, the obscurity of Mr Barratt's original comic intent notwithstanding. He was gratified, since it was usually just Johnson who responded to his drollery. By the end of the meal Mr Richards was in similar spirits to Barratt and Captain Billings and there was some talk of impromptu shooting, "a fellow ought to be able to shoot what he wants on his own property, after all", and of the whole party staying for supper before Miss Lucy was obliged to remind her host and fellow guests that a specific chore needed to be done and that while the hospitality of Captain and Mrs Billings was exemplary and that nothing would have given her greater pleasure than to spend several days in her first home, now swaddled in the White Ensign, it was imperative that they returned to B_____ that afternoon, as the ball was just ten days hence, a large number of subscriptions had already been received and the decorations must be refreshed where necessary and arrayed and that there was simply no time to lose. Captain Billings called this the finest disquisition he had ever heard and worthy of a Wellington or even of Lord Nelson himself and declared, furthermore, that had Lucy Walker ever taken to sea she would have made a fine, fighting commodore. He used rather fewer words to convey this meaning, of course.

The cart was loaded with swags and drapes and baubles, and a number of coloured candles and tablecloths, punchbowls and fascinating mirrored objects brought over from Venice. The gentleman swigged coffee to sustain them on the journey home and fond farewells were entered into. Miss Lucy wept again as Meadholme disappeared behind the trees and the two eldest Billings girls sighed as the broad shoulders of Mr Richards ceased to be visible.

Mr Barratt, once more stationed on his cushions but surrounded now with all manner of additional finery, had the last view of the place.

"It is beautiful, my Lucy," he said. The young lady turned to thank him but saw that he was asleep once more, long before they had reached the gatehouse.

XXVII

THE CART WAS unloaded by Mr Richards and Broady, who they found waiting on the steps of the Corn Exchange. Mr Richards then drove Miss Lucy to the Rectory, Mr Barratt having indicated that he would walk home momentarily. Once the young people were at a distance Broady handed a parcel to Mr Barratt.

"Tell Mr Johnson that my wife has laundered and pressed those garments herself," Broady said, "and thank him for me."

"He will appreciate that," said Barratt.

"The information you asked for is also there." Mr Barratt nodded.

"Thank you. Broady, given how you and I have started off this may seem peculiar, but hang it, I am thirsty. Would you join me for a small beer?" Broady hesitated, and played with his hat. "It is not a test, Sir," said Barratt. "I had wine with my luncheon and I am now troubled by its effects. I need something to calm the storm."

"In which case, yes," Broady said.

They entered The Bull, which was quiet, as the afternoon and week, indeed, were young. Mr Barratt ducked beneath the lintel and was barely able to stand upright within. They made their way through a series of low, dark spaces to a lighter area, behind the taproom. Mr Barratt ordered two small beers and they sat.

"Where did you go to school?" Barratt asked.

"I did not attend a school, Sir," said Broady.

"And yet Mrs Broady assures me that you have your letters, and are quick with your sums and so on. I am sure that she has not misled me."

"No, Mr Barratt. It was my father who taught me to read and

write, and to count, and about the price of eggs, and rates of interest."

"Of course, you have had some good fortune in life. I am sorry for the reversals you have suffered."

"Thank you," said Broady, raising his glass.

"Mr Broady, I mean to do something for the people of Butcher's Green, for the poor of B_____ generally, in fact. At first I thought of opening a print shop, there being none between here and Guildford, but it seems that you are alone among your neighbours in being able to distinguish between the letters. I then thought I might endow the south end with a school of some sort, but that seems a distant solution to an immediate problem."

"What is the problem, as you see it? There are unlettered persons in every corner of the country, no doubt."

"I am not concerned with every corner of the country," said Mr Barratt, "those affairs need occupy His Majesty the King and his government and not a fellow like me. If someone is drowning in the Southern Sea there is nothing I can do to save him. If he falls in the river here I will attempt to drag him out. Besides there are circumstances which affect the poor in this town in a way that is different from London, or Manchester, or Milton, even. Here, things grow and are harvested, the poor live high for a few months then fall back on the parish. Nothing is made in B_____, save for horseshoes."

"Aye," said Broady, nodding slowly, "we are unusually well-provisioned with forges."

"Since there is no manufacturing, no factories or workshops to speak of, there is nothing to sustain the poor over the coldest months other than the parish."

"You need not tell me, Sir," said Broady.

"The poor are excluded, in this sense, from the structure of society. Rents are only affordable to successful tenant farmers, and how can a poor man, never mind how hardworking he may be, acquire the capital to lease land of his own when his work and pay is seasonal?"

"It is impossible," Broady confirmed.

"So we might think," said Mr Barratt. "I have considered the matter and I wonder if our friend, Henry Nicholson, might not have inadvertently provided us with a solution."

"What?" Broady was disgusted by the sound of the man's name. "He is worse than the pox, Sir, if I may speak frankly. He would never think for a moment to help a poor man."

"Under normal circumstances he would not, I agree, but these are difficult times for Mr Nicholson. He hopes for better days in the near future, but we are about to dash his hopes, are we not?"

"God willing," said Broady. Mr Barratt laughed.

"I have rarely seen the Lord's good graces more angrily appealed to," he said. "Listen Broady, I want to see Nicholson punished for his iniquities just as you do, but I suspect it will pain him more to see honest men benefiting from that punishment." Broady smiled, finally, at this.

"Please explain."

Mrs Walker was in a forgiving mood. Her daughter had returned from Meadholme with happy reports of the estate and of Captain Billings and family. A new closeness had developed between Miss Lucy and Mr Richards, and since it was difficult to imagine a more pleasant young man to whom one's daughter might cleave her happiness, his terpsichorean shortcomings notwithstanding, this was also a source of pleasure. Mr Barratt arrived at the Rectory as Mr Richards departed and was admitted to the library, therefore, though the small beers and confabulation he had enjoyed with Broady had restored his spirits to a point of rambunctiousness and he might well have brushed past any protestation or impediment offered by Lottie had any been presented.

Barratt fell to his knees, not without difficulty, and took Mrs Walker's hand. Miss Lucy turned away, giggling.

"A short while ago I begged you to marry me, my only darling," he began. "I could not have anticipated that I would have to beg, so soon, for your forgiveness." Mrs Walker appeared unmoved by this but did not withdraw her hand. "Please excuse my hastiness, my lack of sensibility, of delicacy. I have never pretended, I think, to be anything other than a blunt sort of fellow, and that bluntness often pervades my behaviour as well as my speech. Generally I only hold it as a slight flaw, and one remarked as suchby those whose good opinion is of little importance to me. However on this occasion it has revealed itself as the gravest of imperfections, obvious to the person whose esteem I hold most precious, and now to me. I must seem an oaf to you, my dearest Susannah, but should you find a way to pardon my recent follies I will strive to be better."

"Get up, Charles," said Mrs Walker. "You really have been too much i' the sun." Barratt, using the arm of the chaise for support, got slowly to his feet. "Lucy, will you excuse us?" Miss Lucy scuttled from the room, blushing. Mrs Walker gestured to the chaise. "Sit with me, we must talk." Barratt's knees complained once more as he lowered himself into the settee's slack embrace, but he was happy as his fiancée sat beside him, sensing that a full rapprochement was likely.

"This business with Nicholson is almost concluded," he said.

"I do not care about Henry Nicholson," said Mrs Walker, sitting. "I am only concerned that we already seem prone to disagreements, Charles, and we have yet to decide upon a date for our wedding. There will be times in any marriage where husband and wife do not see eye to eye."

"It is inevitable," said Barratt.

"However, one might expect the period of courtship, and

betrothal, to be one of general accord, no? It is customary to leave any acrimony until after the honeymoon. I appreciate that you have a less jaded view of the connubial state than I do, and will understand, therefore, that these are not the suppositions of a hopeless optimist."

"No indeed."

"What does that mean?" Mrs Walker said quickly.

"Nothing," said Barratt. "Only that despite your youthful appearance no-one would mistake you for anything other than a person equipped with a great deal of good sense and wisdom."

"You will recall that any wisdom I possess relating to marriage was hard-earned, Charles. I cannot spend whatever remains of my life in a situation of emotional uncertainty."

"Nor would I ask you to, my darling," Barratt said. "I am at fault here, entirely, but I think that we have both grown unused to having to accommodate the feelings and actions of any other person."

"That may be true of you," Mrs Walker replied, "but my first thought is always of Lucy."

"Is that so? I got the impression today that she would much rather have remained at Meadholme."

"Please do not question how I choose to treat my only child, Sir."

"I would never dare to do so, Ma'am, and I have no doubt that you have acted at all times in the young lady's best interests. I meant only to faithfully report what I observed. The question which naturally arises from that observation is whether you placed greater value in your judgment, when removing to B_____, than in Miss Lucy's feelings. And here you are." Mrs Walker was irritated, once more, and Barratt sought to soothe her. "She is perfectly happy here at the Rectory, of course, and has benefited, no doubt, from exposure to a greater breadth of society. Your wisdom is not in question. I have owned that is my clumsiness which has lead to these misunderstandings. You are entitled to act according to your judgment, and I must do my utmost, henceforth, to ensure that my actions do not disturb or discomfit you in any way. I offer no excuse for the inexcusable; I seek only some explanation, in order that I may avoid causing further offence."

"Your implication is that I may continue to do just what I like while you must curb your instincts," said Mrs Walker. "On the face of it this seems like the most generous of accommodations, but in fact it serves to ascribe merit to your actions at the expense of my own." Mr Barratt was bewildered.

"I do not understand," he said.

"You are stripping some gentleman of his estate on a whim whereas I merely moved house. You think me insignificant, Charles."

"My darling, it seems to me that you are determined to be upset with me, for whatever reason, regardless of anything I say or do." He stood. "I came to B_____ to live a quiet life, free from the complications that surround a fellow in London, and for many months I succeeded. Then I had the fortune, good or otherwise, to fall in love. My behaviour since has been informed by that fact. I wanted to appear a better man in your eyes, Susannah, and to improve the lives of those about whom you care so deeply."

"So your actions were not charitable, in that sense, but selfish?"

"I shall make no secret of it. I regret that there are families living in poverty at Butcher's Green, of course, but I might have found a way to overlook their plight had I not come to see them through your eyes, as it were."

"What do you mean?" Mrs Walker asked.

"Our friend Mrs Broady thinks of you as a kind of angel," Barratt said. "I know that you distribute alms in the south end, and that you speak to the people there with care and concern. I meant to assist you, at first, but I then divined that the best way to help would be to restore what Henry Nicholson has taken. To be clear, you bear no responsibility for my manipulation of that gentleman and should have no qualms about it, therefore. Which is not to say that I would have pursued this course had I never met you, I would not. I believe my actions are just, Susannah, and that you have made me a more decent, respectable man." Barratt bowed deeply, turned and made to leave the library.

"Not I," said Mrs Walker. "Only God can mend a man's soul." She watched as Barratt stopped in the doorway, as his great shoulders twitched in a way she had never previously observed, and as he turned, his face a mask of concern.

"There is something else that we should, perhaps, discuss," he said.

Volume the Third

XXVIII

EVEN AS HE stumbled over an explanation of his lack of faith Barratt remarked to himself that what had been straightforward with Broady, where the admission was meant to achieve a specific effect, was infinitely more complex with an audience whose opinion of one's general character and personality was already formed, and whose good opinion one wished to preserve. He had looked into the hallway before he began and heard Miss Lucy and Lottie gossiping at some safe distance, this reconnaissance was succeeded by a series of deep inhalations, as if he were about to dive for some treasure on the seabed. He employed the same words as he had previously, but because he was a great deal more invested in how these words alighted, he delivered them haltingly and in a state of nervousness that was alien to him. He watched as Mrs Walker's expression turned from initial relief - he was not confessing to a murderous past or a string of bigamous marriages - to disquiet, and in the end to tearful confusion.

"What are you telling me, Charles? Does this mean we may not marry? Or that you cannot love me?"

"No, my dear," said Barratt. "This will not prevent us marrying, unless you decide that you do not wish to wed an unbeliever. I would understand, as this is a part of me which I have kept from you. I might only observe that I am the same man that I was before I informed you of my absence of belief." Barratt wondered if this were true, precisely, since he had in some way shared the shock of the moment with Mrs Walker. He did not feel as if he had unburdened himself, as he had hoped he might. Rather he felt that he had simply injured the person he least wished to harm. "As for me loving you, Susannah, know that I spare no affection from you on behalf of any deity, I am all yours, all the love I have to offer is yours, and since I have no hope of Heaven I find my paradise here, with you."

"For how long?"

"For as long as we remain happy and in health, though I will be your companion, nay your lover, whatever fate may bring us."

"How is fate not some implausible superstition, why do you not reject that?"

"Fate is merely a term we apply to that which cannot be seen or anticipated," Barratt said. "It cannot be appealed to, it is indifferent to our actions. It is the same thing as the future, in truth." Mrs Walker was shaken, but wanted to understand.

"Is this not a young man's infatuation, Charles, the allure of whatever is contrary to the common view? Surely you recognise some order to things, some sense of a greater hand at work. Do you not pray?"

"I speak the words of the prayers each Sunday morning, yes. Forgive me, I have seen a great deal more of the world than you, my beloved, and perhaps this has led me to my conclusions. I have seen things which would cause any man to question the benign nature of God. When I found peace and love, and corrected every aspect of my behaviour, when I began to live a blameless Christian life, that was when my happiness was stripped from me, in the most violent and desperate fashion. The misery I had seen in the world was no longer something to be regarded with objectivity; I was part of its total sum. How can a thinking man accommodate such senseless loss within a Christian view of things? The truth is that he cannot, the numbers will not tally. Anyone who has known a share of the agony I have felt, and who continues to believe in a merciful, loving God, in a universe designed for his comfort and pleasure, is lying to himself and all who know him."

"You have lied too," said Mrs Walker. "You sit in church and pretend to be pious. Lord, you read one of my cousin's sermons to his congregation." Barratt smiled in recollection of that particular Sunday morning.

"I understand that it appears hypocritical for me to hold these views, and to attend church. In doing so I injure no-one, however, and I honour the memory of Catherine, who was most a devout person."

"You are lying to God, Charles," Mrs Walker said.

"Well, either he is omniscient, and will choose to forgive or punish me accordingly, though it is hard to imagine how I might deserve greater punishment than that which he has already meted out, or he does not exist, in which case I may as well whisper falsehoods to the wind." Barratt sat after this and found, momentarily, that he could not look at Mrs Walker. Summer noise wafted through the open windows.

"When John called you a non-conformist I presumed that he meant you had some Methodist tendencies, or sympathy for some other sect, not that you rejected God entirely," said Mrs Walker. Her voice exhibited the strain which the conversation had put her under. "I wonder if I am but flesh and bones to you, Charles, is that it? And Miss Lucy, is she just a thing?"

"I will own that for many years after Catherine's death I felt no human connection with anyone, and other people were as objects to me." Mrs Walker stared at Barratt in horror. "I understand that my words frighten you, but having been less than honest with you about this matter I feel it essential that now I answer you in the most comprehensive and truthful manner possible.I was long benighted, but the dawn always arrives. Johnson would be better able to tell you when I began to return to my senses, I only know that it cannot have been more than a few months before my decision to quit London. The people of B_____ are simple, for the most part, if not always kind, and I began to feel a renewed fellowship with my neighbours, and became curious once more about their thoughts and feelings. It was something like a second birth, I suppose, but I found that one part of m   y former self did not revive, not even as I spoke the revelatory words of the Rector, in the house of God. When I met you, Susannah, the restoration of my person was complete. I discovered that not only could I feel again, I could love again, and with a consuming passion. You have saved me. I will not pretend that I do not admire your flesh a very great deal, my love, and am impatient to claim it." He paused in the hope that she would look up at him. Mrs Walker obliged, managing a small laugh, with no obvious bitterness to it, though she continued to weep. "However, I feel the prudent course at present would be to allow you time to think on what I have told you. I hope that you will eventually grant that I could not have done otherwise than reveal myself. I could scarcely have stood beside you in church with this secret darkening my heart. My fear is that I will now lose you, in full knowledge that with you I lose my last chance at happiness. Honesty must be the foundation of any marriage, I think, even if an occasional omission or nuance is necessary to buttress it." He saw her smile again as he got to his feet. "Please find a way to forgive me, my darling, even if my Godlessness prevents our marriage. You have woken my heart and illuminated my life, when once there was only sleep and darkness. My love and gratitude are forever yours." He crossed to her and kissed her hand before turning and departing the Rectory in a few long steps.

"Why does he always have to be so... so overwhelming?" said Mrs Walker. She patted her eyes with a handkerchief while accustoming herself to his absence. For once she found that she did not immediately regret his departure, but felt something closer to relief. Again, as a few minutes earlier, this sense of relief was short-lived. If she were to proceed with their engagement would it always be like this, she wondered, an oscillation between distress and reconciliation, like waves crashing then rolling back over the shingle?

The sun was at its westernmost point and lit the fields beyond the Rectory garden as if they were aflame. Mrs Walker generally only drank milk and warm water before her supper but she found that her nerves had been particularly affected by the interview with Mr Barratt. So when Reverend Archer returned from a parochial visit a short while later he found his cousin on the chaise, with Miss Lucy's head in her lap. Mrs Walker stroked her daughter's hair with one hand. In the other she held the dregs of a large glass of sherry. The three of them ate a simple supper of braised meat and potatoes and spent the rest of the evening engaged in separate, solitary pursuits. Mrs Walker pretended to read while contemplating her future with Mr Barratt, Miss Lucy sewed and unpicked some embroidery work while contemplating her future with Mr Richards and the Rector did in fact read several pages of Ricardo, on comparative advantage, before conceding that he had understood none of it and starting the chapter anew. There were knocks at the door and on each occasion the two women started, but these were only subscribers to Miss Lucy's ball, leaving their details and suggested contributions to the Trust.

Across the high street Mr Barratt sat in the parlour and watched for any sign of Nicholson or the gentleman in the wide-brimmed hat. He refilled his pipe from time to time and looked out of the window until all the lights in the Rectory were extinguished.

"What a woman she is!" he thought. She had not rejected him completely: there was still hope that she might come to understand or tolerate their differences relating to the matter of faith. Nor had she dismissed his admission as trivial. This would have disappointed him more, he realised, than being summarily cast out. It would never do to pretend that how one felt about God was not important. Even to an unbeliever it was a thing of some significance. The intelligence and gravity of her response was all that he could have hoped for or expected. He noted too a certain perversity in his response to her pain; he had never felt so strong a desire to possess her as when she sobbed before him. There was a cruelty about this which he did not recognise, but that was God for you, to Barratt's mind nothing more than some invisible agent which tended to exaggerate a person's most obscure qualities. He emptied his pipe into the firebox, tapping the bowl on its edge, then made his way up the broad stairs to bed.

XXIX

PUZZLEMENT REIGNED once more over the two households. Mr Richards, having no further reason to remain at the Martyrs, removed to the Red House, his worldly possessions fitting neatly into a battered trunk which he carried up to his room on the second floor. From his window he could see over the Rectory to the fields which stretched away evenly to the east. Upon his return from Milton he remarked a change in relations with the residents of that building. Mr Barratt seemed to be avoiding everyone, and as preparations for the ball continued Miss Lucy became increasingly attentive to Broady, asking him about matters upon which Mr Richards was clearly more able to offer an opinion.

Susannah Walker had recovered from the excitement of her last interview with Mr Barratt and had resolved to put all thoughts of him aside for the moment, since any recollection of what he had related to her caused a rush of unfamiliar emotions. She was successful, for the most part, and her cousin and daughter deferred any attempt to solicit information regarding her feelings where none was offered. Barratt, for his part, spent more time in the garden with his shirtsleeves rolled up, than he did in the parlour. It pained him to look out at the Rectory and to imagine what his beloved might be doing at that moment - this had until recently been a source of illicit delight - and his attention was redirected to any stray flora which he might snip, gouge out or uproot.

Mr Nicholson had gone to ground. Nothing had been heard of him since his appearance at the Rectory a few evenings back. Johnson was deployed to establish his whereabouts but reported that if Nicholson was at Hope Hall, as presumed, he did not step out of his front door for an entire day.

No supper was offered with admission to the ball but Miss Lucy had decided that light refreshments and restorative tit-bits should be made available to subscribers so the kitchens of each opposing property stood ready to prepare dainties of all kinds, and great quantities of flour and butter had been ordered. Preparations were already under way too at Foulke House, whither Barratt, Cunningham and Mr Richards had been invited on the Friday preceding the ball. Sir Clifford's cook lacked the skill of her counterparts at the Red House and Steddon Hall but adjusted for this deficiency by catering in greater quantity.

"Sir Clifford will try to bury you with dumplings," Barratt told Harvey Richards that morning. "Be sure to take a light lunch."

Cunningham had advised that he would collect them in his own carriage and arrived promptly, wearing his better coat. Mr Cunningham's coachman was a fellow of unappealing temperament who swore at his horses often, and in a thick Devonian accent. Fortunately much of this invective was unintelligible, therefore, both to the jehu's passengers and, it may be presumed, to the recalcitrant beasts at which it was directed. Mr Richards was delighted to be in the company of his great-uncle once more and spent much of the journey to Foulke House laughing at Cunningham's various complaints.

"It is a disastrous thing to grow old, Harvey, I counsel strongly against it. One's instincts may remain acute, but the body, favouring inertia, does not allow a person to act upon those instincts. The other day I stepped into the library to consult a book; it was a matter of some importance. After several minutes of fruitless searching I remembered that the volume required was beside my bed, and that in order to retrieve it I would have to climb the stairs, which was impossible to contemplate. I would have sent Mrs Flannery to fetch it, but she has acquired a habit of hiding at the other end of the house and it would be unseemly to shout, I think. I do not possess Mr Barratt's skill for projection, you see. Good fellow, Drury Lane's loss is our gain."

"How is Mrs Flannery?" asked Barratt.

"Elusive, Sir. I see her infrequently, because, she says, the place won't run itself. It is difficult to see why not, it is merely a pile of old stones, after all. I fear I may have frightened her, with certain approaches made in a condition of less than pristine sobriety."

"Oh dear," said Mr Richards.

"Nothing of an ungentlemanly nature, Harvey, I assure you. But I have made it clear that Steddon is hers, if she will have it."

"If she will have you, you mean," said Barratt, laughing. "I presume you have told her that you are not long for this world."

"Indeed, I thought it might prove an inducement. She has a son, a young man of considerable indolence and stupidity, who would inherit all. One might expect the woman to act on his behalf."

"It is a question of patience, Cunningham."

"How long ought a fellow be made to wait, by your estimation?"

"I speak not of your patience but hers," Barratt explained. "She may wish to defer your betrothal until you are rather closer to God. If you were to marry tomorrow she would still be waiting, but in bondage. As things stands she may wait as a woman of liberty."

"There would be little point marrying her if I were no longer fit to consummate the union," Cunningham observed. Mr Richards chuckled freely at this remark.

"May I make a suggestion?" He asked, when his laughter had subsided.

"There will be something put aside for you, boy, never fear," said Cunningham.

"I am entirely ineligible for any further assistance from you, dear Uncle, you have already been far too kind."

"Never mind the fact that he will outlive us all," Barratt interjected, "even Mrs Flannery."

"If she does agree to marry me I will make a point of it."

"Uncle, my advice would be this:if you wish to secure Mrs Flannery's affections promptly you must imitate the actions of the coquette."

"How so, Harvey?"

"Believe me, gentlemen, I do not speak from experience, or not at least from first-hand experience, but I believe it is a common tactic among young women wishing to secure an offer from a vacillating suitor to feign affection for another eligible beau, in order to push things forward." Mr Barratt considered this for a moment, contenting himself that neither his fiancé nor his late, much-adored wife had duped him in this fashion.

"So I should lead Mrs Flannery to believe that I favour another?" Cunningham asked.

"No, Sir," said Mr Richards. "She need only be conscious that she is not the only prize sow at the fair, as it were."

"In that case perhaps I should turn my attentions to Mrs Walker," said Cunningham, grinning. Barratt glared at his elderly associate momentarily before his face relaxed into a smile.

"I am certain that Mrs Walker will be pleased to hear that she has been spoken of in these terms," he said. "As for the estimable Mrs Flannery, well, I will try to ensure that my valet does not sweep the lady out from under your nose. He can be headstrong where matters of the heart are concerned."

The driver brought the horses to a halt with an array of curses and announced their arrival at Foulke House. Mr Richards jumped out as quickly as he was able, full of regret for redirecting their conversation towards this unfortunate terminus. If any hard feeling existed between Barratt and Cunningham, however, it was forgotten in an instant. Mr Barratt assisted his friend's descent from the cab and patted him gently on the shoulder once he had gained *terra firma*.

Sir Clifford's footman, in full livery, bowed deeply as they approached the entrance before opening the door and bowing again as he did so. Mr Cunningham and Barratt, unused to any kind of formality when dining at Foulke House, exchanged a glance of mild perplexity followed by a nod, as they each separately came to understand that the pomp must be for the benefit of other, unknown guests. A butler greeted them within and directed the three gentlemen to a drawing room. A low hum of chatter was audible as they approached and Barratt felt a familiar tightening in his chest. He yearned most powerfully for Mrs Walker, and knew with a kind of punishing certainty how much more tolerable such an occasion would be with her at his side. He supposed that his pride was at fault. He meant always to be honest, his pride would not allow him to make an exception and now he would never know what it might feel like to walk into a room with Susannah Walker, Susannah Barratt indeed, on his arm. Barratt paused to gather himself, and to allow Cunningham to enter first.

Sir Clifford, who was addressing the room while facing away from the door, saw the eyes of his audience move in that direction and turned to greet his newly arrived guests, who stood in a kind of stagger, looking like nothing so much as some parable relating to the perfectibility of male physiognomy.

"Here are two of the most brilliant persons of my acquaintance," Sir Clifford pronounced. Cunningham waved the compliment away.

"You do your acquaintance a disservice, Sir. I imagine we are among the least brilliant persons in this room." This remark, offered as Mr Cunningham performed a sedate bow, endeared the old gentleman to the whole company. Aside from Sir Clifford, Lady Foulke alone had any idea who the gentlemen were, and which of them her husband's epithet was intended to celebrate. She took it upon herself, therefore, to offer a general introduction.

"This is Mr Giacomo Cunningham, of Steddon Hall," she began. "Mr Charles Barratt, and the young gentleman, I presume, is Mr Harvey Richards?" Barratt nodded as his name was announced and Mr Richards bowed crisply, offering a flourish of his remarkable teeth as he straightened.

"I am Harvey Richards," he confirmed, "and I am greatly honoured by your invitation." Barratt, who stood at Mr Richards' shoulder, was afforded a brief glimpse of the world as seen by his young associate, and found it an agreeable place, filled with looks of frank admiration, and free from any kind of anxiety.

Cunningham, Barratt and Mr Richards made up a party of twelve. The servants had been obliged to dust down their finery by the presence of Sir Thomas Dearmont, who was a baronet, but who more importantly was Lady Foulke's younger brother. He was staying at Foulke House along with Lady Dearmont, their little son Francis, and Sir Thomas's ward, a pretty girl of about twenty, who was introduced as Beth. They had escorted Venetia, daughter of Sir Clifford and Lady Foulke, back from the city and this was the ostensible reason for their visit. The season was almost over, Lady Dearmont noted, and Miss Venetia had in any case taken very little interest in society. The reluctant Miss Foulke was lean, like her mother, but otherwise seemed assembled from the less attractive parts of her parents, having her father's high colour and her mother's high forehead, his nose, her chin and so on. In temperament, however, she was utterly unlike of them. Her manner and mode of dress called to mind some puritanical governess, and Barratt suspected that she may have adopted this position in some informal way during her stay in London. Francis treated his cousin more like a servant than a close relation, asking her a series of impertinent questions, pulling at her sleeve and demanding that she retie his bootlaces. The boy was clearly infatuated with Beth, meanwhile, and sat quietly at her feet when she implored him to leave dear Venetia be. The Dearmonts ignored their child entirely, preferring to concentrate on an ongoing squabble whose origins preceded the arrival of the party from B_____. This dispute bubbled to the surface from time to time throughout the evening before subsiding into a hostile silence. Barratt considered it probable that their lives were always like this; it would explain the little boy's misbehaviour, certainly. If Susannah Walker's first marriage hadsomething of this character then it was little wonder that her husband's death was not long mourned. It was unhelpful, Barratt thought, that Mrs Walker made her way into his thoughts a great deal more now, when he could not simply cross the street to pay his respects to her, than she had done in easier times. He felt her absence more keenly too, in the knowledge that her presence was denied to him, and by his own actions.

The beating of a gong summoned them through to the dining room where a great quantity of food already lay on the table.

"Goodness," said Mr Richards.

"It looks like Wenlock Edge, Sir Clifford," said Cunningham. "I congratulate you."

Mr Barratt was seated between Miss Foulke and Mrs Carter, widow of Colonel Carter, who had died at Corunna. The latter lady was an amiable, garrulous sort who laughed as energetically at her own jokes as she did at those of others. She had come from Milton with Miss Reeves, her sister. The two women were of strikingly similar appearance and after Cunningham remarked on this likeness it was admitted that they were twins. So alike were they, indeed, in demeanour as well as looks, that Barratt wondered how the good Colonel had chosen one over the other to marry, and provide a pension for. Mr Richards, who sat beyond Mrs Carter explained that he had himself recently removed from Milton.

"It is a happy spot, is it not, Mr Richards," quoth the widow. "Whereabouts were you staying?"

"At the Martyrs, Ma'am."

"Truly? I have heard that it is haunted."

"I was only there for a matter of months and while I encountered a few lost spirits I am quite certain they were mortal." Mrs Carter took a moment to grasp the meaning of this and laughed appreciatively once she had. She dabbed away the last of her laughter with a napkin.

"What is your profession, Sir?"

"I am that most useless of things, I fear, a gentleman without a gentleman's income. For the moment I am assisting Mr Barratt." Mrs Carter leaned towards Mr Richards and lowered her voice to a whisper.

"He is a most impressive person," she said. "Very rich, I imagine?"

"I know nothing of his financial situation, Ma'am, but I imagine it is secure enough."

"He seems a rather melancholy soul, is he recently widowed?"

"No, his wife died many years ago, but I believe theirs to have been an unusually strong attachment. However..." Mr Barratt had not overheard any part of this exchange but he brought it to a close with a precautionary cough. He had been conversing, in the meanwhile, with Miss Foulke. This young woman had impressed him principally by appearing to be oblivious to the appeal of Mr Richards, and also by the forbearance she demonstrated towards Master Dearmont.

"Miss Foulke, I imagine you are greatly relieved to be home," Barratt said. "I spend very little time in London nowadays, and am always glad to leave the place."

"Sir Thomas and Lady Dearmont were exceedingly kind to have me, Sir, and I was very fortunate to have use of their library and pianoforte. It is true that I do not take the same pleasure in society as other people of my age seem to do and so that aspect of city life was wasted on me. I am happy to able to tell people that I have been in London for the season, nevertheless, and witnessed its grandeur and folly." Barratt noted that the young woman's voice was a great deal more attractive than the rest of her person. There was a calmness to it, which bordered on resignation. He thought she would prove a more suitable companion for an elderly gentleman, Cunningham say, than the flighty Mrs Flannery, being the sort of serious young woman who would read improving literature to a fellow after his eyesight failed.

"It is curious that we have not met before, since I have visited Foulke Hall frequently these past two years," said Barratt.

"I have travelled extensively both in Italy, where a portion of my mother's family is from, and in the Low Countries. You did not visit us at Christmas?" Mr Barratt swallowed a spoonful of soup and thought about this.

"No," he said finally. "Although Sir Clifford did dine with me in January. Twice perhaps."

"I returned from Belgium in the middle of December," Miss Foulke explained. "I am not surprised that my father did not mention me, since I have seldom been at the forefront of his thoughts." Barratt considered the young woman's profile. A father's neglect, real or imagined, was not enough to make a girl plain, but it was possible he supposed to rob a child of their natural vitality, and it was this quality as much as any aesthetic advantage which Miss Foulke lacked, through ignorance, rather as a flower might wilt without sunlight. He was greatly pained, of course, as a result of his personal circumstances, and resolved to bathe the young lady in his attention for that evening, at least. He was civil to Mrs Carter, but answered her questions as economically as possible in order to return his focus to Miss Foulke.

It is possible to fall asleep anywhere - Mr Barratt had recently reclined into the arms of Hypnos on the back of a moving cart - but most frequently we lie down in a bed of some sort and close our eyes in order to sleep. In essence we adopt a position of pretence in expectation of that pretence being realised. Similarly Mr Barratt meant to find something to fascinate him about the unprepossessing Miss Foulke and while her accounts of foreign cities were delivered with no great passion and her questions to him lacked any distinguishing wit or imagination his interest in the young woman grew more sincere and less effortful as their conversation continued.

"Do you feel that your travels have changed you at all, Miss Foulke?" he asked.

"I am more aware of the history, customs and manners of other European nations," Miss Foulke replied.

"What I meant to ask was, I suppose, has your exposure to and awareness of the difference of others, not as a phenomenon rumoured in books but as something you have yourself observed, has it altered the way you think and feel?" Miss Foulke considered her trout with a look of increasing anxiety.

"Ought it to have done?" she asked.

"By no means," said Mr Barratt, essaying a reassuring smile. "The conclusion I reached when I returned from my own adventures was not anything revolutionary, I assure you."

"What was it, Sir?"

"Nothing at all. Nonsense. Anyway, we were speaking of you."

"I will not allow you to escape so easily, Mr Barratt," said Miss Foulke. She smiled at last, a pleasant, self-contained smile, and Barratt saw the light of animation appear in her eyes. "You are a guest, it is true, but you cannot be allowed to unwrap the sweetmeats of your intellect only to snatch them away untasted." Miss Foulke studied Mr Barratt as she spoke, her gaze flickering over his face before settling on his own eyes. He turned back to his plate before chewing and swallowing a deliberate mouthful. He took a sip of Hock and wiped his lips.

"Very well," he said. "When I sailed back to England after some years abroad I determined that the world, and here I mean the human sphere really, is at once much larger and also a good deal smaller than I had previously imagined it to be."

"Is that not a paradox, Sir? You have lied to me, what could be more revolutionary than a paradox?"

"It is not truly a paradox, Miss Foulke, it is merely a way of expressing the fact that I was doubly mistaken in my presumptions. I set off with no understanding of how scattered and various humanity was. I encountered every shade of person, a thousand different sets of habits, modes of dress, beliefs: men who cut and pierce their own flesh or speak without using their tongue, women who stretch their necks with coils of brass, who throw themselves from cliff faces rather than face widowhood, who dance naked to please their God, people who live only by consuming insects or the blubber of whales, who cross vast oceans in hollowed out tree trunks, who attempt flight, tribes who worship the sun, the moon, cats, great stones they have carved themselves, volcanoes..." Barratt paused to draw breath.

"In what sense, then, was the world smaller than you thought?" Miss Foulke asked.

"Having discerned how unalike and unfamiliar these troops of mankind were in certain facets, how apparently random and disordered were their ways of thinking, I noted too that in a great many aspects they were indistinguishable from my neighbours in Finsbury. The things which people fear do not alter whichever continent they are in, nor do the things which they want.

Everything else is trivial, I came to believe, I still believe, in fact." The animation which Barratt had observed in the eyes of Miss Foulke had become a kind of definite excitement. She looked, he thought, like someone who has just mastered the rising trot, or seen the sea for the first time. Miss Foulke placed her hand on the tablecloth, next to his, so that their fingers were almost touching.

"I am with you," she said quietly, leaning towards Mr Barratt. They nodded to one another and withdrew their hands from the table as the meat course was announced.

XXX

"AN EXTRAORDINARY repast," said Cunningham, as the gentlemen set about their pipes and cigars. "You have quite outdone yourself, Sir Clifford."

"Hospitality on the grandest scale," agreed Sir Thomas, who seemed altogether more clubbable in his wife's absence. The host acknowledged these compliments with a wan smile; his attention was fixed on Charles Barratt, who was speaking in confidential tones, as confidential as that gentleman's cavernous chest would allow anyway, with Mr Richards. Barratt became aware of Sir Clifford's scrutiny.

"We must toast Colonel Carter, and all the fallen," Mr Barratt said to Sir Clifford. The five gentlemen passed the port wine around and the fallen were toasted, along with the King and Lord Liverpool. As he emptied his glass Sir Clifford, his face still ruddier than was usual, addressed Mr Barratt.

"I hope that you do not intend to involve my Venetia in any of your scheming, Charles." Mr Barratt cleared his throat.

"My closest friends are in this room and only one is blessed with a child. It is natural that I should wish to become acquainted with that young person, I would have thought." This was not the reassurance of innocent intent which Sir Clifford sought, yet he was too placid by nature to demand anything further. Barratt chose to relieve him. "Fear not, Sir, we spoke of her travels and of my own. She is an intelligent and accomplished young woman of whom you must be tremendously proud."

"True," added Sir Thomas, who had been ushered into the realms of complete amiability by the port. "She was with us for a six-month and we barely noticed she was there. A meek child, but very ladylike."

"The misdeeds of your former associate were not mentioned," said Barratt. Sir Clifford attempted a frown of censure at Mr Barratt, but his brother-in-law had either not heard this last remark or was not sufficiently inquisitive to seek an explanation. Mr Barratt returned his friend's look with an easy smile. "That matter is all but concluded in any case, and I hope, to the satisfaction of all parties." A volley of screams was heard at this point from some nearby spot within the house and Sir Thomas raised his eyebrows and begged to be excused.

"I must put Francis to bed before he injures someone," said the baronet. Once he had left Sir Clifford asked to be appraised of any developments with the Trust and Mr Barratt told him of Nicholson's visit to the Rectory and, to the delight and hilarity of all, of the rabbit-hunting expedition which followed.

"It was then pointed out to us that our approach was unlikely to fetch us any rabbits," said Mr Richards, "as they are by nature very nervous creatures with particularly acute hearing..." Mr Barratt was by this point a similar colour to Sir Clifford. "Hence the big ears." Neither Sir Clifford nor Mr Cunningham had the faintest notion of what the other two found so amusing about this concluding remark but since they had already been richly entertained by these gentlemen and were anyway some degree less than sober they joined in the general uproar. There was some smiting of the table and rattling of silver, another toast was raised, to rabbits, and Lady Foulke was obliged to enter with a reminder that there was a child in the house.

There was no further opportunity for Mr Barratt to speak with Miss Foulke once the whole party reassembled as his company was monopolised by Sir Thomas's ward, Elizabeth, who proved to be as foolish as she was pretty, Mrs Carter and Miss Reeves, who together outflanked their interlocutor by the tallboy in a manoeuvre that Napoleon himself might have attempted. Upon closer observation Barratt determined that the older ladies were in fact easily distinguishable from one another, Miss Reeves being a little more slender, though still stout, in faith, and a good deal less careworn. Mrs Carter was a widow, of course, and for some years both her sons had pursued the same dangerous profession as their father. It was unsurprising, therefore, that time had marked them differently, though Barratt supposed that there were challenges and worries which were specific to spinsterhood. Miss Reeves assured Mr Barratt that she had always lived within her means. The sisters had acquired some capital following the sale of their father's business, it seemed, and the money had been carefully managed.

"They said it went under the market, Sir," Miss Reeves explained, "but we only wanted enough to get by."

"Six months later the first peace was signed, and the company folded soon after," said Mrs Carter gleefully.

"What business was your father in?" Barratt asked. The sisters were astonished.

"Did you never hear of Reeves, the bootmaker?" Mrs Carter demanded. "Supplier of boots to His Majesty's army?"

"My apologies, I was more in the maritime line," said Barratt. Cunningham came to his friend's rescue.

"Come, Charles, we must not outstay our welcome." He, Barratt and Mr Richards then bade their farewells, which were protracted, and Sir Clifford escorted them to Cunningham's carriage, offering further warnings about the character of Henry Nicholson.

"He is a desperate man, and desperate men are dangerous."

"All the more reason to tame him, Sir Clifford," said Barratt. "Besides, I myself am dangerous enough, no?"

Cunningham's coachman was one of those persons whose unpleasant characteristics were softened, rather than exaggerated by drink. He addressed the horses in gentler tones and the short journey to B_____ passed in docile fashion. Barratt was surprised to see tears in the eyes of his elderly friend as they parted at the Red House.

"Look out for him," Cunningham said to Mr Barratt. "He is a particular favourite of mine."

"Indeed," said Barratt. He bowed deeply and pressed the old man's hand between his own and a look of perfect understanding passed between the two gentlemen, neither of whom had a son of their own to admire, to feel proud of and protective towards, on a bright, moonlit night.

Johnson, who had been in London on an errand for his master, had returned that evening and shared a nightcap with Mr Barratt, and young Mr Richards, before they retired, each to their separate apartments.

The next morning an unexpected mist rose, the first seen since April. It was not a harbinger of cooler days, however, and had dissipated entirely by the time Barratt and Mr Richards had completed a lengthy, well-seasoned breakfast and drunk several cups of coffee. Another surprise, in the spritely form of Reverend Archer, was then visited upon the Red House, the Rector arriving as Harvey Richards set out, more gingerly than usual, for his morning perambulation. The two young men bowed to one another *en passant*.

"Good morning, John," said Barratt, appearing in the hallway with a napkin tucked into his collar. "Have you had your breakfast?"

"I have eaten, yes." Barratt directed his friend into the parlour.

"It is something of an honour to receive you on a Saturday. How goes the sermon?"

"Oh, I think it can wait," said Reverend Archer, taking a seat by the window. "It is the fear of God which brings the faithful to St Andrew's, rather than the brilliance of its young cleric."

"Not I," said Barratt.

"No, you are exceptional, Charles, in a number of aspects, though your appreciation for and comprehension of my weekly exegeses may be the least important." The Rector concluded this remark with a pained smile.

"What is it, John? What can be so important that it drags you from your study on a Saturday morning?" Reverend Archer did not reply at once. Instead he looked across the street to the Rectory, and wondered if it were too early to ask for Sherry. The clock on the mantel, as if conscious of the Rector's dilemma, struck ten.

"There is an unhappiness in my home and I feel sure that you are the cause of it." Reverend Archer paused, and turned to Mr Barratt. "I feel no less affection for you, Charles, than I do for Susannah and I understand that whatever has caused this sundering must be an issue of significance, since I do not believe you would allow some childish misunderstanding to persist. You are a proud man, but above all a practical one. I would ask therefore that you speak with Mrs Walker and attempt, between you, to resolve this matter."

"Unfortunately I cannot change what I have already said to Mrs Walker," said Barratt, "nor would I wish to retract those words which have distressed her, since they were truthful, and kindly meant."

"You have distressed her with kindness, Charles? How so?"

"I intended only that she might not be misled, that I should not continue to mislead her, more specifically, about my religious feelings, or lack thereof."

"You told her that you are an atheist," said Reverend Archer, nodding slowly. "Little wonder then that she is half-distracted."

"I determined that I would have to make the admission at some point, and it seemed more honourable to do so before our marriage than after it."

"Susannah likes to affect that she does not feel things deeply, if at all, but it is a mere pretence. She is as sensitive as any of her sex. The revelation must have shocked her, since you give the impression of a man who loves God, not of one who refutes his existence."

"You were not shocked when I told you, John," Barratt remarked. "You were barely even surprised."

"My circle of Oxford friends, whom Susannah occasionally disparages, includes a number of fellows who are sympathetic to Mr Shelley," said the Rector, "some of whom enjoy more prosperous livings than St Andrew's."

"Godlessness in the Anglican church, eh? I am not sure if this is a commendable development. You, at least, are a true believer?"

"Of course," said Reverend Archer, a note of irritation creeping into his voice. He had expected this to be an uncomfortable interview, but had hoped that his friend might behave in a less aggravating fashion. "Mrs Walker has not had the benefit of a gentleman's education, and accordingly has not been exposed to any great diversity of views."

"She does not know her Aristotle from her Empedocles."

"You may wish to put it like that," said the Rector. "Imagine then how she must feel when the person she most admires tells her that the very foundations of her thought are false."

"I do not require Mrs Walker to think as I think, nor to believe what I believe. She is a woman of great wit and imagination and is every bit as capable of forming opinions about such matters as I am."

"Have you told her this?" Reverend Archer asked.

"It was implied," said Barratt. His friend raised an eyebrow.

"You may think that I do not give the fairer sex sufficient credit for their intelligence or perspicacity, and you may feel that the counsel of a bachelor *malgré lui is* beneath your contempt, but my word, Charles, do you not think you might have been more explicit when the happiness of you both hung in the balance?" Mr Barratt knew immediately that the Rector was correct. When he had spoken to Mrs Walker he had thought only of what he wanted to say and not of what the lady needed to hear. He savoured his humiliation for a moment, as if it were a fine claret, then bowed to his friend, smiling.

"It is a great pity that no woman will have you, my friend, as I am sure you would make a marvellous husband to any. I will heed your advice, if you will confirm that Mrs Walker might consider receiving me." Reverend Archer laughed and got to his feet.

"She is not in the best of spirits this morning," he noted. "Perhaps tomorrow, after church?"

"Unless there is some contraindication I shall call on you then," said Barratt. The two gentlemen shook hands. "I have one more thing to ask you, John, if I may. As I practice so must you preach."

"Sorry, I do not grasp your meaning."

"Your visit here has interrupted the composition of your sermon, I suppose," said Barratt. The Rector nodded. "If I am to be more explicit with Mrs Walker perhaps you might consider being more explicit with your parishioners?" Reverend Archer laughed again and raised a hand of farewell. As he crossed towards the Rectory Mr Barratt shouted after him. "Keep it short, John! And speak up!"

XXXI

REVEREND ARCHER'S sermon, as it turned out, would not have been regarded as noteworthy in any other parish church in England, either for its brevity or intelligibility. At St Andrew's however, on a warm, July morning, the homily was held to be the most digestible heard in that blessed space since the previous autumn, when Mr Barratt had thundered away following the incident with the wasp.

Barratt's eyes were fixed upon the profile of Mrs Walker throughout, but she did not turn to look at him at any point, choosing instead to study her hymnal and casting only an occasional glance at her cousin in the pulpit. Mr Barratt thought that a deeper hue was detectable on his beloved's cheek and wondered if she had been spending more time in the Rectory garden, attempting to bend Nature to her will; certainly his own plot at the rear of the Red House had proven a welcome distraction from matters of the heart. He nodded to the Rector at the conclusion of the service and dropped some coins into a collection plate before escaping briskly up the aisle, lifting his hat to the assembled company without acknowledging any person in particular. Johnson and the cook followed a few moments later. Barratt sat in his parlour and waited until he saw that the residents of the Rectory had all returned home. He combed his hair in the vestibule glass, then bent to brush some dust from the toe of his boot. His hand never reached the offending blemish. A pall of utter darkness fell over Mr Barratt and his body fell to the floor with a great noise.

He awoke in the same position, since it would have taken several strong men to shift his lifeless form and several more to get him upstairs to bed. Smith, the apothecary, knelt close to Mr Barratt's head and Mrs Walker, who had chanced to look out of the Rectory door and notice the commotion across the street, lay sobbing across her lover's broad back.

"He lives yet, Ma'am," said the quack, as Mr Barratt opened his eyes. The stricken gentleman surveyed the scene with interest from this novel perspective, the bright flagstones of the hallway and brighter still the noonday street beyond. Through the open door Barratt noticed how the shadows fell and calculated that he could not have long been unconscious; minutes, moments even. He felt no blood running on his scalp nor could he sense any particular site of injury. His shoulder was somewhat sore but he presumed this was a result of his fall. Mr Barratt looked up at the crouching apothecary and wondered if he had suffered some sort of apoplexy. He found that he could speak, which was greatly reassuring, though the words he uttered, "I am quite well," and the unprecedentedly frail manner in which they were expressed seemed to contradict each other. Upon hearing Barratt's voice Mrs Walker stopped her sobbing, lifted herself from his back and threw herself down beside him on the stone floor.

"My love," she said, "my only love." She kissed Barratt's cheek and tears fell from her face on to his. Giving the general impression of some great wounded beast, downed by a distant marksman, Mr Barratt turned slowly so that he lay on his back. Mrs Walker continued to kiss his face until Smith observed that perhaps the gentleman might benefit from being allowed some air, which interjection invited a truly terrifying glance from the lady at whom it was principally addressed. She saw the wisdom in it, after a few uncomfortable seconds for Smith, and said "Of course you are correct, Sir," rising to her knees, while continuing to stroke her lover's hair.

Johnson and the cook then reappeared with salt of hartshorn from Mr Barratt's own medicine chest. Mrs Walker was touched to see the invariably sanguine valet in a state of perturbation.

"He is awake," she said. Johnson exhaled deeply, and bowed, while the cook crossed herself. "Where is Mr Richards?" Mr Barratt, supporting himself on his elbows, spoke next, his voice already somewhat less feeble, but a rumour, yet, of its usual forcefulness.

"I sent Harvey to Hope Hall," he said. "I had a suspicion that Nicholson might act against me, and I wanted him watched." Mrs Walker, whose fingers lay amid Mr Barratt's hair, made a fist so that he appeared alarmed, of a sudden.

"It is the strain of your accursed feud with Henry Nicholson which has brought about this turn, Charles, do you not see it?" Barratt was only conscious of the strain under which his scalp was suffering. "Why do you not let it go?"

"If you will let my hair go, sweetest one, then I will pursue the matter no further, I promise you," said Barratt. "Johnson, perhaps you might retrieve Mr Richards? And please shut the front door." Mrs Walker loosened her grip and Johnson carried out his master's second instruction, shaking his head disparagingly at the crowd of prurient onlookers gathered on the street outside.

They sat Mr Barratt up and between the four of them managed to lift him into a chair brought from the parlour. The cook said that she would bring some beef tea, a measure of which the apothecary unreservedly approved. Smith also prescribed a few days of bed rest, at which point Mr Barratt dismissed him, with an instruction to send his bill in due course, even though he was unclear what ministrations, if any, the quack had performed. Mrs Walker, who could not bear the thought of leaving Mr Barratt's side, asked if Smith would look in at the Rectory to appraise the other residents of the situation, offering some coins which were refused.

Mr Barratt was then visited on his hallway throne by Reverend Archer, Miss Lucy, and Lottie, who kissed his hand and told him not to go around giving people scares. Johnson and Mr Richards returned a short time after the party from the Rectory had departed. They managed to support Mr Barratt between them, in a remarkably lopsided arrangement, and get him to bed.

In spite of a degree of relentlessness which inhered to his personality, Charles Barratt was not, in fact, unaccustomed to intervals of prolonged inactivity. When a project was under way, or a troubling idea occupied his mind Barratt was impatient to achieve some kind of resolution, indeed the problem of Butcher's Green, and the poor of B_____ generally still nagged at him, since he had made several thwarted beginnings, but he was also of a Socratic bent: when one could do nothing, nothing could be done.He put Mrs Broady and her neighbours to the back of his mind, therefore, and contented himself that his preparations for dealing with Mr Nicholson once and for all were complete, he had only to wait. Mrs Walker was with him from dawn to dusk, reading to him from the scandalous volume she had taken from the Rector's library, the tale of a holy man's descent into depravity. They laughed a great deal at the convolutions of the plot and at the unfortunate monk, whose dialogue Mrs Walker performed in the thickest of foreign accents, though she had never travelled abroad.

She remarked in passing that the regular occupants of Barratt's bench in St Andrew's were perhaps the most motley to be found in any church in the land: an atheist, a dogsbody and a Roman Catholic. She then suggested, teasingly, that a woman might not feel at all safe under the same roof as such people. Mr Barratt reassured her that his cook was utterly unlike any of the characters found in Mr Lewis's book and completely respectable in all regards, and that Johnson would follow his mistress's every instruction to the letter. As for his own predilections and peccadilloes, well, his testimony could scarcely be relied upon and Mrs Walker would have to draw her own conclusions. He declared that he had no recollection of intimacy of any kind within the walls of a convent though he did confess to kissing a beautiful woman in the shadow of a nearby church, and that just a few weeks previously. Mrs Walker enquired if the embrace had been satisfactory and Mr Barratt observed that it was not in the nature of such encounters to be satisfactory; they were either disappointing or they left a person wanting more. This particular instance was of the latter case, he was happy to report. Mrs Walker took Mr Barratt's hand and said that it was a great pity that his health would prevent him from seeking such pleasures for the foreseeable future. Mr Barratt smiled and complained that while he knew a lack of vigour would one day prove to be his greatest demerit he had always presumed the day to be some distance in the future.

These were golden hours for them both, the shock of Mr Barratt's syncope notwithstanding. When they wearied of the novel they would speak of their personal histories. Mr Barratt had lived longer and in a greater variety of milieux but Mrs Walker's recollection was much keener and more detailed. She remembered the names and diverse temperaments of each of her ponies, there had been several apparently, while Mr Barratt could only confirm that his father had once owned a horse and that it was piebald. Mr Alexander Barratt was the less-favoured of his parents, and a man with many weaknesses, it was disclosed.

"He would beat me, on occasion, not because of any transgression on my part, but because of some defeat or setback he had experienced in business. One day, some time after my fourteenth birthday, I hit back and knocked him to the ground. I ran out of the house and never returned. He died that winter of consumption."

"You must have despised him," said Mrs Walker.

"I did not admire him, particularly," Barratt admitted, "but he paid for my education, and for that, at least, I was grateful."

"My father was the kindest gentleman I have known," Mrs Walker said. "We were all spoiled by him." Her fiancé smiled and thought of Miss Lucy, a child who had yet to be denied a single thing.

Their conversations did not dwell exclusively on the past although the subject of their engagement was scrupulously avoided. Mrs Walker did ask for Mr Barratt's impressions of Meadholme, which were duly reported, but Barratt was careful to constrain his enthusiasm with regards to the house itself, enthusiasm which might have seemed presumptuous, whereas the great affection which he had developed for the tenants of the property was set forth in the most fulsome terms, being an altogether less perilous field of discourse.

"They are a fine English family and the Captain is a man after your father's heart, very loving and generous towards his daughters."

"I have not met him," said Mrs Walker. "His correspondence is very direct, though perfectly civil."

"As is the gentleman, I assure you, though he does have a habit of speaking, at all times, as if he is issuing orders. You shall meet him at the ball, I dare say." Mention of the ball brought Henry Nicholson to mind and the corners of Barratt's mouth tightened. Mrs Walker guessed at the cause of her fiancé's change in demeanour but thought it politic not to further harangue him,accordingly Mr Barratt's spirits, and the pleasant tone of their discussion soon revived.

After so many hours thus spent in uninterrupted company they came to know a great deal about one other, but just as discussion of the future was taboo so was any prolonged reflection on their previous espousals, each party having different reasons for steering around the subject. Mr Barratt did not wish Mrs Walker to believe, as she once had, that his heart would only ever belong to Catherine Barratt, and he was aware that when he spoke of his late wife such an impression was ever likely to be formed. For her part Mrs Walker saw no benefit in recalling to mind a period of her life which was distinguished by a combination of cruelty and neglect. She had frequently wished her husband dead, and while he had fulfilled these wishes, rather earlier than might have been hoped or expected, she was certain that the memory of those unhappy years spent in his company, alleviated only partially by the arrival of her beloved daughter, might prejudice her against the idea of remarrying. Mrs Walker loved Barratt, with a passion that had not wavered since his proposal, but she knew, as all women must, that we marry most favourably with the head as well as the heart. Charles Barratt was in almost every particular a decent, upstanding Christian gentleman, well made, if a little heavy, and perfectly amiable, if a little loud. The time she had spent with him since his collapse had only confirmed her earliest assessment, but of course this image of the man was at best incomplete and at worst a falsehood. Susannah Walker knew this - how she wished she did not! - and could not at present see how such knowledge might be disregarded.

On the third morning after the incident, a sultry Wednesday, Mr Barratt found that he could rest no longer. Had it not been for the soothing and almost permanent presence of Mrs Walker at his bedside the degree of impatience provoked by an unfinished stratagem would have compelled him to rise far sooner, of course, though Mr Richards was an able deputy and had been poised to act swiftly on Mr Barratt's behalf if the need arose and Johnson was available in the event that a less gentlemanly hand was required. No further emergency sprang from the first, however.

Barratt got up before Mrs Walker arrived. He pulled off the bedclothes, which were anyway in need of changing, and arranged them in an approximate circle on the floor around his feet. He then performed a series of sudden bends, almost touching his toes, and raising his body abruptly upright each time. He felt no ill effect from these exertions and declared himself fully recovered, therefore. He called for Johnson to bring him his usual morning attire and drew the curtains open. The sun was already high in the sky, it being little more than a fortnight past midsummer, and Mr Barratt lifted the sash and perched himself on the window sill, as a warm breeze dried the perspiration from his nightclothes. He felt renewed, as if the apoplexy or fainting fit or whatever it was had somehow marked an end to a defined period of his life. Mrs Walker had acted as his Virgil, guiding him back to the light. He reclined against the frame of the window and looked north, past the handsome old church, to the countless greens of the English countryside. He heard the persistent chirruping of swallows from beneath the eaves. It was on a morning of such perfection and clarity as this that Barratt might, perhaps, have succumbed to the notion of a divine creator, an epiphany which would have doubly comforted him, providing hope of true felicity in this life, since it would mean that he might marry his beloved without scruple, and in the next. Mr Barratt's great misfortune was that he could not simply believe, however, so while he was sensitive to the beauty of a Surrey morn, and felt the thrill of it as deeply as any man might, he saw no reason to seek an explanation, divine or otherwise, for the brilliance of the sky or the sweetness of the air. For him these things were the way they were because they were the way they were, and not because an unseen deity had willed it.

He leant forward, out of the window, and looked upwards to see if he could spy the swallows' nest. As he did so Mrs Walker stepped out from the Rectory and saw Mr Barratt in this somewhat precarious position. She shrieked, loud enough that Barratt started, his hand slipping momentarily on the sill. His predicament, viewed from across the street, appeared more lethal than it was, particularly as Charles Barratt's physique was unusually top heavy, and Mrs Walker offered a sharp encore to her previous exclamation. Barratt was in no real danger, in fact; he steadied himself by grabbing the bottom of the raised sash with his free hand then turned to his fiancée and offered a broad grin. Mrs Walker was not amused, but did not wish to make any more of a scene. She swore quietly, through clenched teeth, that she would exterminate Charles Barratt herself, before regaining her usual composure and making to cross the street. From his eyrie opposite Barratt saw a man approach her, moving quickly, a familiar figure in a wide-brimmed hat. When he reached Mrs Walker he took her wrist – she gasped again – and pressed a note into her hand. The man then jumped nimbly over the church wall and ran off through the churchyard. Barratt shouted for one of the gentlemen of the house to retrieve Mrs Walker. Moments later Mr Richards escorted the lady across the street and into the parlour. She sat beside the fireplace and turned the note in her fingers without opening it. Mr Barratt stepped into the room, still dressing himself, and took the missive from her. He unfolded the paper. Five words were written upon it in a strange ink, of a deep rust colour, the letters scribbled in haste, great anger or fear and unblotted, so that a ghostly, mirrored impression was visible on the other side of the fold. It looked, for all the world, like the work of a deranged mind.

"What does it say?" Mrs Walker asked. Barratt considered some invention, some ruse which might allow him to destroy the note without her seeing it, but reasoned that half-truths or outright dishonesties had not helped their relationship thus far. He handed the paper back to her and she cast her eyes across it. It read, "TELL BARRATT HE MUST STOP."

XXXII

THE BUSIEST residents of B_____ were, undoubtedly, Mr Broady and Mr Richards. For the moment each man served two masters, though Broady's situation was more straightforward. He worked in the fields from dawn until mid-afternoon, returned home briefly, then placed himself at the disposal of Miss Lucy. Harvey Richards, meanwhile, was expected to attend to the whims and wishes of this young lady and those of Mr Barratt simultaneously.

Their ordeal was almost over, however. The morning of the ball had arrived and within a few hours both Broady and Richards would be allowed to auction off at least one of their respective commissions. A few simple tasks remained to be performed. Refreshments needed to be safely transported from the kitchens of the Rectory and the Red House to the Corn Exchange. Mr Richards had been asked to oversee these preparations. Broady was to recruit a number of temporary ostlers, on the understanding that they would be paid by those attending the ball and not by the Trust itself.

The Rectory was a site of considerable activity, therefore, when Harvey Richards announced himself an hour before noon. Musicians were rehearsing in the library, an odour of spice wafted along the scullery passage and the ceilings were rattled by excited footsteps on the upper floors as final fittings of evening wear took place. Mr Richards put his nose into the kitchen but was warned away by Mrs Walker's cook.

"Is that Mr Richards?" shouted Miss Lucy. "I cannot come down, I am not decent." The young lady concealed herself behind the newel post at the top of the stairwell. "Mama and I are checking that we can still squeeze into our dresses," she explained. "What are you wearing this evening, Sir?" Mr Richards indicated, with an economical gesture, that his attire would not alter. "Really, you are not going to change?"

"I might put on a clean shirt," he said. "Since I will not be dancing it scarcely matters what I wear. One does not need a dress uniform to sip punch."

"You might at least attempt to dance," Miss Lucy cried.

"I have attempted it, more than once, and found it impossible.

Never fear, Miss Walker, there will be many other young gentlemen who shall consider it the honour of their life to take a turn on the floor with you. Better to enjoy their skill and enthusiasm than to suffer a fellow who dances reluctantly and very ill indeed."

A barking sound from the kitchen summoned him away, several hundred tiny pies having cooled sufficiently to be safely transported along the high street, and Miss Lucy was left to remark to herself only that there would be no other person attending the ball so worthy of her admiration as Harvey Richards.

Mr Barratt, like his young associate, would not be dancing. He was quite certain that he was fit enough, but Mrs Walker did not share this opinion and since a further cooling of relations between the two of them seemed to threaten following the intervention of the man in the wide-brimmed hat Barratt had pledged to engage in no more taxing an activity than a tap of the foot or nod of the head. He had not attended a ball for many years but his figure had not greatly altered during that time. Nevertheless the morning of the ball found him in items of evening wear, now somewhat démodé, but this was to allow Johnson to buff his slippers and to take a stiff brush to his frock coat. A halo of very dark grime materialised on the lime floorboards as the valet worked. This substance was proper London soot, Barratt determined, and meant to remark upon the fact but Johnson had disappeared in search of a dustpan.

It was to be an important evening for Charles Barratt. First he would bring his business with Henry Nicholson to a conclusion. It was not quite checkmate, but the endgame would look unpropitious for any sensible opponent. Nicholson was no such a person, Barratt had concluded, but he might be prevailed upon to see sense if the true helplessness of his situation were demonstrated to him with sufficient force. It was then Mr Barratt's intention to press his suit with Mrs Walker once more, provided the other matter was concluded successfully. He would renew his proposal, offering to undertake religious instruction from Reverend Archer, if it might influence her to accept him. In truth he rather hoped this measure would not be necessary, since he saw little personal benefit in it, and he had yet to consult the Rector to ensure his co-operation. This morning, however, a rather more pleasant, or at least less complex task awaited him. He was to call on Miss

Foulke with some books he had promised to loan her, among them Mr Paine's *Age of Reason*, which Barratt had, as a precautionary measure, rebound within another less interesting tome. Johnson saddled the larger mare for his master, who headed for Foulke House at a gentle trot.

Sir Clifford greeted his friend with an energetic handshake.

"You are quite recovered, then, Charles? You look very well indeed."

"I am in rude health, Sir," said Barratt. "Thank you for your concern."

"I heard of your illness from a most unexpected source, you know," Sir Clifford said.

"Really? I presumed that Lottie must have told everyone within five leagues."

"The Rector's maid? She is as loose-tongued as any good servant can be, though a shrewd thing with it. My information came from your Narcissus, Mr Nicholson." Mr Barratt raised an eyebrow. "He did not call upon me, you understand," Sir Clifford continued, "but upon Venetia. She is the belle of the county, it seems, all of a sudden."

"I did not know that Miss Foulke and Mr Nicholson were acquainted," said Barratt, coldly.

"They have known each other since childhood, Charles, and he was not such a bad fellow in those days. His mother's death affected him deeply, I believe. Grief acts on us all in different ways." Sir Clifford's observation was hardly revelatory but Mr Barratt recognised the truth in it. He considered the implications of this sentiment, if indeed there were any, on his plan of action. Was Nicholson someone to be pitied or censured? As ever, when Barratt had any doubt about the rectitude of his campaign against that gentleman he called to mind little Catherine Broady, whose future Henry Nicholson had stolen, who lived in squalor because of his licentiousness and bitter nature.

"Here is Miss Foulke!" Barratt said, as the young lady emerged from the library. Her father's remark about her sudden beauty had been meant playfully but it did appear that the unwonted attention she had recently received had encouraged Miss Foulke to pay greater attention to her dress and toilet, and may indeed have caused some perceptible change to the light in her eyes. She remained too thin and oddly put together to ever be considered beautiful or pretty even, other than by a parent or a particularly devoted lover, but if a Frenchman were to visit Foulke House (none ever had) he might describe the daughter of that property as *jolie laide*. Mr Barratt's voice, in common with the rest of the man, had regained its natural puissance, so that Miss Foulke was considerably startled upon hearing her name so boldly pronounced, but recognising the gentleman of whom she had recently grown so fond she soon recovered her composure and offered a smile of frank delight.

"Mr Barratt, I had heard that you were sick and here you are looking very well indeed. What a relief it is to see you!" Mr Barratt bowed deeply.

"Miss Foulke, it is a pleasure to see you. Have the Dearmonts returned to London?" "They have," said Sir Clifford, "and taken that hellchild with them, thank God."

"Francis is a very spirited young man," Miss Foulke admitted. "Though Lady Dearmont does not pay him the attention he deserves, perhaps."

"She is devoted to that foolish girl, Beth, meantime. Seems to think they are like sisters." Sir Clifford seemed to regard companionship between women of differing ages as wholly unnatural.

"I'm sure Mr Barratt has no interest in the strife and struggles of our family, Papa. Will you join us for lunch, Sir?" Barratt had not considered the possibility. As he did so he felt a hot, sharp sensation in his chest.

"No, I must away. Here are your books." Miss Foulke took the parcel without looking at it, her gaze remained fixed on Mr Barratt. She looked at him with an expression of lively pleasure which caused the gentleman to forget the promise he had made to Mrs Walker altogether.

"I know you do not particularly enjoy dancing, Miss Foulke," said Barratt, "but perhaps you would consider me for your first turn this evening, and we can forgive each other's lack of technique."

"I would be delighted to, Mr Barratt, however that dubious honour has already been awarded elsewhere." This response surprised Barratt but did not displease him, ultimately, since it appeared to confirm that Henry Nicholson would come to the ball. The whole affair had been organised for the benefit, and in the name of Mr Nicholson's Trust, but so erratic and unpredictable was his behaviour that his attendance at the event, affirmed in writing to Miss Lucy, was not strictly guaranteed. Another one of Mr Barratt's concerns was alleviated. The separate parts of his plan need now only fall into place, like a child's puzzle, and Nicholson's fate would be decided.

XXXIII

CHARLES BARRATT rode home at a still more sedentary pace allowing the mare to stop and graze from time to time. As he slouched in the saddle his mind drifted from one idea to another. He was aggravated by a half-remembered notion which related back to a conversation that had taken place during his last visit to Foulke House and began to wonder if his mental faculties were deteriorating. Then it came back to him: boots. Mr Reeves had not needed to diversify as peace seemed a distant prospect. His business did one thing, and did it well. Well enough for the common foot soldier at least. Reeves and his daughters had escaped the consequences of their short-sightedness, but no doubt someone had suffered. A little imagination might have kept the business afloat. Barratt imagined that the raw material, skills and equipment required to manufacture an infantryman's boots were largely the same as those used for fancy Hessians, dancing slippers or certain types of ladies' shoes. It was something worth investigating, he decided. He would speak with Mr Richards about it at the earliest opportunity.

Harvey Richards would not be available to discuss such matters that afternoon, however, since he was still engaged with last minute arrangements for the ball. In between ferrying refreshments to the Corn Exchange he was preparing accounts for the Trust. A considerable profit had already been made, by his calculations, despite Miss Lucy's insistence on the provision of small comestibles, and this figure would doubtless increase, as surcharges were applied for those wishing to attend who had not purchased tickets in advance. Richards was loath to questionMr Barratt's judgment but was concerned that the funds which he, among others, had worked so tirelessly to raise would somehow end up in the hands of Henry Nicholson. Were he to admit any doubts to Barratt he knew that they would be blithely dismissed. "Nicholson will not see a penny of the proceeds," he imagined Mr Barratt declaring, "unless I am struck down by a lightning bolt, and as you can see, Harvey, the sky is clear." His Mentor had no fewer shortcomings than any man, though they were trivial for the most part, Mr Richards believed, and more than outweighed by Barratt's qualities. The one serious flaw in Mr Barratt's character, his hamartia, as the Rector might term it, was a general lack of caution. The consequence of this was an obliviousness to the ramifications of his actions, Mr Richards had come to realise, particularly as they affected everyone other than himself. It sometimes happened that the prudent course was the one soonest taken and most energetically pursued, but this was not usually the case. It was Mr Barratt's habit to bring pressure to bear on an undesirable situation in order to resolve it. If he encountered an unstable brick wall, for instance, he would certainly push on it to see if it fell before considering any safer method by which it might be made secure, and would never think to discover what might lie on the other side. This mental image, of Mr Charles Barratt visiting terror upon the residents of Surrey by collapsing their decrepit boundary markers like some haphazard Joshua, made young Mr Richards laugh aloud. He looked over the figures once more, chuckling occasionally as he did so, then put down his quill and blotted the page.

The long, slow days of early summer had bred among the people of B_____ and its environs an impatience for excitement and a number of carriages rolled up to the Corn Exchange ahead of the appointed hour. Miss Lucy had anticipated this eventuality and the early birds were greeted and welcomed into the main hall, where Odd Jake and his ensemble played at a reduced tempo, as if they were still familiarising themselves with their instruments. Surrey finery was not London finery, being a degree less ridiculous, but a crowd soon gathered at the steps of the building to admire the guests as they descended from barouche or phaeton, offering murmurs of approval or disdain to each arrival. Broady directed the traffic himself, sending the carriages in broad circles towards the Bull where a crew of rough-looking fellows waited to attend to them. Within a few minutes the hall was alive with the sound of conversation and half an hour later it was very full indeed and some souls, seeking peace, made their way to the upper balcony.

Harvey Richards was quite correct. The best young men in the county made themselves known to Miss Lucy at the first opportunity, employing a range of complimentary phrases, some extemporised, others clearly rehearsed over a period of days, and her dance card was soon full. She could not have distinguished one gentleman from another, nor did she take any great satisfaction from her popularity. It was enough that the ball was a success, which it showed every sign of being, and that the aforementioned Mr Richards was granted an opportunity to see her in her best ballgown. If she were in the company of some handsome bachelor of good fortune when this encounter occurred so much the better. Richards, exhausted by his efforts over the past few days, was fast asleep meanwhile, as was Mr Barratt. The latter gentleman had at least dressed in readiness for the evening's festivities and sat snoring, at customary volume, in his favourite armchair in the parlour. Mr Richards had yet to change. He lay abed on the second floor, in his shirtsleeves, a tuneless whistle emanating every few seconds from his finely shaped lips. Johnson had polished and dressed the cart that morning so that its appearance was somewhat less agricultural and had even brushed down his own livery but Mr Barratt had assured his man that he would be attending the ball as a guest. "My understanding is that Mrs Flannery will be also be present in this capacity," Barratt had explained. "Take the night off."

Mr Barratt had offered two of the remaining rooms at the Red House to Captain Billings who was attending the ball with Mrs Billings and their two eldest daughters and it was the arrival of this party which roused the somnolent gentlemen within.

"We are late," Mrs Billings whispered to her host in the hallway. "Captain Billings will be in a rage." Barratt found the Captain to be his usual, implacable self however, when he followed his wife inside. "Very good to see you, Barratt. What a smart little house. Absolutely spotless, I perceive, very shipshape." Mr Barratt bowed and told the Captain that he was altogether too kind, and might wish to examine his accommodation before passing judgment. "What? I'll sleep in a hammock, Sir. Just string it from the bedposts!" Barratt assured him that such a measure ought not to be necessary, though he could not absolutely vouch for the bed having never slept in it himself.

The ladies were ready in a little under half an hour and proceeded the short distance to the Corn Exchange in Captain Billings' carriage. Johnson poured each of the gentlemen a healthy glass of Sherry, to be consumed while they waited for the carriage to return.

"You're the fellow who needs some Dutch courage," Barratt remarked, and Johnson poured himself a glass, smiling. He would hardly be noticed in present company, of course: two giants and a sea captain who, even without his uniform, had the bearing one would expect of a national hero. Captain Billings addressed Johnson as if he were a valued lieutenant and the valet was reminded that he had always rather admired naval folk. He recharged the sailor's glass, and his own, before the coachman announced his return.

It was a warm evening, free from rain, and the sky blurred from blue above to pink westwards. A queue had formed along the high street as guests were deposited in front of the hall. Mr Barratt, who sat on the near side of the carriage, facing the driver, leaned out to determine what was holding up the traffic. Two substantial ladies were being assisted down from their carriage by an anxious fellow in yellow breeches. They made their way inside, eventually, and then Barratt saw Henry Nicholson jump from his own, marvellous landau. Nicholson hurried into the building and the queue moved forwards. Buller, Nicholson's occasional jehu, turned the fine black vehicle sharply around and headed back north, lifting his wide-brimmed hat to the occupants of Captain Billings' carriage as he passed. Mr Richards nodded, compelled by natural courtesy to do so, and Johnson scowled at his counterpart. Mr Barratt ignored Buller entirely as he continued to stare at the doorway into which Nicholson had just passed.

"Who was that irregular-looking cove?" Captain Billings asked.

"A person of no importance," Barratt replied, without shifting his gaze. As Mr Barratt spoke these words an unseasonal shiver, the cause of which could not readily be determined, ran through his body.

Dancing had already commenced when the four men from the Red House made their way into the hall. Mrs Billings seized her husband and breathlessly explained that both Philomena and Jane had already found partners for the Roger De Coverley, several sets of which were under way at the centre of the hall.Mr Barratt perceived the pride in Mrs Billings' eyes as she watched her eldest girls dance, and was almost overtaken by a familiar, though unwelcome rush of emotion. Mrs Walker found him in this somewhat parlous condition, with his own eyes glowing.

"Charles, my darling, are you quite well?"

"What a thing it must be to love a child," said Barratt. "You are most fortunate."

"So I am," said Mrs Walker, squeezing his hand. "You must know, my heart, that Lucy loves you as much as any child might love a father. In fact I believe she cares for you more than I do." They laughed together at this last remark.

"She is all the daughter I could ever imagine having," said Barratt.

"And yet she is not yours." Mrs Walker raised a hand to stroke her fiancé's cheek. Barratt enjoyed the caress for a few moments then took Mrs Walker's hand and kissed it.

"Excuse me," he said. Mr Barratt began to move around the perimeter of the room. His height, as ever, was something of an advantage as he picked out the faces he wished to see. There was Cunningham, resplendent in his very best wig, speaking to another fellow of similar vintage. Broady, dressed once again in Johnson's clothes, stood sentry by the door. Across the floor Mr Richards was engaged in a similar pursuit to Mr Barratt. When the two gentlemen caught each other's eye Barratt nodded and Mr Richards raised four fingers, before gesturing towards the low dais at the front of the room where the musicians were at work. There stood Henry Nicholson, apparently in the easiest of moods, smiling and conversing with a young woman. Mr Barratt approached Nicholson from his side of the floor, and saw Mr Richards move in the same direction. Barratt shook his head and Mr Richards retraced his steps.

Nicholson looked up as Barratt was almost upon him, and the young lady turned, following his gaze.

"Why, Mr Barratt!" said Miss Foulke. "Allow me to introduce my dear friend Henry Nicholson." The music stopped at that moment and the dancers began to applaud. Mr Barratt waited for the noise to subside before speaking.

"Mr Nicholson and I are already acquainted, Miss Foulke. Can this be the gentleman whose attention precedes my own?" Nicholson appeared to be confused by this question and a hint of the wildness which sometimes overcame his expression was momentarily detectable.

"You are a veritable Torquemada, Mr Barratt, and you have grasped my terrible secret," Miss Foulke said. "Come, Henry, let us dance the next set." She dragged Nicholson towards the centre of the room where couples were already arranging themselves into sixes, likes spots on a die. Barratt bowed neatly and turned towards a table full of small pies, prepared in his own kitchen. He took one and bit into it, offered a blessing to his cook, and nodded his head in time to the music, as it began again.

XXXIV

"I HAVE FOUNDYOU!" said Mrs Walker, taking Barratt's arm. "I guessed that you might be sampling your own wares." Mr Barratt was unable to respond immediately, having bolted an entire pie as his fiancée approached. He nodded instead and attempted to smile without opening his mouth. Mrs Walker dusted some crumbs from the lapels of his jacket. "What a pity that you are not yet well enough to dance, Charles!" Barratt raised his shoulders and displayed the palms of his hands, intending to indicate, wordlessly, that the situation was regrettable but beyond immediate remedy. The pie in his mouth seemed reluctant to disintegrate, he found, which gave rise to the suspicion that it had originated in the Rectory kitchen rather than his own, in fact, a suspicion which he might well have relayed to Mrs Walker had the inhibiting presence of the intact pastry not prevented any communication of a verbal nature. Mr Barratt continued to nod until rescued, several awkward moments later, by Reverend Archer who dragged his cousin away to make up a quadrille. Barratt, relieved, began to work at the edge of the pie, an activity which gave him the appearance of some mighty ruminant, contemplating the weighty questions of the day. Having swallowed, eventually, the last of the recalcitrant pastry Mr Barratt helped himself to some punch to aid its digestion.

The dance which had just begun seemed rather complex to Barratt, and utterly bewildering to Harvey Richards, who joined him at the punch bowl. Hopping was involved, clapping too, though at seemingly arbitrary intervals. Mr Richards studied the closest set, growing ever more certain that the arcane rules which governed dance generally, and the placement of one's limbs in particular, would never be remotely comprehensible to him. Just as some children are said to be letter blind so was he dance blind, he decided. He thought to share this observation with Mr Barratt but saw that such trifling chatter would not be welcomed if it were heard at all. Barratt was staring, narrow-eyed, at Mr Nicholson, as if he wished to set him ablaze through the sheer fixity and concentration of his glare. Mr Richards had always previously assumed that there was no element of personal vindictiveness in Barratt's plan to bring Henry Nicholson to book. He believed, rather, that Mr Barratt meant only to restore the lawful order of things. It was no straightforward matter to reconcile this position with the evident antipathy in Barratt's gaze. The immediate cause of this ill-feeling was obvious enough, indeed Mr Nicholson seemed intent upon making an exhibition of himself, leaping higher, clapping harder and laughing louder than any other gentleman in the room. He whispered delightedly in Miss Foulke's ear each time they crossed and then cackled anew. Mr Richards sensed some danger in this.

"Mr Barratt," he said, and was ignored. "Mr Barratt. Charles!" Barratt turned at last, his face still marked by enmity. "It is not my place perhaps to offer counsel, Sir, but I think we are most likely to achieve the desired outcome if we approach Mr Nicholson in a spirit of reconciliation, rather than anger." Mr Barratt sighed and placed a hand on Mr Richards arm.

"Wise fellow," said Barratt. "I was almost persuaded to destroy him, the prancing fool, no matter the cost. I shall calm myself."

This crisis averted Mr Richards turned his attention to Venetia Foulke, who seemed to him a respectable young woman, if somewhat plain and unengaging. Watching as she moved around the floor, Mr Richards was unable to comprehend the fascination which she apparently provoked in Mr Barratt. She danced well enough, by his estimate, but without distinguishing herself in any way. Instead, he thought, she seemed to carry out the movements in a half-hearted, mechanical fashion. Her appeal lay in some vibrant aspect of her personality, he supposed, though when they had conversed briefly at Foulke House he had found her rather abrupt and indifferent, traits which he attributed to a certain reticence in the lady's nature. Perhaps she possessed some ineffable quality which was beyond his detection but evident to others, as sounds of higher pitch were said to be audible only to dogs. Mr Richards sipped from his glass of punch and considered the matter.

The quadrille concluded at last and Odd Jake announced that there would be a short intermission. Mr Barratt approached Henry Nicholson.

"I wonder if you would mind walking a few paces with me, Mr Nicholson," he said. "I have information to impart which should interest you, and may ultimately prove to be to your advantage."

"Tell me here," said Nicholson, "I have nothing to hide from Miss Foulke."

"Very well," said Barratt. "I do not pretend to be fully cognizant of the scope of your vices, Nicholson, but I do know that they have so reduced your finances that you have embezzled funds from the Old B_____ Charitable Trust in order to avoid bankruptcy and also, presumably, to feed your deplorable habits."

"That is an absurd and slanderous accusation, Sir," hissed Nicholson. "I demand that you withdraw it, and offer an immediate apology."

"It is indeed absurd that I should have to confront you in order to bring your criminal behaviour to an end," Barratt replied. "My allegation cannot be slanderous, however, if there is evidence to prove it. I am in possession of that evidence. And I am no lawyer, Sir, but I assume that the threshold for slander requires that at least one other person hears the defamatory statement." Nicholson turned to where Miss Foulke had been standing moments earlier but she was gone, swept away by Mr Cunningham and now engaged *tête-à-tête* with the old gentleman. "I do have a voice which tends to carry, or so I am told," Barratt continued. "Perhaps we might step up to the balcony. It will be a little warm up there but it is less likely that we will be overheard." Mr Nicholson hesitated. "I do not wish to broadcast your secrets, Henry, nor do I mean to extort a penny from you that is not owed. I am offering a solution to your problems, that is all, a path back from the dreadful place to which your misdeeds have brought you. Come."

Nicholson preceded Barratt towards the entrance and up the stone stairs to the balcony. The two men followed the curved walk to the end so that they stood above and to the side of the stage. Mr Nicholson turned and spoke first.

"Why should I listen to your lies, Barratt?"

"I am a terrible liar, in fact, perhaps through lack of practice. That is one reason why I do not play at cards. We are wasting time, however, as you must know the truth of my accusation, unless you are mentally afflicted." As he spoke these words Mr Barratt examined Nicholson, whose eyes were now undisguisedly wild, but could not determine if this wildness was the product of fear or a kind of crazed defiance. "Allow me to explain the situation, as I understand it," Barratt said, "and then perhaps a way can be found to extricate ourselves therefrom." Nicholson began to pace back and forth, like a caged beast. Mr Barratt continued. "Hope Hall is mortgaged, the estate has no tenants and is in a ruinous condition, through your negligence. You are indebted to a number of people, including most of your fellow board members at the Trust. Four of those gentlemen are downstairs, incidentally, five if you include Reverend Archer. A quorum, indeed, sufficient to propose, second and vote upon your dismissal as chairman. You also seem to be in thrall to your coachman, a person called Buller, who I presume shares certain of your vices. He has ridden off with your carriage and pair, along with that stick of yours. I have advised him that he may retain these articles and consider whatever debt is owed to him discharged." Mr Nicholson stopped pacing for a moment and pulled at his hair.

"How dare you?" he exclaimed. Barratt raised a conciliatory hand and went on.

"As to the Trust, well, that debt is less easily repaid. I have obtained certified copies of the Trust's ledgers dating back to your father's death."

"Those copies were illegally obtained, Sir, through burglary!" said Nicholson. "They would not be permitted in the High Court."

"Again, I know little of the law Mr Nicholson, but I do have a receipt, signed by you, for the sum of ten pounds, here I quote, 'to obtain and peruse the accounts of the Old B_____ Charitable Trust' and there is no evidence of any burglary having taken place."

"There was a boy," said Nicholson. "He saw you going in, or coming out."

"I do not dispute that there may have been a boy who saw someone, at some point, either entering or leaving the Trust's offices, but that person was there, presumably, on your authority."

"Why would I knowingly grant access to the ledgers if I thought they might incriminate me?" asked Nicholson.

"Why would you not, unless they contained information you did not wish to disclose? Anyway, the copies are now in my possession, and they indicate that a number of deposits were made to Irving's Bank in Guildford. I have established, however, that these payments are fictitious."

"How so? Surely that information is privileged."

"Here, I admit, I was fortunate. Mr Irving is an old friend of Giacomo Cunningham, and the two venerable gentlemen are at present in the company of Miss Foulke." Barratt gestured towards Cunningham's vivid coat. Nicholson leant on the balcony rail and stared. "There is also the question of your character to consider. If you look to the door you may see a person called Matthew Broady." Nicholson groaned. "I understand you dismissed that gentleman and his father from your employment because you were jealous of his marriage to a young woman. Mr Broady claims additionally that you forced yourself upon his wife."

"Rebekah? I have not touched her, Sir. We were lovers, it is true, but that was many months before she married that fool. I loved her."

"Nevertheless, when there is an accusation of this kind, Nicholson, very little attention is paid to the order of events, and scarcely more to the actual facts. Gentlemen will fear for their wives and wives will fear for themselves. You will be regarded as a fox in the henhouse." The wildness had dissipated from Henry Nicholson's eyes, Barratt noted, and his face wore a less predatory expression than was generally the case. He had never looked less like a fox, actually, and might almost have been pitied.

"Gad, is there anything else?"

"I fear so," said Barratt. "There is a man of uncertain origin secured in my coal cellar who claims to be a haberdasher but who, in addition to acting as a pawnbroker, also procures and deals in what might most politely be termed illegal commodities. He has indicated his willingness to speak against you in order to save his own skin." Mr Barratt paused. "I want him out of my house, Nicholson, since I have other, more respectable guests staying with me. I do not wish to expose you, since to do so would not benefit those who have already suffered because of your selfishness, but you should not doubt that I will, without hesitation, if you choose not to comply."

"What do you want me to do?" asked Nicholson, his face now a picture of defeat.

"Firstly, step away from the balcony rail. We do not want an accident to occur and for everyone to be cheated of their just desserts. Secondly, in the interval between the next dances you must announce your resignation from the board of the Trust and nominate Harvey Richards as your successor. Explain that you have plans for your estate which require your complete attention. Thank Miss Lucy Walker for her efforts on behalf of the Trust. That is all you need do this evening. Tomorrow you will appoint Broady as your land agent."

"No," said Nicholson, "I cannot do it."

"You killed his father, Henry, not with a single blow, or gunshot, but you are responsible for the man's death. It may be the worst of your actions. Besides, Broady will not be working for you, he will be working for the Trust."

"I do not understand."

"Until you have repaid the money which you have stolen all excess revenue from Hope Hall will pass directly to the Trust," said Barratt. "You will be provided with a stipend and allowed to live at the Hall. Once your debt is repaid you will be able to collect your own rents again." Nicholson's lips moved but no words came forth. "I have considered the matter for several months, Henry, and this is the only solution. Justice is served, and you are saved from ignominy."

Nicholson nodded and walked past Mr Barratt, towards the stairs. He turned and spoke.

"I wonder, what has any of this to do with you?" Charles Barratt smiled.

"I have sometimes asked myself the same question," he said. "I think, perhaps, I was simply in the wrong place at the correct moment."

XXXV

THE LADIES OF the Rectory were disappointed, once again, with the conduct of the gentlemen of the Red House. Harvey Richards had arrived late and had ignored Miss Lucy altogether, even when she was dancing, preferring to skulk around at the edge of the room, conversing briefly with a number of yeoman types before conspiring with Mr Barratt. His attention had then turned to Miss Foulke, with whom he was now exercising his considerable charm, though to little apparent effect, Miss Lucy was pleased to note. She thought that Miss Foulke resembled one of those large African birds, with her long neck, curious posture, and permanent look of mild disapproval. Mrs Walker had begun to regret prohibiting Mr Barratt from dancing, since he appeared to be using this embargo as an excuse to overeat and to resume his feud with Henry Nicholson. She was surprised, therefore, when these two gentlemen reappeared at the far end of the hall, conversing without hostility. Mr Nicholson's expression was hard to read, but Mr Barratt, whose face she had studied with a lover's intensity, disguised in Mrs Walker's case only partially by her ironic disposition, for several months, glowed with a unmistakable sense of triumph, so that it was possible to imagine a laurel wreath nestling on his head. He was explaining something to Nicholson and using a great many emphatic gestures. Mr Nicholson was nodding along more in a spirit of obedience, it seemed, than enthusiasm. The two men approached Mrs Walker and Mr Nicholson asserted, in a somewhat vacant fashion, that Mrs Walker looked more lovely than ever and that he would consider it the greatest of honours if she would consent to dance the next set with him. The request was unexpected and Mrs Walker's eyes flickered to Mr Barratt, who smiled as if to indicate his consent. This in turn provoked a brief look of anger from his fiancée which communicated the idea, in the most succinct manner possible, that she would dance with whoever she chose whenever she chose and did not require his approval. She offered her hand to Nicholson without casting a further glance at Mr Barratt; had she done so she would have observed that his smile had not disappeared but had instead broadened into a grin of frank admiration.

Miss Lucy was also making her way to the centre of the room, where a bright-skinned young man, the only son of a particularly prosperous farmer, awaited her. She passed Harvey Richards, who bowed briskly. Miss Lucy turned and told Mr Richards that he should ask Miss Foulke to dance, since she was obviously an object of great interest to him. Mr Richards thought that it was perhaps rather unfair of Miss Lucy to categorise Miss Foulke as an object, and expressed this view with his usual lightness of tone. Miss Lucy disliked his response, however and pouted. Mr Richards then offered his assurances that he had no intention of dancing with Miss Foulke or indeed of dancing at all, adding that if he were to stand up with any young woman on Earth it would certainly be Miss Lucy herself. This remark was rather more warmly received and might have ensured a full restoration of the young lady's partiality had Richards not insisted on offering a entirely superfluous appendix to his compliment, in which he explained that Miss Lucy was unique in so far as she was the only person he had ever consented to dance with and would therefore be alone in anticipating and accommodating his shortcomings, which were not inconsiderable, where that discipline was concerned. Fortunately for Mr Richards, perhaps, Miss Lucy was only vexed by this qualification for a brief moment, pursing her lips anew, before bestowing a pert blow to his chest and skipping away towards the farmer's boy.

Mrs Walker was pleased to discover that Henry Nicholson, despite being one of those men who were all knees and elbows, was a very competent partner, though his steps lacked the exuberance previouslydisplayed in the quadrille. As she moved about the floor she felt Charles Barratt's gaze upon her like a kind of embrace, as if they were engaged in a waltz rather than standing yards apart. Whenever her husband had watched her dance his scrutiny had been inhibiting, and his own movements mean and crab-like. The memory upset her, and sensing that the emotion might be evident in her expression she turned to happier thoughts. Mr Barratt was not a graceful man, but he danced as he did most things, with energy and enthusiasm. She recalled the thunderous noise that he and Mr Richards had made between them on the library floor, the trembling bookcases, the fiddler rendered inaudible almost, and her smile was soon restored.

The dance concluded. Henry Nicholson bowed to Mrs Walker then stepped towards the front of the hall and up onto the low stage. Mr Nicholson was capable of expressing himself with a degree of elegance and did so now. Miss Lucy Walker was compared variously with Queen Elizabeth, Boadicea and Helen of Troy but none of these legendary ladies, Nicholson explained, could match B_____'s own princess for determination and pluck. Furthermore not one could hope to emulate her skill at a Scottish reel. Nicholson gestured to Miss Lucy, bright red but delighted, who waved and curtseyed to widespread applause and some isolated whistling from her agricultural suitors. Since almost no-one, not even the other trustees, knew precisely what the Chairman of the Trust did Mr Nicholson's resignation from this position created no great disturbance among those present at its announcement, nor was this information of a kind which might be readily celebrated. Having walked away, figuratively speaking, from the one thing which afforded him the slightest respectability therefore Nicholson now began his literal escape into the heady, silent air of the Corn Exchange interrupted only by a meaningful cough from Mr Barratt: Nicholson had yet to propose that Harvey Richards should succeed him. Mr Nicholson corrected this omission, opining that Mr Richards was just the fellow to bring the Trust into the nineteenth century. Mr Cunningham would remark later that Nicholson, with his long, dark hair and sense of sombre self-importance, had reminded him somewhat of Charles the First, the tyrant turned martyr, and Mr Barratt had responded with some remark about Cunningham being very nearly old enough to have witnessed the king's execution.

A slender minority of those attending the ball had heard of Harvey Richards, but almost everyone recognised him – that very handsome young fellow – when he replaced Mr Nicholson on the dais. He thanked Nicholson for his service, spoke briefly but in the most glowing terms about the efforts of Miss Lucy while minimising the importance of his own contributions to the evening's success, then instructed Odd Jake to strike up the band once more, creating the general impression that he had in fact masterminded every aspect of the festivities but was far too modest and courteous an individual to take credit for it.

Mrs Walker was perplexed. "A few days ago, Charles, you promised me that you would take no further action against Henry Nicholson and now, suddenly, it seems that he has withdrawn from public life, at your insistence I presume. Have you no respect for my wishes?"

"I should first mention, dearest one, that the promise to which you allude was made under some duress. The case against Mr Nicholson was already established at that point, it only needed the gentleman himself to be persuaded into the best course of action. Since you had forbidden me from pursuing the matter I was obliged to wait until I saw Nicholson again. I did not go running after him, I simply explained the predicament he was in and offered a means of escape. I have acted for Mr Nicholson, not against him."

"Was he offered a choice?" Mrs Walker asked.

"We considered various options, yes," said Mr Barratt. "Mr Nicholson and I have agreed on what I think, what we think, is the most prudent way forward." Barratt took Mrs Walker's hand. "Susannah, it is finished. I apologise for allowing myself to become preoccupied with the matter, my concern was only for the poor." He considered this statement momentarily before correcting himself. "That is not entirely true, I confess. My motives were a good deal more complex. There was the matter of waste, for instance. Not simply the funds of the Trust being squandered on Nicholson's predilections, but the whole estate at Hope Hall left uncultivated. I know that you have experienced deep unhappiness, my darling, but never deprivation or hunger. I felt the poverty of Butcher's Green like a ravenous discomfort, and I was enraged, but I know too that I wished to see things done better and my egotism could not allow the situation to persist when it was within my power to put it right. Neither could I see you and my beloved Lucy associating with someone I knew to be cruel without attempting to curb the worst of his behaviour, though I see now that in attempting to protect you I have instead managed to provoke Mr Nicholson. Again, it is finished, and you need not fear him." Mrs Walker raised her hand so that Mr Barratt might kiss it.

"You are certain?" she asked.

"He is weak, rather than wicked," said Barratt. "He was overindulged as the only surviving child of doting parents, perhaps, then permitted to associate with the wrong kind of men. His cruelty is not innate, of that I am certain."

"No child is born cruel, surely," said Mrs Walker, and Mr Barratt, who held a rather different opinion but chose on this occasion not to divulge it, smiled and kissed her hand once more. It was enough, for the moment, that he had persuaded Mrs Walker to put aside any ill feeling regarding his behaviour towards Nicholson. There would be many more warm evenings on which to consider their future. They sat together and watched the last of the dances, Mr Barratt rested a hand on Mrs Walker's bare shoulder and a thrill passed through each of them. Barratt smiled broadly and reflected that whatever the outcome of their courtship he was very fortunate to experience these sensations, to love a woman who was in many ways his superior, and to feel beloved by her, for the second time in his life. Mrs Walker's feelings at that moment were rather more unsettled, and not simply because Mr Barratt's lack of faith presented an obstacle to their future happiness. She was more concerned for her daughter, who moved among the other young people at the centre of the room with as much grace as her frame would allow. Miss Lucy was the focus of a great deal of male attention, and the evening had been a triumph, but her mother sensed that Harvey Richards' affections (which were all that Lucy cared about)while openly bestowed would never be anything other than fraternal in nature. Mr Richards loved Miss Lucy, but he did not love her as a husband ought to love a wife. He was too proud a man to wed in these circumstances, Mrs Walker, suspected, even having walked the halls of Meadholme. She could not imagine her daughter happily married as Mrs Harvey Richards and Lucy could not, at present, imagine anything else. Mrs Walker sighed,Mr Barratt enquired as to her wellbeing and she said that she was perhaps a little tired, but not so much so that she felt unable to wait for the scheduled arrival of their carriage, and besides, it would take more than a cousin's fatigue to drag Reverend Archer from the floor.

XXXVI

STORMS LOWERED over the Surrey countryside in the week following the ball keeping many people indoors, but Reverend Archer had only to traverse the high street to call upon his friend Charles Barratt and managed to do so, between hail showers, on Wednesday morning.

"Here is an intrepid fellow!" said Barratt, opening the front door himself. "What do you make of this weather, John? Should we expect frogs next, or locusts?"

"I suppose hail is more common in June than July," said the Rector, "but spring was late this year."

"Quite right, Sir. For a moment I was concerned that the Lord was punishing us for putting on frivolous entertainments, but I suppose there is no real harm in it."

"Indeed," said Reverend Archer. "The Lord is merciful and we have not yet strayed as far from the path as those in the Cities of the Plain."

"Towards whom God was not especially merciful, as I recall," said Barratt, grinning. "Can I interest you in coffee?"

"Thank you, Charles." The two men stepped into the parlour, and moments later the cook appeared, unbidden seemingly, with a coffee pot and cups on a tray. "What is your opinion of Miss Foulke?"

"Why do you ask, John?"

"I ask because I am looking for a respectable woman, one perhaps who has some income of her own, who might consent to marry a priest." Mr Barratt chuckled.

"How extraordinary, you have never once asked my opinion of any person."

"I understand that you are well acquainted with Miss Foulke, that you are fond of one another, indeed."

"I suppose we are," admitted Barratt. "I confess that I am curious as to the source of your intelligence. Have you spoken with Sir Clifford?"

"I have, but only in the most general terms, not as a prospective son-in-law."

"I am sure Sir Clifford would be honoured to consider you in that light, John. He is a vain fellow and you are from an excellent family. As for your personal qualities, well, if my own daughter had lived I could hardly imagine a more welcome suitor for her than you." Mr Barratt meant this remark sincerely but the faintest hint of a smirk appeared at the corner of his mouth.

"I sense some caveat, which you are reluctant to disclose," said the Rector.

"Not at all," said Barratt. "If Miss Foulke is content to marry you and you are content to marry her there is no reason why you may not be wed."

"Is it her friendship with Henry Nicholson which gives you pause? I saw them together at the ball. I sense no romantic attachment between them, and the association is not, in itself, an impediment to our happiness."

"You speak already of 'our happiness', then!" Barratt exclaimed, laughing. "Have you exchanged more than two words with the lady?"

"Our conversation has been limited, it is true, but like you, Charles, I see much to admire in Miss Foulke."

"You asked my opinion and now I understand why. She is a perfectly admirable young woman, of course. Her family seems unexceptionable and she is just the right age to marry a gentleman like you. She is calm, intelligent. She might, perhaps, be a little too serious for you, but married couples can suffer from a surfeit of similar instincts, I suppose. I am all for the match."

"Still, Charles, there is something which you are not telling me. Do you think I am too short for her?"

"I never think of you as short," said Barratt. You are not Mr Richards' equal in that regard, it is true, but he lacks your wit and is a veritable oaf when it comes to dancing."

"Why do you mention Mr Richards, has he taken an interest in Miss Foulke?" The Rector exhibited an unusual degree of anxiety, Barratt thought, at the mere mention of Harvey Richards' name.

"He was the first prodigiously tall person I thought of. Harvey is as interested in Miss Foulke as everyone else seems to be of a sudden, but here I can offer you some encouragement: she seems oblivious to him."

"She enjoys the company of men, though?" Reverend Archer asked.

"That is a strange question, John, an Oxford question, one might almost say. She seems to enjoy my company, certainly." The Rector looked downcast. "It is quite possible that I am mistaken," Barratt continued, "but I have the impression that Miss Foulke is unlikely to marry a man of the cloth. So you see it is not your person, but your profession, which might fail to appeal to her."

"You have discussed the matter, then?"

"Never," admitted Mr Barratt. "Again, I am merely relaying an impression I have, which may be incorrect. There are many advantages to the match, I have yet to meet a person who did not like you, John, and you seem to have formed an attachment to the young lady. Have at it, my friend. You will wait a long time for Miss Foulke to set her cap at you, so you must act first. Pick her some flowers from the Rectory garden, Lord knows it is overly abundant."

Mr Barratt had offered little in the way of encouragement to his friend, in truth, but Reverend Archer seemed more than satisfied with his visit. The clergyman thanked his host then crossed back to the Rectory, his movements light and neat as ever. Barratt wondered, unusually, if he had done the right thing. He suspected that Miss Foulke felt as he did about spiritual matters, and that this might preclude her from a union with John Archer, but she had never stated her position explicitly. Even had she done so Mr Barratt would have presumed this a confidence, and he had said as much as he dared without risking a betrayal. In the end though he wondered if it mattered at all, this business of belief. It was not important to him, obviously, though Mrs Walker was rather more scrupulous. Would Miss Foulke consider marrying a man with opposing religious views? In some ways Reverend Archer wore his faith more lightly than Susannah Walker did, his clerical garb notwithstanding. Why then, he wondered, had he, Barratt, never been perturbed by his fiancée's godliness? Why should an absence of belief be scorned by the faithful and simple conformity privileged? The word itself, faithful, had somehow come to connote all manner of positive qualities which had nothing to do with belief in God. Conversely to be faithless was to be a scoundrel of some sort or another, rather than simply an unbeliever. Barratt mused on the injustice of this, before remembering that despite the great tragedy which had befallen him his life remained very comfortable, and the greatest concession he made to the idea of God was one he himself had imposed. What was an hour of Reverend Archer's Byzantine reflections on a Sunday morning compared with the privations of the hindoo in Bombay, praying to several Gods and ignored by them all, starving to death in the street?

Mr Barratt found that he was angry, not at his own plight necessarily, but at every petty misunderstanding, every Holy War and all the human misery suffered in the name of God. As ever, when he was angry he had to act. The storm had recommenced and Barratt arrived at the Rectory door with hailstones in his hair and on his shoulders like scattered seed. Lottie answered the door, neglecting to disguise her amusement at Mr Barratt's appearance.

"Hurry in, Sir, we have no fire for you to thaw yourself in front of, it being the middle of July."

"Thank you, Lottie," said Barratt. "Is Reverend Archer in his study?"

"I believe so, Mr Barratt. Was the Reverend not just with you?"

"Yes indeed, but there is something important I have neglected to mention to him."

"Go on through," said Lottie. "I dare say you will encounter the ladies of the house in the library." Mrs Walker was brushing her daughter's hair when Barratt entered the room. He bowed and offered a curt greeting before knocking on the study door.

"Come in, Charles," called the Rector from within.

"How did you know it was me?" Barratt asked, stooping into the low space.

"Who else knocks on a door as if they mean to remove it from its hinges? What is it, my dear friend? Some further demerit of mine has occurred to you, no doubt, which must be swiftly brought to my attention before I throw myself at Sophia FitzClarence, or the Countess of Liverpool."

"I do not grasp your meaning, John, forgive me. I feel that I was insufficiently supportive of your suit towards Miss Foulke." The Rector had grown used to his friend's occasionally mercurial nature, which had emerged, he thought, just as his relationship with Mrs Walker had blossomed, such was the transformative nature of love, but he could not begin to guess why Barratt had wanted to correct himself so soon after their last interview. Reverend Archer attempted to communicate his curiosity by smiling and at the same time raising his eyebrows towards one another. Mr Barratt misinterpreted his expression. "I see that you are aggrieved, my friend," he said. "I should not have offered an opinion where I was not qualified to give one, I am quite ashamed."

"But Charles, you merely suggested that Miss Foulke may not wish to marry a clergyman. There is nothing unnatural in that; people are allowed different tastes, even God-fearing people."

"It was a baseless supposition, though," said Barratt. "A remark born of a strange kind of jealousy, I suppose."

"You have feelings for Miss Foulke, then?"

"What, no!" Mr Barratt said. "I am in love with your cousin, Sir. I meant only that I would be jealous of your company, John, if you were to marry, and I wished to dissuade you while at the same time appearing to offer encouragement."

"I am somewhat confused, Charles," Reverend Archer said. "Am I to believe that I should pursue Miss Foulke, in your opinion, or do I risk destroying our friendship, as if we were two young ladies of Bath in one of Mrs Walker's novels?" The Rector offered this remark with the broadest of grins, which even Barratt could not miss the meaning of.

"You must think me very foolish," he said. "I have asked the Foulkes to dine with me on Friday. The weather ought to have improved by then. Perhaps you, Susannah and Miss Lucy would care to join us? Cunningham will also be there, of course." Reverend Archer rested a thumb beneath his bottom lip and looked up at Barratt, resembling some mendicant puppy. "I shall send Mr Richards away for the evening. I am sure the young ladies of Meadholme would be delighted to see him, and I have a gift for Captain Billings." The Rector stood and shook Mr Barratt's hand.

"Thank you, Charles, I think I can speak for the ladies, and we would be delighted to attend."

Mr Barratt nodded and excused himself, slipping out through the study door as quietly as his great frame would allow. Mrs

Walker, who had not moved from the chaise, coughed meaningfully as Barratt made to escape the library with the mere lifting of an imaginary hat. Mr Barratt proceeded into the hallway, however, saying "Reverend Archer will explain all," over his shoulder as he opened the front door and leaned into the storm.

XXXVII

THE WEATHER HAD indeed improved by the time Harvey Richards set out for Meadholme two days later but the great quantity of precipitation which had fallen earlier in the week had thickened the roads with mud and strong winds had brought branches down at various places along the route. Mr Richards, who was entirely ignorant of Reverend Archer's affection for Miss Foulke, wondered why Mr Barratt had insisted that the pair of ebony elephants, betusked in ivory, were conveyed to Captain Billings with such urgency. It was not in the young gentleman's nature to complain, however, and he set out in the cart in the latter part of the afternoon, carrying also the decorative items employed at the ball, which were to be returned to the dry vaults at Meadholme.

The high street was also somewhat treacherous under foot and Johnson was despatched across to the Rectory an hour before Barratt expected his guests, armed with two bushels of sawdust and woodbark with which to form a safe path across the larger thoroughfare.

Mr Cunningham, keen as ever to sample the delights of Barratt's cellar, arrived first. It soon became apparent, however, that the old gentleman was almost as thirsty for information as he was for Mr Barratt's venerable Burgundian wines.

"How did you do it, Sir? I was sure that snake Nicholson would wriggle from your grasp."

"I think, in the end, he did not need a great deal of persuading," said Barratt. "I made certain claims, involving your friend, the banker, and Mr Broady which would not have stood up to serious interrogation. Their presence was enough, I suppose, to convince him to give it up. The sense of being surrounded by his misdeeds, of having past actions closing in on him was sufficiently compelling, but it was a gamble, of course."

"So in a sense, he wanted to be caught?" Cunningham asked.

"Not to be caught, perhaps, but to be relieved of a burden."

"How will you calculate his debt?"

"That is straightforward enough," said Barratt. "With Mr

Richards as Chair and Treasurer we will have access to receipts, ledgers and the Trust's bank account. We will gather the information after the fact, as it were."

"The gentleman will pay," said Johnson, entering the parlour at that moment bearing a thickly dusted bottle upon a tray. He and Cunningham retained a grudging mutual respect despite their rivalry for the affections of Mrs Flannery, and acknowledged one another with a bend of the neck.

"That will do," Mr Barratt said, nodding. Johnson disappeared and the sound of horses turned the gentlemen's attention to the parlour window. Sir Clifford offered a regal wave from the carriage which halted beyond the open sash.

"Here he is," said Cunningham. "Our own Earl of Shelburne." Barratt took this remark to mean that Sir Clifford's instinct to maintain peace and quiet at all costs was one with which Mr Cunningham, *agent provocateur*, did not necessarily agree.

"We ought not to mention Mr Richardson again," said Barratt. "Miss Foulke is fond of him."

"I know, I know," Cunningham replied. "I am not some catechumen, Sir."

"No indeed," said his friend. They proceeded into the hallway to greet the newly arrived guests. Lady Foulke and her daughter had not previously visited the Red House and each of them spent some polite moments admiring the marble, the looking-glass, the lowboy and the scent of the sweet peas arranged in a trio of narrow vases thereon.

"Surely a woman's hand is behind this!" Lady Foulke exclaimed.

"This is not the kind of flower which my cook prefers to work with," said Barratt, "and she is the only woman within these walls." Lady Foulke looked at him blankly for a moment before registering this *jeu de mots* - which Mr Barratt himself would scarcely have claimed to be among his very best efforts - then made a sound something like a snort, but also not unlike a cackle, which resounded around the stone walls of the vestibule. The noise, which issued unexpectedly, perhaps, from the sister of a baronet, was repeated twice, and echoed twice more, much to the apparent chagrin of Sir Clifford and his daughter. Cunningham, on the other hand, was delighted.

"What a pleasure it is to hear you laugh, Maria," he said. "And what a pity that Miss Foulke monopolised Mr Barratt's company when we were last at Foulke Hall. He is the most amusing gentleman in Surrey."

Mr Barratt laughed at the absurdity of his friend's remark which in turn provoked another bout of uncontrolled exclamation from Lady Foulke, who explained, once she had quite recovered her equilibrium, that her occasionally excitable nature came from her mother's side of the family: the Italian side. The party from the Rectory arrived as the honourable lady concluded her apologia so that the hallway, grand and uncluttered as it generally was, now seemed almost crowded. Reverend Archer made no attempt to disguise his nervous animation, or if he did the effort was in vain, and he bounced from host to each fellow guest on tiptoes, offering cordialities with air of a person who had very recently been freed from a long imprisonment. Miss Lucy's excitement was tempered by the realisation that Mr Richards was not present, and she was just proud enough not to enquire as to his whereabouts. Both she and Mrs Walker were keen to make a study of Miss Foulke, who seemed, to the ladies of the Rectory at least, to have cast a spell over the gentlemen of B_____, since it was not apparent otherwise how her looks, character or demeanour might garner the level of attention she presently enjoyed.

"How pretty this little piece is," Miss Foulke remarked, inviting Mrs Walker to consider the lowboy. What the younger lady meant to communicate with this observation, we may assume, is that she was aware of the understanding between Mrs Walker and Mr Barratt, and that she felt the gentleman's choice of fiancée exhibited a refinement which was also evident in his choice of furniture. This was altogether too subtle for Mrs Walker, who acknowledged that the thing was well made but to her mind resembled a headless dog."Oh, yes!" Miss Foulke said. "Now that you say it I see it completely. You have ruined it it for me, Mrs Walker, absolutely."

Miss Foulke was neither little nor pretty, and it would take more than a few sweet peas to convince a person that she was. She did possess a kind of heightened gentility, and a pleasant, pliable nature, it seemed, which might appeal to a thin-blooded man in search of a wife to support him in all his follies. So judged

Susannah Walker, attempting to puzzle out Reverend Archer's fascination with her fellow guest. What might Miss Foulke see in him? Mrs Walker was fond of her cousin but not blind to those factors which might deter a young woman from accepting his suit. There were several more obviously attractive members of his congregation who would have welcomed any preferential regard from the Reverend Archer, simply because of his family and income. Miss Foulke was perhaps wealthier than the Rector, and her connections were more than respectable. These were not inconsiderable qualities, of course, but would not interest John, Mrs Walker felt sure, any more than the rustic pulchritude of the various Hettys, Annies and Janes who made eyes at the Rector every Sunday morning. She presumed that the attraction was somehow intellectual, though as far as she was aware Reverend Archer and Miss Foulke had only conversed once, briefly, at the ball.

Miss Lucy thought that Miss Foulke looked plainer still than she had in her ballgown. Her face was pink even though she had not been dancing, her dress was the colour of an old bone, her hair was done carelessly, and she said everything in the same lifeless tone of voice, as if she wished only to be allowed to sit in a corner with some terribly boring book and be left alone. It was true that Miss Foulke had a long neck and that she, Miss Lucy, was somewhat deficient in this area but it was simply incomprehensible that any gentleman of spirit might favour a stooping, stuffy young woman with a few hundred pounds over the heiress to Meadholme.

Mr Barratt, who had only intended to make Miss Foulke feel more visible in her own home was gratified, if a little nonplussed, at the result of his efforts. In the space of a fortnight she had become the still centre of a whirl of attention. It was possible, he considered, that it was always this way in small towns. He had himself been subjected to the scrutiny of B_____ society for a period, not once but twice, and on each occasion interest had soon wained. Miss Foulke was more socially accomplished than Barratt might ever have dreamed of being and thus better equipped, he hoped, to enjoy her moment in the popular glare.

They went into the parlour where there were but six seats, so Barratt and Sir Clifford were obliged to remain standing. Mr Barratt talked his friend through the menu, though Sir Clifford was a glutton, in truth, principally concerned with the quantity of potatoes that would be served, rather than the quality of the fish course. He listened patiently enough, leaning on the mantel shelf while regarding his daughter with an admiration which was entirely novel. Miss Foulke sat between Mrs Walker and Giacomo Cunningham on a small settee, undergoing a gentle inquisition from the lady to her right. Reverend Archer, who had occupied Barratt's usual chair by the window strained to hear their conversation, as did Cunningham, despite his immediate proximity to it, though the old fellow nodded occasionally, to indicate that he agreed with whatever was being said, though he had little idea of its actual substance.

"I have never travelled abroad," said Mrs Walker. "I suppose I ought to regret the fact, but there is plenty to occupy my time and imagination here in B_____, I find."

"I was very fortunate to have the opportunity," Miss Foulke replied, "but like you I am sure I would have valued the time equally had I spent it here." Reverend Archer, whose hearing was keen enough to absorb this exchange in its entirety, could not restrain himself.

"But surely, in addition to the aesthetic pleasures it affords, the sights one sees and so on, travel broadens our understanding of humanity, in all its glorious variety, which in turn brings us closer to God."

"Is your congregation at St Andrew's insufficiently various then, John?" Mrs Walker asked. "We shall have to summon some Lascars and Visigoths from the Surrey countryside."

"Mr Barratt and I discussed this very idea," said Miss Foulke. Barratt, who had been staring into the hallway, wondering when Johnson would reappear to serve Sherry, turned at the sound of his name. Miss Foulke was smiling at him in a faintly conspiratorial fashion, while Mrs Walker and Reverend Archer fixed him with expressions of disapproval and confusion respectively.

"And what conclusion, if any, did you reach?" asked the Rector.

"We decided that one might allow travel to inspire one as comprehensively or as little as one chose, I think," said Miss Foulke. "That is about the shape of it, Mr Barratt, is it not?" Barratt took a moment to orient himself, and to recall the conversation.

"I, for one, am edified," said Mrs Walker, in a tone of voice which made it rather difficult to tell whether she was being sincere or satirical. This aggravated Mr Barratt somewhat but Miss Foulke once again steered towards calmer waters.

"Reverend Archer is the authority on such matters, of course," she said. "I am sure that the sermons he delivered while I was away from this parish would have provided a great deal more nourishment for the intellect than the canals and cathedrals of Europe, however picturesque they may be." Barratt considered a quip about the digestibility of the nourishment in question but glimpsed the look of unalloyed delight in the Rector's face and swallowed the remark.

"I have yet to see you at St Andrew's, Miss Foulke," said Cunningham, who had at last gleaned some notion of what his fellow guests were discussing.

"You are seldom seen in church yourself, Cunningham," said Barratt.

"Steddon Hall lies in the parish of All Saints, strictly speaking," Cunningham replied, "though I never go there. Nay, Mrs Flannery disapproves of established religion, you see, so I am prevented from worshipping more often than once a month."

"I favour private prayer myself," said Miss Foulke, "but a church is about more than worship, of course."

"If you think of a parish as a cartwheel then the church is at its hub," said the Rector. "Which is where the spokes meet the axle, and where the energy of the horse is transferred into motion." This appeared to be the definitive statement on the subject, certainly there was no other person present who might sensibly comment on the intersection between physics and metaphysics. Happily, Johnson arrived at that moment with a very large bottle of Amontillado and the room was spared even a second of awkwardness.

The parlour was connected to the dining room by a pair of tall doors which were rarely opened, indeed a small table stood usually where the doors met on the parlour side. This had been removed, and when Johnson had poured the last of the Sherry he unlocked and opened the doors so that they swung back against the west wall of the parlour. The portrait of Catherine Barratt loomed into view. Miss Foulke and her mother had not seen the painting before, and

Sir Clifford had failed to warn them of its unsettling effect. Lady Foulke gasped when she saw Mrs Barratt floating above the dining table, Miss Foulke's eyes widened considerably and both ladies looked towards their host as if the presence of the portrait required an explanation. Barratt, as ever, had his back to the image of his late wife so that he failed to comprehend immediately what had agitated the ladies of Foulke Hall. Once Miss Foulke guided his attention to the picture by staring at it with her mouth slightly open Barratt explained who the subject was.

"It is tremendously lifelike," said Lady Foulke. "I feel almost as if I might reach out and take her hand."

"She had pretty hands," said Mr Barratt, "slender, but not all bones like some hands are." This remark, delivered calmly but with a hint of wistfulness, caused all four ladies, and Reverend Archer, to consider their own fingers momentarily. "We do not have a gong, perhaps we might step through to the dining room?"

The presence of the late Catherine Barratt, rendered with almost supernatural skill by some disciple of Mr Lawrence, had often, as previously noted, restricted the sense of conviviality at her husband's table. She seemed a less portentous figure once Lady Foulke had recovered her nerves, some spell had been broken perhaps, and the meal passed in the most comfortable of spirits. Reverend Archer was coaxed into telling a couple of the more universally palatable tales from his time at Exeter College, the perch was superb, and at the arrival of duck upon the table Mrs Walker recalled the first time that Mr Barratt had dined at the Rectory, managing to impress upon those of her fellow diners who had not been present just how execrable the food had been. The Rector was rather ashamed and Miss Lucy, who had spent too much of the evening feeling overlookedand was beyond the moderating grasp of her mother, teased Reverend Archer mercilessly, suggesting that he had employed the cook not for her skill but instead on the basis that he might receive change from a half crown. Mr Barratt interceded, declaring that the hospitality he had received at the Rectory and the company he had enjoyed that evening were worth more than all the rubies in India. He did not remember any indifferent duck, moreover, only the delight he felt at making the acquaintance ofMiss Lucy and Mrs Walker, two of the loveliest ladies, unquestionably, in the whole kingdom.

Besides, he noted, thrift was only the neighbour of prudence, and ought generally to be considered a commendable trait.

Barratt's cook had baked and stuffed apples for dessert and had also provided jellies made with gin and barberries, as these were a favourite of Mr Cunningham. The host asked that Johnson bring up a bottle of Moscadello from the coolest part of the cellar.

"Now, Madam, we shall try a wine of similar provenance to your good self," Barratt announced to Lady Foulke, who sat beside him. "Sweet, fair, and Italian." Mrs Walker squeezed her fiancé's hand in approbation; it was better all round that these innocent flirtations were addressed to mother rather than daughter. Mr Barratt then turned to Mrs Walker and asked if she would accompany him into the garden for two short minutes as he had a horticultural or perhaps botanical query which required her expertise as a matter of urgency. Mrs Walker protested that it was very nearly dark but Barratt was already on his feet, pulling her from the table, almost. As they descended into the garden he placed a large hand at her waist and said "There is no wine to compare you with, Susannah, my only love, not one in the world. You are more delicious and more intoxicating than any nectar that can be imagined."

"Fool!" said Mrs Walker.

They returned to the dining room and retook their seats moments later, smiling, but with eyes downcast. Mr Cunningham winked at Barratt and Sir Clifford cleared his throat.

"Did Mrs Walker provide a satisfactory response to your query, Sir?" Mr Barratt folded and unfolded his napkin before looking up.

"Well," said Barratt, "it seems that the lady would prefer spring flowers at her wedding."

Harvey Richards returned at noon three days later with a quantity of rum and a sheepskin for Miss Lucy. The young gentleman admitted that he might have stayed longer, so perfectly was he indulged at Meadholme, had he not received a summoning missive from Mr Barratt, and offered his congratulations on the happy news conveyed therein.Mr Richards carried a note from Captain Billings, thanking Barratt for his hospitality and assuring him that it had not been necessary to swing a hammock in the larger guest room. There was another letter, on hot-pressed paper, folded and sealed. It was addressed, in an unfamiliar hand, thus:

MR BARRATT
THE RED HOUSE

To be opened in the happy event of his marriage.

"What is this?" Barratt asked. Mr Richards smiled.

"It is a letter of some sort."

"Of a most peculiar sort. Who gave it to you?"

"I would rather you did not ask," said Mr Richards. "I do not wish to defy you, nor to betray the author, who has sworn me to secrecy."

"Very well," said Barratt, tossing the letter into a drawer of his bureau. "Consider the question withdrawn. How are things at Meadholme?"

"All very orderly, as you might expect. Captain Billings runs a tight ship. There is a degree of restlessness among the younger folk, as it is summer and they are rather isolated."

"No threat of mutiny, though?"

"None," said Mr Richards.

"Thank you, Harvey. I am sure you have things to do."

"Indeed so, I must haste to the Rectory with this," Mr Richards brandished the sheepskin. And there is another letter. You are not the only resident of B_____ with an admirer at Meadholme, it seems." Barratt was discomfited.

"What? Has one of those girls set their cap at Reverend Archer?" Mr Richards smiled again.

"Not to my knowledge, Sir. This *billet-doux* is addressed to Lucy Walker."

"The midshipman, is it?" Mr Richards nodded. "Saucy dog."

"His family is noble," Mr Richards observed. "More noble than yours or mine at any rate."

"Still, we are decent-sized fellows, Harvey, are we not, and gentlemen with it. Not pipsqueak fifth sons of some moorland Duchy!" They laughed together for a moment before Mr Barratt dismissed his protégé with a thump on the shoulder. He followed Mr Richards into the hallway then stepped into the parlour. The front door closed and Barratt watched the young man cross the road, his figure erect, his stride as purposeful as ever.

XXXVIII

AUTUMN CAME, a season of brief plenty for the poor of B_____ and of more sustained comfort for the rest of that prosperous little town. Harvey Richards was elected Chairman of the Old B_____ Charitable Trust. The organisation's coffers had been swelled by the proceeds from Miss Lucy's ball and the long-promised disbursements of Sir Clifford, Cunningham and Mr Barratt, so that funds were available for the relocation of a number of families from Butcher's Green to properties on the estate of Hope Hall. Most of the expense involved went on refurbishing these cottages, which had fallen into varying states of dereliction following the death of Henry Nicholson's father and the Exodus of tenant farmers which his successor had brought about. Here, Mr Broady proved himself invaluable; he had followed his father 'like a little terrier dog', by his own account and knew every square yard of the land and every brick of each building. Rents were set at the same figure as those paid for the hovels by the riverside. The sudden, resultant loss of income caused some aggravation to the landlord of Butcher's Green but also meant that Mr Barratt was able to buy the land there at a considerably reduced rate. Barratt continued to collect rent from those whose stubbornness or infirmities kept them in those sad quarters but these funds were spent on improving the occupied structures and razing the rest, so that the lot of the remaining residents was generally improved.

On the first cold morning of October Mr Barratt swallowed a mouthful of smoked mackerel and addressed his valet.

"Should I build myself a house there, Johnson? What do you think?"

"Where?" Johnson asked.

"Butcher's Green."

"Aye, Sir, if you wish to die of the Roman Sickness or some other marshy ailment."

"Perhaps you are correct," said Barratt. "We are quite comfortable here, are we not?" Johnson nodded and poured more coffee. "It is possible, in any case, that Mrs Walker may wish to return to Meadholme, particularly if Miss Lucy marries."

"The impression I have received," Johnson began, "is that despite its charms Mrs Walker feels no great attachment to Meadholme." Mr Barratt nodded. "The house in Whitecross Street is very comfortable and convenient but I don't suppose you miss it, Sir."

"No," said Barratt. "I would not return to Finsbury under any circumstances."

"Perhaps we might consider letting the property, then, to offset some of our expenses here?"

"I think it is time we did, yes. A capital idea, will you see to it?"

"It is all in hand," said Johnson, "awaiting only your instruction." Mr Barratt chuckled.

"You have lead me on, Bill, like an ass to the well."

"There is no harm in it, if the ass is thirsty," Johnson said, grinning.

Mr Broady brought his family home. The agent's house was the newest on the estate, and had required less reparatory work than many of the other buildings; some windows were reglazed and slates replaced and the place was inhabitable. The property, which stood three furlongs or even a half mile from Hope Hall itself, along the B_____ road, was modest enough. There was a small garden behind the house and the boys now had a room of their own in which they continued to fight, almost without interruption. Mrs Broady was delighted with the place, even though she must at some point have dreamed of being mistress of the whole estate, and was happier still when a cartload of furniture, retrieved from Mr Barratt's London home, was delivered and installed by Johnson and Mr Richards.

Broady drew a wage from the Trust and walked the land as if it were his own, indeed in an obscure sense it seemed that it might be, he being an hereditary custodian, in effect. His new neighbours were his old neighbours, but all now lived at a healthier remove from one another, and breathed healthier air. They were tenants and Broady had no land of his own to speak of, so no resentment arose between the agent and those from whom he collected rent, or if it did it went unvoiced, since no hierarchy could be clearly established. Broady's income was subsidised from time to time by

Mr Barratt, who employed him on an informal basis to keep an eye on Mr Nicholson. Mrs Broady was similarly tasked, though her intelligence was generally more useful, and more generously rewarded, as she was able to speak with Nicholson and to assess his mood, to ask him questions, make suggestions and so on. Broady was still unable to communicate in a civil fashion with the person he believed responsible for his father's premature death.

And what of him, Henry Nicholson? In the weeks following the ball he had quarantined himself with the walls of Hope Hall. This, we may assume, was an agonising period for the young gentleman, in which he attempted to adjust to a sudden, if not indefinite change in circumstances. His only visitor during this period was Miss Foulke, whom he addressed in the most unfriendly terms and sent away, and Smith the apothecary, despatched thither subsequently by Miss Foulke. Smith reported that Nicholson had grown a beard, was living on fruit, biscuit and dry sausage, and might possibly have lost his mind. It was an altogether more sane and stable Nicholson who emerged from this retreat, however. He wrote to Miss Foulke, offering an effusive apology and asking that he be allowed to call on her to reiterate his remorse in person. Mr Nicholson arrived at Foulke House thinner and more pale than ever. He was clean shaven, his manners seemed softened, his whole being, in fact had lost its prickliness. A further apology was issued to Rebekah Broady, in the form of a rather longer letter, and though Nicholson only acknowledged his past offences in the broadest terms it was clear that his penitence was sincere. Mrs Broady had loved him once, and accordingly had no wish to see him suffer. After her family was settled in the agent's house and when Broady was at home, as often as twice a week, she would carry Catherine up to the hall to visit Mr Nicholson. Mrs Broady was concerned for Nicholson at first, but as the days shortened and his strength improved these visits became more of an excuse to escape her warring sons and to enjoy the company of someone who admired her yet. She and Mr Nicholson would sometimes recollect an incident from the early days of their courtship and take delight in it; somehow the unhappy ending towards which these events had inexorably led did not taint the pleasure that these memories afforded. Mrs Broady would return to her family with a heavier heart oft-times, and little

Catherine too would seem more of a burden on the walk back from Hope Hall. Nevertheless she persisted, recognising that a degree of melancholy served as a reminder of her selfhood. If she could still feel then she was still Rebekah, and not simply someone's wife or someone's mother.

Henry Nicholson was conscious of the pain he had caused to Mrs Broady and her husband. The new tenants on his estate had also suffered, though less directly and entirely unknowingly, because of his past malfeasance, which Mr Barratt had kept to himself. Nicholson was greeted by the former residents of Butcher's Green, wherever he encountered them therefore, as a noble benefactor. Caps were hastily doffed, hands pressed together as if in prayer, crude curtseys attempted. Mr Nicholson was mortified each time, of course, and wondered if this was not some part of Barratt's plan, that he might be tortured by his past even as he attempted to escape it. Nor did he have the means to make amends to those he had wronged. Whatever income he received from the Trust went towards basic sustenance, upkeep of the hall and his various debts. High were the walls of the prison which Mr Barratt had erected.

Harvey Richards received no financial assistance from the Trust; the role of Chairman was intended for a gentleman of means and leisure and was voluntary, the innovations of Mr Nicholson notwithstanding. Richards depended on ad hoc payments from Mr Barratt and the odd guinea from Mr Cunningham. He was happy enough with this arrangement and as a result of his cohabitation with Barratt he ate and drank rather better than most young men in similar circumstances.

Inevitably perhaps, in his efforts to reorganise the Trust along more accountable lines Mr Richards had uncovered further iniquities. A fellow called Jeffers had been put in charge of the rents which the Trust collected from stallholders on market day, the license to do so being essential to the charity's viability. Richards calculated that Jeffers had been diverting a significant proportion of this revenue into his own pocket for at least two years. It was no small sum but Jeffers was the brother-in-law of Reverend Archer's church warden and could not simply be pilloried. When presented with evidence of his misdemeanours Jeffers denied everything and some words of encouragement from

Johnson were required before he resigned his role. Rents were now collected monthly rather than weekly, and by Mr Richards himself rather than a paid intermediary. The increased efficiency of the Trust effected by this and other measures put in place by Richards in the first months of his Chairmanship did not improve the young gentleman's financial situation, naturally, and Mr Barratt was alarmed to perceive a hole in the toe of Mr Richards' boot as they crossed to St Andrew's on the second Sunday of Advent.

"Must you wear those rotten old boots, Harvey? No-one approves more of thrifty measures than I, but we would not wish to be misjudged."

"Mr Barratt, I am certain that you are not perturbed by the judgments of any man. Besides, these are the only boots I own." Mr Barratt raised an eyebrow but did not respond.

The two gentlemen were to dine that evening at the Rectory so they returned to the Red House after the service, Reverend Archer's sermon having explored the mysteries of water, prophecy and the cleansing of sin in a somewhat obfuscating fashion which had left certain parishioners unsure if John the Baptist and the Holy Ghost were indeed separate entities. Barratt was enough of a heathen to attend to correspondence on a Sunday afternoon and Mr Richards kept him company, as it was already rather cold and fires burned only in the kitchen and library. Mr Barratt signed a letter, stowed his quill and turned in his chair.

"If you were to marry Lucy Walker you might purchase as many boots as you like," he said. "I know you are fond of her, even if you do not admire her exactly, and many marriages have survived quite well on less."

"You believe I should propose to Miss Lucy?"

"I do not have a cock in the pit," said Barratt, unhelpfully. "I was thinking only of your shoe leather."

"I get the impression that Mrs Walker does not approve of me," said Mr Richards.

"That is her way, I fear," Barratt replied. "I sometimes wonder if she likes me at all and we are to be married in a few months."

"Anyway I would prefer not to be dependent on my wife. It is undignified."

"So are your boots, alas. Listen, Harvey, I made my own way in life because there was no alternative. Lucy Walker is a pleasant, prosperous young woman who loves you. You need not be dependent upon her, my hope is that we will go into business together as partners rather than in our present arrangement, and you will have a healthy income of your own if we are successful. What I am telling you is that your scruples need not prevent you from marrying Miss Walker." Mr Richards did not reply. "You do not love her then," said Barratt, "nor can you imagine ever loving her."

"She is pretty, of course," admitted Mr Richards. "I only wonder if we could ever share a life of the mind."

"Miss Lucy is no fool, one need only consider her success with the ball."

"I did not suggest that she was a fool, Sir, it is just that we have little in common, in terms of the things with which we are preoccupied. Miss Foulke, meanwhile..."

"Miss Foulke may share certain of your interests but she is not interested in you, Harvey, perhaps for the same reason that you profess no interest in Lucy Walker. She thinks you pretty but insubstantial. There is no kinder way of putting it."

"Did she tell you this?" Mr Richards asked.

"She has never asked me a single question about you," Barratt replied. He watched as Mr Richards endured a rare moment of self-doubt. "Miss Foulke is mistaken, my dear fellow, about your character. You are a good deal more sophisticated than her, I suspect. As is Miss Lucy, in her own way. She is a little younger than Miss Foulke too, we should remember, and at an age where the difference of a couple of years is more marked." Barratt got to his feet. "Still, the heart wants what it wants," he said. "It would be a kindness though, I think, if you were to explain to Miss Lucy Walker that she has no prospect of becoming Mrs Harvey Richards, since at present that is the only future she imagines for herself. Unless, of course, you think a change of heart is possible." Mr Richards shook his head. "You are a good man, Harvey, I am sure you will do the right thing."

XXXIX

MR RICHARDS did nothing that evening. He behaved towards Miss Lucy as he had always done, with the warm, indulgent air of a kindly elder brother. Reverend Archer talked through the intricacies and ironies of the church at Christmas. Once outside the pulpit his wit shone as distinctly as ever so that his guests wondered anew how such a mind could produce sermons of such surpassing opacity. The conversation then turned to more personal matters. The Rector now dined frequently at Foulke House and spoke with affection of Sir Clifford and his household.

"Here is a true Christian," he observed. "A generous spirit, incapable of anger, conscious always of causing the very least trouble."

"Blessed are the peacemakers," said Barratt.

"Precisely," said Reverend Archer.

"I think it is better to do things," Miss Lucy said. "Surely it is more important to help people, or to prevent them doing ill than to sit around pretending everything is perfect. If children are hungry we should make sure they are fed. We should be angry that they are starving in the first place."

"You feel that I do not do enough for the poor, cousin?"

"I meant my remark to be general, John," said Miss Lucy. "No-one could reproach you for your efforts on behalf of your parishioners. I cannot understand how certain prosperous families can simply sit in a big house on a hill, doing nothing other than eating great quantities of mashed potato while babies go hungry not two miles away."

"If you are speaking of Foulke House..." the Rector began.

"I was speaking generally, cousin," said Miss Lucy.

"We should remember that Sir Clifford has recently made a generous donation to Mr Richards' Trust," said Barratt, who was delighted to see Miss Lucy exhibiting something of her mother's fierce energy.

"You twisted his arm, no doubt," Miss Lucy replied. "I doubt that he has ever set foot in Butcher's Green." This remark appeared to confirm that Miss Lucy had been referring to Foulke House, in fact, and her complexion took on a slightly deeper hue, so that she was almost as pink as Miss Foulke. That young lady might as well have been present at the Rectory dining table at that moment, so prominent was her position in the minds of those who actually surrounded it.

"Do you think we shall have snow, Charles?" asked Mrs Walker, after a prolonged pause.

"No doubt of it, my dearest," Barratt replied, smiling broadly. "Snow shall fall."

The lovers excused themselves from the table ahead of the younger diners, declaring that they could not manage even the smallest slice of cake. Mrs Walker sat beside Barratt on the chaise in the library.

"I should feign some injury, perhaps, so that we can spend more time in each other's company," said Barratt.

"We see more than enough of one another, Charles, it would be a pity if we grew jaded before we are even married."

"I am not in a position to speak for you," he replied, "but I cannot imagine ever being anything but thrilled to be in your presence."

"Really? Even when I am reading a frivolous novel and ignoring you completely?" Barratt placed a hand at Mrs Walker's waist and squeezed her against his side.

"Particularly then, my love! What could be more exciting than to pit oneself against the forces of fiction?" Mrs Walker was delighted but made every effort to disguise this feeling.

"Release me, Sir," she said. "I am not yours yet."

Lottie entered the room feigning a cough, as if there was a danger that she might discover the affianced parties *in flagrante delicto*.

"Was there anything else you were wanting? Lottie asked. Mrs Walker removed Mr Barratt's hand from her waist and shook her head.

"I am neither hungry nor thirsty, Lottie," said Barratt with a grin, "though I am certainly yearning for some sensation which remains, for the moment, beyond my grasp." Lottie giggled and blushed and Mrs Walker delivered a sharp elbow to the ribs of Mr Barratt, with the practiced aim of a Royal Artilleryman.

Miss Lucy, Reverend Archer and Mr Richards joined them then from the dining room and the rest of the evening was spent in amicable conversation, no further reference being made to Foulke Hall or its residents.

A pair of new boots appeared at the foot of Harvey Richards' bed on Christmas morning, a timely arrival, since he was to ride home that day to his mother, Mr Cunningham's niece, in Clandon. He pulled them on before dressing and found that not only did they fit perfectly but the uppers were of such quality that they assumed the shape of his feet as if he had worn them for six months. He had bought Mr Barratt a folding device in silver and steel for cleaning the bowl of one's pipe. Barratt declared himself delighted with this object when he opened the box at breakfast. Mr Richards ate in haste, and Barratt winced rather at the thought of a long, cold ride accompanied only by indigestion. He and Johnson would take the cart over to Steddon Hall later that morning to eat a goose with Mr Cunningham and Mrs Flannery. The cook had returned to London until the New Year; she too had not seen her family for many months. As Barratt stood on the steps of the Red House and watched Mr Richards disappear in the direction of Portsmouth he shivered, though he was not cold by any means. Had he been a superstitious man he might have thought this spasm to be some kind of augury or premonition. Instead he determined that some part of his mind wished to draw his attention to something, something which he had forgotten and ought to remember. Barratt looked south, waiting for the memory to come to him. A vain effort, he decided eventually, stepping inside and closing the door. Whatever he was supposed to recollect, the loose thread, the thing that pulled mutely at his coattails, had ridden off with Mr Richards.

It was the first mild winter for many years. The roads and ponds barely froze, and then for a few days rather than for weeks. At the start of March Mr Barratt deferred the sowing of lettuce seeds in the garden of the Red House fearing that frostier weather must return but it never did, and he cursed the weeks lost. At Hope Hall the new tenants turned the soil in fields long left fallow, acre upon acre of weeds transforming into ridges and troughs for potatoes, onions and leek. In the larger fields wheat and barley was sown. Henry Nicholson, who had by now become accustomed to the unearned deference shown by the Trust's tenants, visited each

smallholding regularly, on fine days at least, offering
encouragement where he was quite unable to offer advice. Barratt
rode out to call on Mr Nicholson from time to time and found the
gentleman greatly changed in manners and demeanour. Where
once he had seemed nervous and protean he now evinced a calm
melancholy, which Barratt associated with those who deprive
themselves of life's pleasures through choice: monks, ascetics and
so forth.

"Do you resent me, or my actions?" Barratt asked Nicholson,
finding him at home one bright morning a few days after Easter.

"I suppose I might, if I thought about it long enough. I try not
to, you see. I try not to think about the past. It is difficult. I am glad
that my father did not live to see what happened to Hope Hall."

"I am sure it will be a handsome estate once more," said
Barratt. "It will be yours again, of course, before very long."

"And I will wonder how I deserve it," Nicholson replied.

"How are you getting along with Broady?"

"I keep out of his way, wherever possible. He continues to
look at me as if he wishes my head would fall off, which is his
prerogative, I suppose. His wife is very kind. I believe she has
almost forgiven me."

"You will have to tolerate him a while longer, I fear," said
Barratt. "His tenure can only be terminated with the agreement of
the Trust, you will recall."

"Indeed," said Nicholson. "There are elements of this bondage
from which I will never be free."

"Once the mortgage is paid and your other obligation settled
you may wish to sell Hope Hall. The agreement with the Trust is
unlikely to be negotiable. Surely it is better that this place remains
with you and any heir, however, rather than ending up in the hands
of Mr Irving and his bank."

"Better for who, exactly?" said Nicholson. "*Cui bono*? Only
you, perhaps, Mr Barratt, in that you can walk away confident that
you took the right course of action."

"If you were to renege on the mortgage no-one would benefit,
other than an old man who is already far too rich."

"Never fear, Sir," said Nicholson, with a wan smile. "I will
wear the yoke."

The wedding date was set. Mrs Walker and Mr Barratt would

marry on the first Saturday in May with their two households in attendance. Reverend Archer read the Banns for the first time a month before, raising his eyes to the prospective bride and groom in turn as he announced their names. Bell ringers were engaged. Almost as soon as the appointment was fixed it was put back, however, since a shortage of a particular fabric, in a particular colour, meant that Mrs Walker's dress would not be ready in time. A further four weeks were required. Mr Barratt was philosophical about this deferral, telling his bride-to-be that he had already waited a lifetime for her, so a few more days did not signify, but in fact wrestled with a mischievous urge to suggest that their marriage would still be legal if she were to wear a dress which she already owned. Discussions about domestic arrangements continued meanwhile, since there were a number of complications to unravel which were specific, if not unique, to the conjugation of the Rectory and the Red House.

Reverend Archer had become accustomed to the delights produced by Mrs Walker's cook, but he did not employ her, or rather he did, but was only able to because of the stipend provided by his cousin which would necessarily cease once she moved across the street. Where would Miss Lucy and Harvey Richards live? The latter person might have been expected to return to The Martyrs, or similar lodgings somewhere in B_____, the Rectory was suggested as a more convenient situation for the young gentleman, though some tension persisted between Mr Richards and the Rector. Steddon Hall was also considered a possible mooring, though Mr Cunningham's hospitality had its limits, even for poor relations, and the house was almost as far off as Milton. Miss Lucy still had hopes of setting up home with Mr Richards but they had yet to reach anything approaching an understanding. He had treated her with greater respect since the autumn and the scales had fallen from his eyes where Venetia Foulke was concerned, it seemed, but a proposal remained a distant prospect. Miss Lucy was very fond of Mr Barratt too, of course, but did not relish the idea of being beneath his roof, being startled intermittently by some sonorous exclamation or other, for an indefinite period.

Had some nimble bookkeeper attempted to total the various calculations relating to these matters, a task to tax some clerical titan like a labour of Hercules, their efforts would have been for naught, however. Plans for the wedding day, and for the lives to be lived thereafter, were soon to be halted, by a terrible and bloody event.

XL

THE WORLD WAS wide and various enough that at any point in time some atrocity or other was being committed somewhere. Charles Barratt, a well-travelled gentleman who as a rule chose not to ignore the savagery of humankind, knew this as well as anyone. Riding out on the last morning of April with no particular destination in mind, however, he cannot have imagined that he would encounter the most appalling brutality on a day of such perfect Spring splendour. The trees were heavy with blossom, some of which drifted in the scented air. The sun warmed his neck, a lark sang somewhere above and a sense of well-being pervaded his mind and body. He passed the gate beyond which the road sloped down to Hope Hall then turned the big mare around. He had no wish to see Henry Nicholson - their last interview had left Barratt with a sense of vague unease - but a few moments spent in the company of Rebekah Broady, he felt, might enhance his mood still further.

The agent's house stood empty. Mr Barratt put his head in at the kitchen door. There was a smell of baking, but none of the incessant row generated by Mrs Broady's boys. He considered returning to the London Road but the lark sang again, if indeed it was the same bird, in the direction of the hall so Mr Barratt pulled the reins westwards. After a furlong the house came into view and on the road, halfway between Hope Hall and his own position Barratt saw the figure of a woman carrying a bundle against her breast, and moving erratically towards him. She wore a smock which must once have been white but was now splashed with crimson. Barratt kicked the mare and approached the woman at a brisk canter. It was Mrs Broady, he established. He climbed down from his horse and placed a hand on her shoulder.

"What, are you hurt Madam? Is it little Catherine?"Mrs Broady, her face marked by terror, looked up at him.

"It is you, Mr Barratt, Sir. Nay, my baby sleeps. It is Henry, he is murdered!"

"Take the child home, Mrs Broady. Burn your dress, it will not wash. Where does he lay?"

"Inside the door, Mr Barratt. I held him to see if he would wake but he is dead, quite dead." Barratt thought for a moment then remounted his horse.

"Where are your sons?" he asked.

"They have gone to the market with their father, Sir."

"If anyone should ask you, Mrs Broady, tell them that we discovered Mr Nicholson together." She did not respond but regarded Barratt with an expression of confusion. "I am certain that I know who committed this act, Madam, but if that person is not quickly apprehended suspicion will fall elsewhere. It is for your own protection." Mrs Broady nodded and turned away. Mr Barratt flicked the reins and rode down to Hope Hall.

Nicholson's body lay on its back on the chequered marble of the hallway. Given the condition of Mrs Broady's smock Barratt had expected more blood. He estimated that there was but a single wound, on the left side of Nicholson's head, since this was where the blood had collected. The gentleman's hair, thick and dark as it was, made it impossible to determine without closer inspection. Mr Barratt was not squeamish by nature but he took a breath and like Odysseus, returning to Ithaca, reminded himself that he had seen worse things. He knelt beside the corpse keeping his riding breeches away from the puddle of blood, which seemed vivid and freshly shed. Barratt took a handkerchief from his pocket and put it over his fingers, before touching the side of the dead man's head. The wound was in front of Nicholson's ear, a round concavity an inch and a half wide perhaps and half as deep. Barratt pushed a shrouded fingertip into the wound to establish this latter dimension and as he did so the body twitched and Nicholson's eyes, lifeless a moment earlier, turned to Barratt with a look of agony and anguish combined. Mr Barratt made an incoherent sound and sprang to his feet in alarm.

"My God, he lives!" Barratt exclaimed, kneeling again, this time with no regard to the condition of his clothing. "Henry, it is Charles Barratt. I must leave you for a period, but I will send someone to look over you. I will bring a doctor." If Nicholson understood these words he was unable to respond. He continued to stare at Barratt with horror in his eyes and Mr Barratt felt unable to leave the stricken man, fearing that the idea of being abandoned might cause Nicholson's condition to deteriorate. There had been very few occasions in Charles Barratt's life when had not known what to do, but this was one such moment. It did not last. Mr Nicholson's eyes closed. As Barratt leant over to check that he was still breathing Broady appeared at the door.

"Broady, good fellow, do you know where Dr Pearson lives?" Broady nodded.

"Rebekah says Nicholson is dead."

"She is mistaken, though he may not live long without your help," said Barratt. Take my horse and find the Doctor. Tell him it is a heavy blow to the head."

A small blanket lay folded on the floor at the foot of the stairs, placed there by Mrs Broady, Barratt assumed, for little Catherine's comfort. Mr Barratt lifted Nicholson's head as little and as gently as he could and slid the blanket beneath it. He sat on the floor beside Mr Nicholson, putting a hand close to the mouth and nose of the injured man from time to time to check his breathing. The marble was cool and Mr Barratt was not altogether comfortable. His greatest concern was for Nicholson, of course, but he thought there must be a cushion nearby which might provide some relief to his posterior. As he climbed to his feet Barratt remarked some object glinting behind the open door and knew immediately what he would find there. Mr Nicholson's stick, its black wood polished to a brilliant lustre, rested against an angle of the wainscot, with a smear of red matter visible on one side of its silver head. It must have been placed there by a steady hand, Barratt thought, positioned by a person in complete charge of their senses. The idea unsettled him, and he returned to Nicholson's side, forgetting altogether about his quest for a cushion.

Dr Pearson was the very best kind of physician, in that he understood the narrow limits of his capabilities, and did not exceed them to the detriment of those under his care. He tranquilised Mr Nicholson, supervised his removal to a shabby daybed in one of the downstairs rooms, then cleaned and dressed his wound. He recommended that Nicholson be watched night and day, that two guardian angels were required, ideally a lady and a gentleman, and that Mr Nicholson must be fed with liquids, since the act of chewing would prove more painful than it was possible to consider. The good doctor rode off to his next patient a few moments later, having handed a bill to Mr Barratt, who looked more likely to settle it than Broady.

"I will stay with him, Sir," said Broady.

"You are a good man," replied Mr Barratt. "Be sure you do not finish him off."

"He is part of the Estate," said Broady, smiling. "I am duty bound to take care of him, whatever my feelings may be."

Barratt rode back to the Red House then despatched Johnson and the cook to assist Broady. He contemplated a visit to the Rectory but presumed, correctly, that Mrs Walker would already have heard of the outrage at Hope Hall and would hold him accountable in some way. It was true, he acknowledged, that he had provided the assailant with the weapon used to strike down Henry Nicholson. A more important fact to be borne in mind, he felt, was that this was the only possible terminal point for someone of Nicholson's character, and he, Barratt, had been the only fellow bold enough to divert the gentleman from this sorrowful path, or at least to attempt it. He sensed that Mrs Walker might not be entirely sympathetic to this point of view, however, and was very glad that she was unaware it was he who had placed Mr Nicholson's stick in Buller's hands.

It was now four in the afternoon, by Mr Barratt's watch, and he had not eaten lunch. The events of the day had suppressed his appetite entirely but had left him rather tired. He sat in a low chair in the parlour, therefore, and fell asleep immediately. He was woken little more than an hour later by the return of Johnson and the cook. They had been dismissed by Miss Foulke. The lady had learned about Mr Nicholson's injury from one of her servants, who had spoken to Dr Pearson's maid at the market.

"I had already prepared some soup," said the cook. "Beef, it was."

Miss Venetia Foulke began her vigil that afternoon, only quitting Mr Nicholson's side momentarily when it would have been unladylike not to do so. She slept in a chair beside the daybed and sent Broady out for provisions from Foulke House. Dr Pearson visited daily, at first; as Mr Nicholson's situation improved he returned less frequently. After a fortnight Lady Foulke came to see her daughter, hoping to take her home and leave the invalid in the hands of a kitchen servant. Mr Nicholson was sitting up by this point, but his head was still heavily bandaged, giving him the appearance, so Lady Foulke thought, of some Sahib in the East India Company who had adopted the local custom.

"How are you, Mr Nicholson? We are all very concerned for you." Nicholson answered only with a pained smile.

"Mr Nicholson cannot speak, mother," explained Miss Foulke. "I am able to comprehend his needs as we have established a series of looks and simple gestures via which he can communicate. Henry understands me very well, of course."

"I am relieved that someone does, my dear," said Lady Foulke.

"You are most kind to bring the items I requested, Mama, and Jessie too, but I simply cannot abandon Mr Nicholson until he is quite well. Mr Barratt is here often and provides all kinds of assistance. Please do not worry yourself."

"Good morning, Madam," said Barratt, stepping out from a darkened corner of the room and startlingLady Foulke considerably. "Rest assured,Miss Foulke has either myself or Mr Broady at her disposal throughout the day."

"You conceal yourself remarkably well, for such a gigantic person," said Lady Foulke. Mr Barratt smiled and bowed.

"My man would be surprised to hear you say so, Lady Foulke." She stepped forward, kissed her daughter and departed.

Barratt had grown to admire the forbearance shown by Nicholson in coping with his newly reduced state and felt responsible, to some degree, for the gentleman's condition. He wished to be of assistance both to Mr Nicholson and Miss Foulke, therefore, though the young lady's devotion to her patient presented a further complication, Barratt suspected, in affairs between him and his fiancée. An added benefit of putting himself at the service of Nicholson was that it allowed Mr Barratt to avoid Mrs Walker, but this ruse would not work indefinitely; they were due to be married in two weeks, after all, and at some point he would have to face a reckoning.

XLI

THE MOOD WHICH prevailed at the Rectory was one of nervous excitement, though it appeared that Mrs Walker, whose impending nuptials inspired this giddiness, did not share in it. Lottie spent her time removing dust from every surface, largely oblivious to the fact that the age of the building and its furnishings, combined with a heightened degree of human activity, meant that each stratum she wiped away was quickly replaced. The young servant had a habit of singing to herself as she worked. Her voice was very pleasant and the few simple country airs which she knew only added to the spirit of celebration which pervaded the property. Miss Lucy hoped that Mr Richards, who had become noticeably more solicitous towards her in recent weeks without ever actually presenting himself as a suitor, might be caught up in this matrimonial whirl. Accordingly she dressed and performed her toilet each morning with the focus and attention to detail of a young lady who expects, that very day, to receive a proposal. Harvey Richards appeared at the Rectory every other morning, it seemed, ostensibly to offer apologies on behalf of Mr Barratt for his protracted presence at Hope Hall. These visits were interpreted by Miss Lucy as a summoning of nerve by Mr Richards which would lead, undoubtedly, to a satisfactory climax. The uncomfortable implication of this idea, perhaps, was that Mr Richards was exploiting the near-fatal assault on Henry Nicholson for his own romantic ends. Miss Lucy was not an unimaginative young woman, as we have seen, but she did possess a tendency towards self-regard so this possibility did not occur to her.

Reverend Archer had also visited Hope Hall and had found Miss Foulke still more captivating presented as Epione. The Rector observed a new tenderness to her character as she ministered to Mr Nicholson. He had long admired the young lady's patience, of course, but this aspect of her personality came as a pleasant surprise and Reverend Archer felt increasingly that it would be a grave disappointment if he were to fail to secure her hand in marriage. Just as the Rector's feelings developed, however, so did Miss Foulke's attachment to Henry Nicholson.

Charles Barratt believed that this bond was devotional in

nature, and that there was no erotic element to it at all. Miss Foulke had religious doubts but she was also an unusually serious young woman, and craved that connection with the sublime which others seemed to achieve by surrendering to God. The self-sacrifice inherent in making the care of an invalid the central fact of one's existence appealed to her for this reason, Barratt supposed. It was not an instinct he shared, but one he understood. If a person rejected the myths of the pulpit it was not unreasonable for them to seek meaning elsewhere. This was the plain on which instinct and reason did battle and for the very great majority of people instinct won out. Mr Barratt was a man guided by his instincts generally, and in fact there was no contradiction in his atheism. It was no more reasonable to believe that the universe was godless because Catherine had been taken from him than it was to have believed the opposite while she lived. What he had experienced was not so much a loss of faith as a change of heart. The kind of devotion exhibited by Miss Foulke presented more of an obstacle to Reverend Archer, Barratt calculated, than if she had been in love with Henry Nicholson, since it was less prone to sudden change or reversal. She would remain steadfast. Neither her heart, nor her mind would change.

Mr Barratt left the Red House very early each morning, calling first on the Broadys and then on Miss Foulke and Mr Nicholson. He usually brought something to Hope Hall, either food prepared by his cook or something from his library for Miss Foulke to read to her patient. The dull hours spent waiting to be relieved by Mr Broady were Barratt's own act of penance, naturally, though he resented himself somewhat, and experienced none of the transcendent glow of dutiful selflessness which illuminated Miss Foulke from within.

After two weeks Mr Nicholson's condition began to improve. He could not talk, still, and Dr Pearson confided to Mr Barratt that he might never speak again, an opinion which caused Barratt a familiar shudder. Nicholson could write, however, which seemed almost miraculous. He gestured for a quill one morning and Miss Foulke provided the necessary stationery. The first question he wrote down, "Where is Buller, is he taken?" confirmed to Miss Foulke what Mr Barratt already knew. She showed the note to Barratt, who pulled up a chair beside the daybed. Over the next hour the story behind Buller's savage assault was slowly and painstakingly related.

Mr Nicholson had not owned the superb carriage and the pair of black geldings outright. They were not his entirely to give away, in fact he owned little more than a wheel, and a leg of each horse due to some novel arrangement made with the vendor of each. Buller, needing ready money, had attempted to sell the creatures and the carriage for a great deal less than they were worth. This aroused the suspicions of one prospective buyer, who had surveyed the carriage and established its provenance. The buyer, a scrupulous gentleman whose name was Wolfe, then contacted the coachbuilders in the hope that they would provide an estimate as to the true value of the landau, and a further sequence of events was set in train. The coachbuilders confirmed that they had sold the carriage to a Mr Henry Nicholson, who still owed them a considerable portion of the selling price. The two geldings had been procured by the same company on Nicholson's behalf and they were repossessed along with the carriage. Buller was apprehended despite protesting, truthfully almost, that he had been given them in lieu of money owed to him by Nicholson, and was only released when he agreed to abandon any claim upon both beasts and conveyance. Humiliated, his pockets empty, he set out on foot in the direction of B_____, with Nicholson's stick in hand.

"I will find him, Sir," said Barratt, as he read the last of Mr Nicholson's account. "Fear not, I have already sent Johnson out after him. He will be transported for this." Miss Foulke looked alarmed at this possibility while Nicholson, exhausted by the unaccustomed effort of relaying information, closed his eyes and slept. "I do not thirst for vengeance, Miss Foulke," said Barratt, as quietly as he could. "This person, Buller, is responsible not just for this recent assault, I suspect, but also for other ills which have afflicted Mr Nicholson and those around him for some years. He is like some poisonous plant in one's garden, he must be uprooted and destroyed." Miss Foulke's eyes widened further. "I would not worry yourself with the matter. Johnson will ensure that Mr Buller does not escape justice. Your only concern need be Mr Nicholson. Ah, here is Broady."

Mrs Walker considered writing a note to her fiancé but decided instead that she would confront him without advance warning. She strode across the high street at two in the afternoon and yanked at the bell-pull of the Red House. Harvey Richards answered the door.

"Mrs Walker, do come in."

"Is Mr Barratt at home?"

"No..."

"...Is he expected?"

"He often returns home at this hour," Mr Richards admitted. "Would you like to come in and wait for him? I can ask the cook to make tea." Mrs Walker did not answer, but stepped past Mr Richards into the hallway and then entered the parlour. She sat in Mr Barratt's favoured chair, by the window, having turned it towards the centre of the room, where Mr Richards stood with his palms pressed together.

"Why is Mr Barratt avoiding me?" she asked. Few people regarded Mrs Walker with quite the same frank admiration evinced by Mr Richards – aside from her own particular qualities she bore a passing resemblance to his mother, though she was rather younger, and a good deal more forceful by nature – but even he felt that this question was unfair.

"I am sure that Mr Barratt is not avoiding you, Madam. He is much occupied at Hope Hall, of course."

"Why is that?"

"I do not understand you," said Mr Richards. Mrs Walker offered an impatient sigh.

"Why is Mr Barratt spending half the day, every day at Hope Hall?" she asked. Mr Richards sensed that a trap had been set but could not discern whether it lay before or behind him. He opted for retreat.

"A very serious assault was carried out on Mr Nicholson. He was fortunate to survive and would not have, as I understand it, without the quick thinking of Mr Barratt."

"Yes, yes," said Mrs Walker. "That neither explains his constant presence at Hope Hall nor excuses his absence from the Rectory. What is going on, Harvey?" Mr Richards jolted at the familiarity. He looked at Mrs Walker for a moment before responding. She was as fierce a woman as he had ever met, but was by no means the most inscrutable. She is jealous, he thought to himself, simply because Miss Foulke is young. This in turn was a simplification, because Mr Richards was himself young, but there was a kernel of truth in his assessment. He smiled at Mrs Walker in a way that he hoped would not provoke her.

"Mr Barratt says that Miss Foulke has become so devoted to Mr Nicholson, her very being so entwined with the idea of his recovery that she barely registers whether he or Mr Broady stand ready to assist her." This arrow reached its mark and Mrs Walker seemed calmer in an instant.

"If it matters not who is at Hope Hall why does Charles, who is due to marry in less than a fortnight, insist that he be there?" Mrs Walker seemed to address this query to herself, rather as a tragedian might. It was either the seemingly rhetorical nature of the question, perhaps, or instead the softening of Mrs Walker's tone which caused Mr Richards to step directly into the very same snare he had taken pains to avoid moments earlier.

"It is possible that Mr Barratt feels some sense of responsibility for Henry Nicholson's plight," said Mr Richards.

"Indeed he would have to be some kind of a monster, certainly, if he did not feel responsible for bringing the young gentleman so low," Mrs Walker replied, with a gleam of triumph in her eyes. Harvey Richards, appreciating that he had been outmanoeuvred, sat down.

"You cannot think him monstrous, Madam," he said quietly. "You have agreed to marry him, after all." As Mrs Walker prepared her response to this impertinence she heard heavy footsteps from the dining room. Mr Barratt put his head around the door frame a moment later.

"Here is a long overdue *tête-à-tête*," said Barratt. "I should not interrupt you."

"Stay," said Mrs Walker. "We have a great deal to discuss."

XLII

THEY WERE NOT of an age, either of them, at which they might have expected their hearts to be overtaken by the strongest feelings, and were both accustomed to ordering their lives free of any grand passions, so it was readily foreseeable that when Mr Barratt and Mrs Walker were thus afflicted they would each struggle to adapt to the novel situation. Barratt had lived in near isolation for two decades. His principal companions during this period were grief, for the loss of his wife Catherineand their child, who died without a name, and anger at the injustice of their deaths. These emotions visited him less frequently, of course, over the years, but never abandoned him.As these associations wained nothing grew in their stead; Mr Barratt saw out each day in a state of numbness, performing actions and making decisions as if sleepwalking. He did not recall exactly who or what had provoked his removal from London but he was very grateful to have settled in B_____, and more grateful still to have met Susannah Walker, who had revived a part of his spirit which had long been dormant, and restored his sense of purpose along with it. While a new tenderness suffused his person Barratt remained impatient, impulsive and prone to saying or doing the wrong thing. Love may enhance a person's qualities, good or bad, but only in the rarest of cases does it alter them entirely.

Mrs Walker was perhaps a more unlikely candidate, still, to fall under love's spell, her relative youthfulness notwithstanding. Her marriage had not been happy, and her husband's death was a source of relief rather than misery, both to his new widow and the staff at Meadholme, who had held Mr Walker in no great esteem. Miss Lucy had loved her father, oblivious to his faults as young children tend to be, and he had had the good grace to expire before she became conscious of the unpleasant, condescending fashion in which he chose to treat everyone but her. Mr Walker's employees remembered him more fondly than they had served him, and Miss Lucy never heard a harsh word about her father from any of them, nor did Mrs Walker speak ill of her late helpmate. She could not neither forget nor forgive his bullying nature, and general lack of kindness, even as she concealed these characteristics from her daughter. Sometimes the memory of some particularly cruel word or action of his would engulf Mrs Walker as she walked along the high street, or moved from room to room and she would be obliged to steady herself until her breathing returned to its normal rhythm. It seemed improbable, therefore, that she might attach herself to another older gentleman, particularly one whose manner, while fundamentally kind, could also be overbearing.

Once she had allowed her heart to overrule her head Mrs Walker found that the everyday pursuits with which she had filled her time before meeting Mr Barratt no longer satisfied her. She craved his company and attention in a way that she suspected was unhealthy, and disliked herself for it. The situation was complicated by the fact that Barratt, who prior to their engagement seemed to spend weeks doing nothing at all, had become preoccupied with a variety of schemes which kept him from her. The situation had improved during the winter months, as Mr Barratt basked in his triumph over Mr Nicholson, but there had been a sudden reversal, in terrible circumstances, and he had disappeared from her life once more in the days before their wedding. It could not be tolerated.

"Harvey, perhaps you could give us a few minutes," said Mr Barratt.

"You are very welcome to stay and to hear what I have to say, Mr Richards," said Mrs Walker. "It is not confidential, though it may make for uncomfortable listening." Mr Barratt flashed a look of panic at his young friend and Mr Richards nodded quickly.

"I have some urgent business to attend to, Madam. I hope you will not think me rude if I excuse myself, it really is a most pressing matter." Mrs Walker waved him away, exhibiting her indifference with a slackened wrist. "Thank you," said Mr Richards. He ran from the room, almost, and the large front door slammed shut seconds later. Mr Barratt sat in the chair which Mr Richards had vacated and took two deep breaths.

"Susannah, allow me to apologise," Barratt began. Mrs Walker raised a hand.

"It is too late, Charles. I refuse to be treated like this. Where have you been for the last two weeks?"

"I have been spending much of my time at Hope Hall, as you

know, assisting Miss Foulke." Mrs Walker shook her head.

"Were you there from dawn to sunset?" she asked. "What prevented you from calling at the Rectory when you returned each day?"

"I assure you that I have been very busy," Barratt replied, as if trying to convince himself that this sufficed as an excuse.

"On the contrary, *I* have been very busy, attempting to arrange our lives after the wedding. There were a number of things I wished to discuss with you, Charles, but you seemed wilfully to be making yourself unavailable. You were avoiding me, were you not?" Mr Barratt stared at the floor without answering. He wished that he were wearing his best boots. "I admit that I was a trifle confused," Mrs Walker continued, "since you purport to love me and to grow anxious when you do not see me for a few hours..." Mr Barratt made a noise as if he wished to interrupt but Mrs Walker would not allow it. "Yes, you have told me that on more than one occasion in recent months. So what am I to make of this recent, self-imposed interdiction, why does Charles Barratt abhor my presence suddenly?

"I know you to be a kind, warm-hearted gentleman, so I presumed that there must be a simple explanation, that I was somehow misinterpreting your absence as a meanness, and then I realised that it was perfectly sensible for you not to involve yourself in planning a wedding, a marriage indeed, which you knew would never come to pass. Are your feet cold, Charles? Do you regret proposing to me?"

"Certainly not, my darling," said Barratt. "I want you to be my wife. I have never known a moment's doubt."

"You doubt the existence of God, yet you attend church each Sunday. You admit no doubt in loving me yet you will not cross the threshold of the Rectory. This is madness!"

"I was not at church last Sunday," said Mr Barratt.

"You dared not show your face, I suggest, for fear of having to speak to me. I will not be silent, do you understand?" Mr Barratt nodded.

"I am sorry for not having called upon you," he said. "It was cowardly of me. I feared that we might have a conversation like this, so naturally I avoided it."

"This is no pleasure for me either," said Mrs Walker.

"Anyhow, we have scarcely begun. You told me that you were acting on Mr Nicholson's behalf, saving him from himself, in effect. Now he is struck dumb and a violent criminal is abroad, how did this happen?" Mr Barratt then explained Buller's actions and the motive behind them, as Mrs Walker clasped her hands together and rocked back and forwards slightly in her chair. "This person, Buller, he remains at liberty? How do we know that we are safe from him?"

"Johnson will locate him," said Barratt. "He will be arrested and charged and then he will be transported."

"There is the cost of your actions, Charles: one man left mute and another sent to die in another country."

"There was little hope for Mr Nicholson or Buller even had I not intervened. Their vices would have brought about a violent end."

"Why involve yourself, then?" Mrs Walker demanded. "Why not alert the courts, instead?"

"I believed that my solution would prove more beneficial to more people than any the High Court might propose."

"The lives of two men are destroyed, Charles, because you think you know better than anyone, any lawyer or judge, better than any mortal man or God himself, even."

"I regret that Mr Nicholson has been injured but no-one should shed a tear for Buller," said Mr Barratt, whose mood had moved from penitence to irritation. "You say I have destroyed these men's lives, but if I have done so they themselves haveably assisted in their downfall. Consider the lives saved, Madam, those lifted out of poverty in Butcher's Green and into clean, decent homes at Hope Hall. Think of the lost children of Rebekah Broady, taken before they could pronounce their mother's name, and of Catherine, who will grow up on the estate that her grandfather was cast out from." Mrs Walker was not cowed by Barratt's defiance.

"What of the pain you have caused to my cousin, the sweetest, most decent man any woman could hope to meet? You encouraged his pursuit of Miss Foulke.Now, because of your actions, she is devoted to Henry Nicholson, and poor John is invisible to the woman he loves. Do you still defend your actions?"

"I meant only to bring happiness to Reverend Archer, as you must be aware."

"I am aware of this, Charles," Mrs Walker replied, "that good intentions count for very little when one is heartbroken."

"I am truly sorry for any distress I have caused you or John," said Barratt, calming himself.

"You would do it again though, would you not, even knowing the consequences?" Mr Barratt considered this for a moment.

"It is impossible to take into account all the possible consequences of any action," he said. "I acted with a clear mind and a true heart, and I would do the same again, yes." Mrs Walker sighed.

"You are a kind man, my love, but you are careless. You respect no authority but your own, and not because of your Godlessness, which I have struggled to accept. Rather it is a symptom of your self-regard: you reject God because you cannot conceive of a being greater than yourself. I presume you reject the King, the Prince Regent and the Prime Minister too." Mr Barratt considered interjecting at this point but determined that to do so would reinforce Mrs Walker's argument. "You are remarkable, of course, and a person worthy of admiration. I understand that the years you spent alone have shaped your sense of singularity. This lack of care, this thoughtlessness does not prevent me loving you, but, I am sorry, it will prevent me from marrying you."

"No!" said Barratt, slipping from his chair and on to his knees. "Please, Susannah!" Mrs Walker's eyes filled with tears.

"This is what you want, Charles. You may not be aware of it, you may even try to explain your absence from the Rectory as simply being fearful of this very discussion, but I do not believe it. If you wished to marry me you would not have disappeared for two weeks immediately before our wedding day." She stood and placed a hand on Mr Barratt's bowed head.

"I am sorry," she said again. Mr Barratt remained kneeling on the Persian carpet, examining the intricacies of its pattern, until he heard Mrs Walker's footsteps in the hallway and the opening and closing of the front door.

XLIII

MRS WALKER WAS able to contain her emotions as she returned to the Rectory but as is often the case it was the kind word which undid her. She dried her eyes on her handkerchief before crossing the high street, this measure did not disguise her distress entirely, however, and when Lottie enquired as to her mistress's well-being Mrs Walker burst into a fit of violent sobbing, punctuated by an occasional wail. She ran upstairs to her bedroom and locked the door, refusing to answer the concerned entreaties of Lottie, Miss Lucy and Reverend Archer in turn.

The Rector, unable to comfort his cousin, determined at least to discover the cause of her sorrow (to some degree this warm-hearted gentleman may have wished additionally to escape the terrible clamour audible behind Mrs Walker's bedroom door and throughout the building.) The cook opened the door to the Red House and waved Reverend Archer towards the parlour. Mr Barratt was slumped in an armchair as if he had been shot.

"John!" he said, suddenly reanimated. "How are you?"

"I am quite well, thank you Charles. Tell me, has a further misunderstanding arisen between Mrs Walker and yourself?"

"Yes, in fact. She thinks I am careless and refuses to marry me."

"That hardly seems sufficient grounds for abnegating one's future happiness,"Reverend Archer observed.

"She blames me for the injuries sustained by Henry Nicholson, and for destroying your hopes with Miss Foulke." The Rector considered this information for a moment.

"You are not to blame in law," he said. "I suppose it is possible that you bear some moral responsibility for Mr Nicholson's situation, but it is by no means an uncomplicated matter. As for Miss Foulke, well, if ever there was a young woman waiting to rescue someone it is she. For a while I thought I might appear desperate enough to satisfy her instincts but I have been trumped by our friend Nicholson." The two gentlemen managed a bitter laugh at this remark, but a certain discomfort remained between them.

"Mrs Walker is quite correct, I fear," said Barratt. "I have acted impulsively and without sufficient consideration of others. I am sorry, John."

"I know that your intentions were beyond reproach," said the Rector. "Susannah will forgive you." Mr Barratt shook his head.

"She may, but she is determined that we shall not marry. In any case it seemed unwise to contradict her." The two gentlemen smiled at one another, their unrestrained amity largely restored in a moment.

"That is a pity," said Reverend Archer ruefully. "I was rather looking forward to you becoming part of the family."

Though it was just after three in the afternoon it was deemed necessary to bless the continuity of their friendship with a large glass of Amontillado. As they sipped the wine Mr Barratt attempted to persuade himself that he would have been quite happy to have spent the last year and a half enjoying the occasional company of Reverend Archer, and that his adventures with Mrs Walker and Mr Nicholson were merely distractions from the true bond he shared with the young clergyman. He was heartsick, in truth, and a little ashamed, so this proved a vain effort.

Mr Richards returned from his fictitious business and joined the Rector and Mr Barratt in consuming the last of the Sherry. Mr Barratt located another bottle and convinced his guests that it should be opened, if only to assess the quality of its content. He was pleased to observe that Reverend Archer and Mr Richards now conversed in an easy, jocular fashion, the inhibiting factor to their friendship, Miss Foulke, no longer being in play. They sighed, shrugged and laughed like two fellows who had been thrown from the same horse. Reverend Archer declined a third glass of wine, remarking that his sermon was barely half written. He was obliged, therefore, to *revient à nos moutons*, or otherwise risk the disapprobation of his flock. A moment passed in which Mr Barratt managed to avoid choking on his Sherry as he registered the comic ingenuity of the Rector's remark. Barratt's laughter then unrolled like a tuneless peal of bells. Mr Richards, who did not understand a single word of French, laughed along nevertheless, so captivating and contagious was Mr Barratt's hilarity.

"You should put that in your sermon," said Barratt, perhaps overestimating the linguistic diversity of his fellow parishioners, "there are some lost sheep in the bible, as I recall."

"I am sure the Reverend will find them, if anyone can," said Mr Richards. This remark, which was by no means the most dazzling ever uttered by Harvey Richards, produced another bout of delighted convulsions from Mr Barratt. The Rector took this as his cue to leave and both Barratt and Mr Richards bowed and shook his hand as if newly acquainted with some person of great esteem.

"I hope that your interview with Mrs Walker concluded in a warmer spirit than that in which it began," said Mr Richards, once Reverend Archer had departed.

"It was all quite upsetting but it is over now," said Mr Barratt. "We need not speak of it again." This response did not clarify matters particularly, Mr Richards felt, but he was sensible enough to heed Barratt's wishes. He watched as the older gentleman stared intently at the toe of his right boot. Mr Barratt's features were of the expressive kind and he was seemingly incapable of disguising his emotions. It was as well that he did not play cards, Mr Richards reflected, observing a distinct change in Barratt's face, as if he had been dealt a particularly advantageous hand at whist. Mr Barratt lifted his gaze.

"Do you remember Miss Reeves, Harvey?"

"Of course, and her sister, Mrs Carter. We met at Foulke Hall last spring."

"Her late father had a business selling boots, you will recall. Not boots as you or I would wear, but military boots, for infantrymen. Clever Miss Reeves sold the business a few months before Wellington's triumph."

"A tactical withdrawal," said Mr Richards.

"Indeed. I have been wondering about the land at Butcher's Green. Most of the hovels have been cleared, I understand?"

"Yes. There are but two remaining tenants, to the west, at the furthest point from the road. One of the other buildings is illegally occupied, but there seems little point involving the Sherriff until the whole area can be raised. I have written to Mr Nicholson with a view to building a terrace of cottages at Hope Hall. What has this to do with Miss Reeves?"

"An excellent question," said Mr Barratt. "If I wished to involve myself in the manufacture of boots, slippers and so forth, I would do well to seek the advice of a person familiar with the process. Do you know anything about shoemaking, Sir?"

"Not a thing," admitted Mr Richards.

"We can assume, I think, that it requires a different degree of literacy from printing. The skills involved may be more difficult to learn than the alphabet, however."

"I doubt that Miss Reeves has ever stitched a boot herself."

"No, but I imagine she knows a number of people who have, and who may wish for steady employment, rather than whatever piecework they are presently dependent on. Carter, Reeves and Richards, shoemakers, what do you think?" Mr Richards thought it sounded like a firm of rustic lawyers, or undertakers, and was suspicious as to why Mr Barratt would not lend his own name to the enterprise. "Barratt does not fit with shoes, you see, and I think we should honour the late Colonel."

"Splendid," said Mr Richards. "You mean to construct a factory, then?"

"We will start small, Harvey, but we have some space to expand into if we are successful. That area is anyway better suited for industry than for habitation. Come into the library, I shall write to Miss Reeves directly."

Barratt was determined not to allow any depression of his present mood and took the second Sherry bottle with him. He looked in the bureau for notepaper, pulling out a sheet large enough for his purpose. Upon it sat the letter which Mr Richards had brought back from Meadholme the previous summer. Mr Barratt turned the letter over in his fingers, noting the conditions in which it might be opened. Since Mrs Walker had insisted that she would not marry him the prescription seemed moot. He sighed and broke the seal.

Dear Mr Barratt,

I learned from Mr Richards that you are to be married in the spring and I offer my congratulations, though I confess I do so with a heavy heart. You will think me foolish for writing this but I wished you to know how greatly you are admired here at Meadholme. Harvey says that Mrs Walker is a most admirable lady and we are all agreed that it is just as well she is, as it would disappoint us greatly were you not to find someone suitable as a companion. I understand that she is not particularly young, cannot be, in fact, as Miss Lucy is her daughter. It is very noble of you to marry her, I am sure, and she is very fortunate. Many gentlemen might have sought a younger wife, who would provide them with children and succour them in old age. Mrs Walker must be the happiest person alive. This is written hastily because Mr Richards is to leave within the hour so I apologise for not expressing myself clearly or elegantly. We have met only twice but I have been impressed on each occasion by how handsome and natural your manners and person are, and my father often remarks on what a gentlemanly fellow you are, even though you sailed with the Company, which would normally mean he would disdain you somewhat. Just yesterday he said that it was a great pity that you were unable to accompany Mr Richards to Meadholme on this occasion. I must conclude as my script is impossible to read when crossed. I wish you every happiness and hope that you think of me from time to time.

Your fond admirer,

Philomena Billings

Mr Barratt pouted as he finished reading the letter, as if he might whistle, but no sound was forthcoming. Mr Richards had a notion of the letter's content, as it had been pressed into his hand by the author. Barratt cleared his throat, then stood and went in search of his pipe. He returned and sat once more at the bureau, then filled the pipe and lit it.

"We were speaking earlier of an evening at Foulke House, perhaps ten months ago," he said.

"Yes," Mr Richards replied. "It was the evening we met Miss

Reeves and Mrs Carter."

"And Miss Foulke, of course. Surely you have not forgotten her, Harvey?"

"I have not, Sir." Mr Barratt smiled and continued.

"Perhaps you recall a conversation with Mr Cunningham and myself that took place en route?"

"I remember that we were all in very good spirits. And that Mr Cunningham's driver was an ill-tempered fellow."

"Let me remind, you," said Barratt. "We were discussing Cunningham's relationship with his housekeeper, Mrs Flannery." Mr Richards nodded.

"Yes! I suggested to my dear uncle that if he wished to secure Mrs Flannery's hand he ought to pretend that some other eligible lady had caught his eye." Mr Barratt chuckled, handed the letter to Mr Richards and waited for him to read it.

"You have spent enough time at Meadholme to make an educated assessment, what is your opinion of Philomena Billings?" asked Barratt.

"She is as she seems in this letter, Sir: a simple, unaffected creature. Not a beauty, perhaps, but a healthy young woman."

"No, none of them are particularly striking, but all appear to be honest, dutiful girls.Now, you will think me dull or inattentive at least, but I must ask, which one is she? I know that two young women stayed here for the ball, and at least one of them was this Philomena."

"She is the eldest of Captain Billings' daughters," said Mr Richards. "Miss Jane is prettier, I would say, but Miss Philomena is taller, with a very attractive frame."

"The dark-haired girl? Yes, she will do very well indeed." Mr Richards handed back the letter and Barratt replaced it in the drawer of the bureau. "I shall write to Miss Reeves, and then, Harvey, we shall see about securing an invitation to Meadholme. Johnson tells me that Mrs Walker is not fond of her property, but I have nothing but pleasant feelings towards the place. What do you say?"

Mr Richards considered Mr Barratt for a moment. He knew that for a long period Barratt had not possessed this irrepressible spirit, that for many years he had hidden from life and that he had arrived in B_____ seeking greater obscurity. He had not found it, instead Mr Barratt's world had expanded, and he had found a way to accommodate that change. Mr Richards thought of a rowing boat caught on an upswell, its prow pointing to the sky, which manages to ride the wave as it collapses and is then propelled towards its destination. The important thing, even at the most precarious moment, was not to panic, or to question why one was at sea in the first place, but instead to keep pulling the oars.

"We are moving forwards," said Mr Richards.

"We certainly are," said Barratt.

T H E   E N D

Printed in Great Britain
by Amazon

83450589R00140